For all the shy kids in the world

What's the opposite of a bucket list? You know what I
mean by a bucket list, right? It's a list of all the things
you want to do before you die. Which when you're only
a twelve-year-old boy could be quite a long list actually,
as you haven't really done ANYTHING yet. But, to
tell you the truth, I don't want to do anything much. It's
easier and less scary to stay at home in my room on my
computer.

So what would you call the opposite of a bucket list?
A list of all the things you want to make sure you
NEVER. EVER. DO. **EVER.** All the awful, terrible,
horrible, embarrassing, dangerous, scary, dumb things
you need to avoid. Like, I know I never want to do
anything where you might have to use a parachute.
I mean, why would anyone want to throw themselves
out of an aeroplane? That's just stupid. And hot-air
ballooning. How is it possible to make something that is

really boring and really dangerous at the same time? OK. Let's be clear. I want to avoid going up in the air in the first place. Actually, it's not so much the going up that worries me – it's the coming down.

What else? Anything where I might come across dangerous animals is right out. Obviously. Swimming with whales? No. Going anywhere near sharks? No. Canoeing up the Amazon? No. The Amazon rainforest is full of snakes, spiders, piranhas, crocodiles and those fish that swim up your willy if you have a pee in the water.

Backpacking in Australia?

NO. NO. NO. NO. NO.

Did you know that twenty-one of the world's twenty-five most poisonous snakes live there? And they have crocodiles. And spiders the size of footballs. And killer jellyfish. Plus they have a massive hole in the ozone layer so you basically shrivel up into a crisp and drop dead if you go outside. Australia is very far away and, as far as I'm concerned, it can stay there.

What else?

I definitely want to steer clear of octopuses.

And . . .

Well, maybe I should just show you my list.

Except I don't know what to call it.

Not a bucket list . . . The only words I can think of to call my list are a bit rude, but . . .

Oh yes. I know – duck it!

A DUCK-IT list.

So here's my duck-it list. Ten things to avoid at all costs (there's a law that says lists should always be ten things). Actually, I think most of the things on my duck-it list are things other people would probably put on their bucket lists, but I really hope I never have to do any of the following . . .

STAN'S DUCK-IT LIST

1. Bungee jumping.
2. Anything where you have to use a parachute.
3. Dancing.
4. Dancing in public.
5. Going on Strictly Come Dancing.
6. White-water rafting.
7. Fire-eating.
8. Alligator wrestling.
9. Kissing.
10. Going on holiday with people you don't know.
11. Octopuses.

All right, sorry – it's not ten things. I had to add number eleven in at the last minute. I panicked.

I panic a lot.

I'm panicking right now.

Why?

Because number ten is happening . . .

I'm going on holiday with people I don't know.

This shouldn't be happening to me. It's an absolute DISASTER.

I keep thinking about how on earth I got here. 'Here' being the Shopping Maze Of Doom at Stansted Airport, completely lost at four o'clock in the morning. I wonder what I could have done differently – how I could have stopped this happening.

All right. Calm down, Stan.

Maybe I'm being overdramatic. I'm not actually going on holiday with complete strangers. I'm going on holiday with Felix, who is my best friend.

OK, to tell you the truth, Felix is not *exactly* my best friend. I don't really have a *best* friend. I have five friends and Felix is one of them. They're all about equal on the friend scale, I suppose. Sometimes I like one of them better than the others. You know how it is. Every now and then I'll have a fight with one of them and then we aren't friends for a bit, but it doesn't usually last long and mostly we forget what the fight was about. Right now, though, I'm having to pretend that Felix is my best friend, because his mum and dad are taking me on holiday to Italy for two weeks.

So, when I get there, if anyone asks me who I am, I've got to say, 'I'm Felix's best friend, Stan.'

Which will be a bit of a lie. To be honest, if I was forced to rank my friends in order, Felix would probably be number five. I don't mean to be rude, but we're not actually that friendly. And if you'd asked Felix before if I was his best friend, he would have said no.

Actually, what he'd have said would have been more like: 'What? Are you mad? Stan? Ha! No way.'

But you see what happened is that Felix was meant to be going on holiday with his *real* best friend, Archie (who is maybe my number four). Archie is really good at football and everybody wants to be his friend, even the girls, but Felix had to make a last-minute change of plan because three weeks ago Archie broke his leg playing football.

Well, he wasn't playing at the time. He was celebrating scoring a goal and tried to do a sort of somersault. He landed funny and there was a loud snapping noise. Like someone shooting a gun in a film. It was really horrible. His bone was sticking out of his leg. I felt sick looking at it. Although it was a little bit cool at the same time. I think Archie might not be able to play football for a while. I wonder if this will make a difference to how many people want to be his friend.

Anyway, Archie's still on crutches, so I've taken his place on the holiday. And I know I wasn't even Felix's first choice of substitute. He asked a few other boys, but they were already going on holiday with their own families.

I didn't have any plans to go on holiday with my family. We don't really go on holiday in the summer because Dad says it's too expensive and crowded everywhere.

'The travel companies really rip you off,' he says every summer as he fills up the plastic paddling pool in our tiny garden with a hose. 'They totally put their prices up in the school holidays. It's criminal. All the airlines and hotels and holiday firms charge twice what they usually do.'

So we normally have our family holiday in the Easter break. We go to Wales. In case you don't know what Wales is, it's a country next to England where it rains all the time. We go to the same cottage every year. It belongs to my Uncle David. I think Uncle David rents it out in the summer, which is why we go at Easter. The cottage smells mouldy, and it never gets warm. Last time we went I recklessly decided to go for a swim in the sea and lost all feeling in my legs.

So this is all a bit different for me. Before today I'd only ever been on an aeroplane once before, when I was ten. Mum's dad, my grandad Johnny, died and left her some money in his will. She wanted to give us all a treat. We went to Spain for a week and Dad got the flu.

All he said about the holiday was: 'Never again.' Even though Mum really enjoyed it. Me too. You could get sausage and chips, it was warm, and you didn't risk acting out the last scene from *Titanic* every time you went in the sea.

Whenever we go to Wales and Dad's not around, Mum looks out at the rain and says, 'Never again,' and we both laugh. It's 'our little joke' (that's what Mum calls it). To tell you the truth, I don't find the joke that funny any more.

So, as I say, we usually spend summer at home in London. But this summer is different because when Felix asked me if I wanted to go on holiday with him I panicked and said yes.

Oh god. What have I done? All I needed to do was to say no and none of this would have happened. I wouldn't be lost in Stansted Airport in the middle of the night.

Maybe you don't just need to avoid going on holiday with people you don't know – maybe you need to avoid going on holiday altogether.

I definitely have to make a new list – REASONS NOT TO GO ON HOLIDAY.

Because this is hell.

Reason 1: Airports

I know I said that all lists should only be ten things, but I can tell that this one is going to be much, much longer. I reckon we'll end up with at least thirty, so I'm calling it '30 Reasons Not To Go On Holiday'.

So, anyway, number one: airports.

What's wrong with airports? I'll tell you what's wrong. Airports cause you to go mad. You want proof? Well, right now, I'm surrounded by people who are shopping, even though it's half past four in the morning. You can't tell it's half past four because there are no windows and the lights are very bright, which is making me feel really weird. The bright lights have obviously sent everyone else round the bend too, otherwise why would they be shopping? It's like some twisted scientific experiment to find out what would happen to people if you made it day all the time. (I can tell you what would happen – they'd go mad and start shopping.)

I mean, you don't go to an airport to do your shopping, do you? You go to an airport to catch a plane. But the people here have a dangerous, deranged look in their eyes and they're buying everything they can get their hands on.

I don't know what to do. I'm wandering around, totally lost, in a sort of maze made from shops. Actually, I can't tell if it's lots of smaller shops or one big one. I don't know where one part ends and another begins. And you can't escape. Everywhere you turn there are bottles of champagne, headphones, sunglasses, foreign plugs and perfume that's been made by pop stars. There's even a gleaming sports car. And why is everything so BIG? There are massive bottles of gin, huge packets of M&M's, giant Toblerones.

And tills. Hundreds of tills.

I'm beginning to crack. I feel an uncontrollable urge to buy something.

ANYTHING . . .

But I mustn't. Mum would kill me.

She gave me some money last night – a twenty-pound note and two twenty-euro notes – but there's a catch . . .

MUM: Here's some money. But whatever you do, don't spend it.

ME: What's the use of money if I can't spend it?

MUM: It's for emergencies.

ME: How will I know if it's an emergency?

MUM: If you're not sure whether it's an emergency, then it's not one. Just don't spend any of it unless it's life or death.

ME: So if I'm dying I'm allowed to spend it. Won't that be a bit late?

MUM: Just don't spend it!

Mum's always worried about me, but she's extra worried about this holiday because she's not going with me. And I'm extra worried because . . . well, because Mum's not with me.

This would be easier and less stressful if I was with Felix, but I'm not travelling with him because he's already out in Italy. His mum and dad own a house there and they're staying in it for most of the summer.

Dad shook his head and let out a long sigh when he heard how long Felix was going to be away.

'That's not right,' he said. 'Not right at all. Everyone knows a summer holiday is two weeks. You go on a Saturday and you come back on a Saturday fourteen days later. A fortnight. Anything else is just showing off. It's not right.'

So, anyway, that's why I'm travelling with Felix's Uncle Simon and Auntie Emma.

I've never met either of them before this morning, and we've already become separated.

Simon and Emma stopped to buy some duty free (which is another name for alcohol), and Simon said I should go on ahead and meet them outside Burger King. I can't see Burger King anywhere and I'm worried I'll never be able to find my way out of the shopping labyrinth. There are even some people sleeping on benches – they look like they've given up and decided to live here.

Maybe I'll end up sleeping on a bench. Maybe I'll end up living here and become an old man with a big beard.

At times like this I wish I wasn't a kid. I can't wait to be grown up and not have to worry about everything all the time. Life is so much easier for grown-ups. They can just walk about the place like they know where they're going, and . . . I don't know . . . buy things and understand the world.

Which way do I go? This would be a whole lot easier if I wasn't so tired.

I had to wake up at three o'clock, which was a bit freaky and sort of a bit exciting at the same time. Mum was already up. In fact, I don't think she'd gone to bed. And I think she'd been crying. I've never really been away from her before. She hugged me for slightly too long when Simon and Emma arrived to pick me up.

'Don't worry, Mrs P,' Simon said as I grabbed my backpack. 'He'll be in safe hands. I've only ever lost three children!'

This was a joke. Simon laughed. Mum didn't laugh. I just smiled. I was too tired to laugh. Mum gave Emma my passport and a special note that says she's allowed to take me abroad as I'm not allowed to travel on my own.

The night got even freakier as Simon drove us through London at half past three in the morning. There were all different people out on the streets and it was like I was seeing a secret world. After a while we left London and got on to the motorway. At one point Simon went to sleep and we nearly crashed. Emma didn't notice – she was listening to her audiobook, and Simon pretended nothing had happened. He made me talk to him after that, though, which was awkward because I'd never met him before and I'm not used to talking to grown-ups, apart from Mum (and sometimes Dad). In the end all I could think of was to tell him the plot of *Guardians of the Galaxy 2*, which I saw the other day.

I don't think he was very interested, but at least he didn't fall asleep again and kill us all.

Wait a minute! There's Burger King! I've made it. I'm free! I've somehow come out of the maze and into a busy area that's surrounded by fast-food places and pubs and bars. Loads of people are eating. There's a queue at Burger King. At this time of the night! Are you even allowed burgers for breakfast? I don't know. But the strangest thing is that the pubs and bars are packed as well. People are drinking wine and champagne and cocktails and pints of beer. I tried beer once and didn't really like the taste and can't imagine why anyone would want to drink it at half past four in the morning.

And the thing that really makes this airport completely insane is that a lot of people are dressed for the beach, in shorts and vests, straw hats and flip-flops, as if they're already on holiday.

This airport has definitely sent everyone bonkers. Like we've all entered some kind of alternative universe where everything's back to front.

And then I see Simon and Emma and I relax a bit.

I won't be fully relaxed until I'm on the plane, though.

Actually, I won't be fully relaxed until we've landed.

Actually, to tell you the truth, I won't be fully relaxed until we get to the house in Italy.

No.

You know what, I don't think I'll be fully relaxed until I'm back in my own room.

At home.

With Mum and Dad.

Reason 2: Flying

So I made it on to the plane and I'm sitting by myself. Well, not exactly by myself. What I mean is, I'm not sitting with Simon and Emma. I'm in the middle of a row between two strangers. An old man with a big belly and a young man with headphones.

I didn't like flying when we went to Spain and I don't like flying now. At least last time I had Mum sitting next to me and she held my hand when we took off (which was scary). And when we landed (which was very scary). And all the bits in between (which were slightly less scary, but still scary).

Flying makes me think of parachutes. And I know they don't have them on passenger planes. I looked it up. I can just imagine the captain coming on over the radio . . .

'Hello, ladies and gentlemen, this is your captain speaking. We are currently flying at 30,000 feet, sorry, 25,000 feet, sorry, 15,000 feet. Sorry . . . we seem to be crashing. There are no parachutes on board, so make yourselves comfortable and the cabin crew will come round with some soft cushions . . .'

I don't think it would go down very well if I asked the old man with the big belly or the young man with headphones to hold my hand. And, to tell you the truth, I don't really want to. The old man looks a bit sweaty, and the young man's hands are really hairy and look like giant spiders.

To try to distract myself from thoughts of doom, I fish out the envelope Mum gave me with the money in. She told me she'd put a note in it. I get it out and look at it.

It's an emergency list – ten holiday dangers and how to survive them – with helpful advice underneath.

I guess this might not distract me as much as I hoped. These are the different headings:

MUM'S HOLIDAY EMERGENCY LIST

1. What to do if attacked by a jellyfish.
2. What to do if attacked by a rabid dog.
3. What to do if attacked by a shark.
4. What to do if attacked by a giant squid.
5. What to do if attacked by seagulls.
6. What to do if left behind by the rest of the group somewhere, e.g. at the beach.
7. What to do if you get food stuck in your throat.
8. What to do if you get food poisoning.
9. What to do if you're abducted by kidnappers.
10. How to survive a tsunami.

I'm not sure how helpful this list is. I know I said I'm scared of jellyfish, but, let's face it, they don't really attack, do they? They just sort of drift about like plastic bags. If you see one on the beach, it's easy to walk round it. You don't need to call in a SWAT team or a bombing raid or anything. And Mum's advice is really complicated and confusing. It's all about 'nematocysts causing venom cells to fire' and 'dispersal of toxins' and 'diphenhydramine cream'. So that's not going to be a lot of use to me.

Her advice on what to do if attacked by a shark is much less complicated . . .

Punch it in the eye.

Yeah, right, like I'm ever going to punch a shark in the eye. I mean, what are the chances of even seeing one? Mum tried to convince me that recently a great white had been spotted in the Mediterranean. I said it was probably a shark tourist that had got lost trying to find Australia, where it was going to hang out with all the other deadly animals.

And giant squid? I don't know if anyone has ever been attacked by a giant squid outside of a pirate film.

OK, so I might get attacked by seagulls. That happens all the time. There are videos on YouTube called things like 'When Seagulls Attack!' but it's not really in the same league as being attacked by a shark. Mum's seagull survival advice is simple: *Move away to somewhere with a roof.* But I think I might just try punching it in the eye. Especially if it's stealing my ice cream.

I'm really not sure about a lot of Mum's advice, to tell you the truth. For choking on food, she advises doing the Heinrich Himmler manoeuvre, but I don't think she's got that quite right.

For being abducted by kidnappers, she says to keep calm and try to befriend them – show them pictures of my family and my dog. Apparently I should talk about my dog and how it will miss me if I never come home. She read somewhere that all kidnappers are sentimental about dogs. The problem is, we don't have a dog so she's put a photograph in the envelope of someone else's dog that she said I need to carry on my person at all times.

I take it out and look at it, then check the money. I wonder if being kidnapped counts as a full emergency? If so, I'm not sure that twenty pounds and forty euros will be enough to pay my ransom. Although, as I'm only twelve and my mum and dad aren't rich, the kidnappers might think that was a good deal.

As for how to survive a tsunami . . . I told Mum I didn't think they had tsunamis in the Mediterranean, but then I said, 'They *do* have earthquakes, though.'

'Oh god,' she said. 'I hadn't thought about that. What do you do if you're in an earthquake?'

'Pray? Scream? Instagram it?'

'You're not helping, Stan. I'll look into it and I'll call you on holiday to let you know what to do.'

I can hardly wait.

You might think that me making a joke with Mum means I'm not worried about things. And all my talk about walking round jellyfish and punching seagulls in the eye makes me look brave and adventurous and heroic. I'm not. It's just my way of not letting Mum's anxiety get to me, because everything she does to try to stop me from worrying just makes me worry more. And I've got enough of my own things to worry about. Proper dangers. Things that might actually happen.

My own emergency list would look more like this:

STAN'S HOLIDAY EMERGENCY LIST

1. What to do if offered weird food.
2. What to do if the toilets are weird.
3. What to do if someone speaks to me in Italian.
4. What to do if I accidentally call Felix's mum 'Mum' in front of everybody.
5. What to do if I dive in the pool and my trunks come off.
6. What to do if I laugh when I'm drinking milk, and milk comes out of my nose.
7. What to do if they have that weird foreign milk that tastes different. And then it comes out of my nose.
8. What to do when I can't reach round my back to put sun cream on when Mum won't be there to do it for me.
9. What to do if we're all watching a DVD and an embarrassing bit comes on where people don't have any clothes on or something.
10. What to do if the plane starts to crash and I shout out something embarrassing.

You're probably thinking I make a lot of lists, but it's something Mum taught me to do. She says that when the world gets on top of you and you're struggling to cope (which is most of the time for me), you just need to put all your problems in a list and it makes them less scary.

It's not working, though. All I can think about is everything that can go wrong and now I'm having a mild panic attack, made worse by the fact that I'm miles up in the air sitting between two strangers inside a thin metal tube without a parachute.

If I was sitting with Felix's Uncle Simon and Auntie Emma I could hold Emma's hand, as long as she promised not to tell anyone. But we've been split up and we're nowhere near each other. The plane is Ryanair and apparently they charge you extra to sit together. It must be quite complicated for Ryanair to work out how to make sure nobody is sitting with a friend or a member of their own family.

Actually, they've probably got an algorithm. Dad says everything is run by algorithms nowadays: 'The robots are taking over, Stan.'

I don't really know what an algorithm is. I'm not sure Dad does either.

If I ever said anything to Dad about algorithms and how robots are taking over, he'd give me a sarcastic look and say, 'Ooh, profound . . .'

It's what he says when anybody says anything that sounds a bit clever. Like if somebody on the TV says something serious, or if me or Mum say something that sounds like we've thought about it for more than about two seconds, or when he's reading things on food packaging . . .

PROFESSOR BRIAN COX (ON THE TV): When we look out into space, we are looking into our own origins, because we are truly children of the stars . . .

DAD: Ooh, profound.

MUM: I sometimes think I've spent half my life doing laundry. I could measure out my days in ironed sheets.

DAD: Ooh, profound.

ME: You know, like, when you're feeling a bit moody and it starts to rain and you think the weather's copying you and sort of crying? They said at school that's called a pathetic fallacy . . .

DAD: Ooh, profound.

JUICE CARTON: Pure natural plant energy from three different types of super fruit and electrolysed smart water to make your life zing!

DAD: Ooh, profound.

You can't ever say anything serious around Dad. He doesn't like anything fancy, anything that sounds like poetry or philosophy, or in any way clever. That's his worst insult. 'Oh dear, Stan, are you trying to be *clever*?' You can get your own back on him, though, because he can talk for hours about football. Or 'the Beautiful Game' as he calls it . . .

DAD: You need depth, Stan. Strength in midfield is all well and good, but you need the support of a solid back line balanced with power and speed up front. Without balance you can't have coherence.

ME: Ooh, profound.

The thing is, I've picked up the habit. I often have to stop myself blurting it out in class, especially when we're doing English. Like Shakespeare or something.

HAMLET: To be, or not to be? That is the question.

ME: Ooh, profound.

Thinking about school makes me feel a little bit homesick, even though I don't really like school that much and I've only been away from home for, like, about five hours. But I just know everything's going to go wrong.

You see when I told Mum not to worry about tsunamis . . . the thing is, I *always* worry about tsunamis – wherever I am. All right, maybe not *actual* tsunamis, but I have a feeling, all the time, that there's a giant wave about to crash over me. That everything's going to go wrong. That I'm going to be drenched and flattened. Even here, on this plane, I can feel the shadow of a huge wave hanging over me, ready to crash down. Just my luck to be the only boy in the history of the world to end up drowned while 30,000 feet up in the air on a Ryanair flight.

I'm distracted from my thoughts by a sudden thump and the plane shudders as if we've just driven over something. For a moment it feels like it's dropping out of the sky, then there's more bumps and shaking. Why is nobody panicking? All that the man with the big belly does is tut and mop up a puddle of spilt drink with a napkin.

'Hello, this is the captain speaking. We've hit a spot of turbulence. So if you could return to your seats and observe the "fasten seat belt" signs . . .'

The captain sounds very calm, but I can picture him opening a window in the cockpit and strapping on the secret parachute he keeps hidden under his seat.

If this is the last you ever hear from me, tell Mum I love her.

And Dad, I suppose.

Reason 3: Mad driving

We're in Italy. We landed safely and I'm still alive.

But at this rate it might not be for very long . . .

Simon is driving and sweating and swearing all at the same time. I'm sitting next to him . . . and also sweating. Partly because it's hot. But mostly because it's terrifying. There are cars and lorries whizzing around us, honking their horns and swerving about. We are on a motorway, or *autostrada*, as the Italians call them. (Simon told me that. He likes to tell me things.)

'In America they call them freeways, Satan.' (Simon thinks it's funny to call me Satan.) 'And in Germany they're called *Autobahns*. Do you know what the German word for a motorway exit is?'

'No.'

'*Ausfahrt!* Ha, ha, ha, ha, ha! *Ausfahrt!*' He laughs – but it's a sort of stressed, manic laugh.

A car comes zooming up very close behind us, flashing its lights, and Simon gets even more stressed out. His face goes all red.

'Look at this idiot, driving right up my bottom.'

Simon actually uses a different, much ruder word, but I know I'm supposed to say 'bottom', or 'bum', or 'behind'. (I think the scientific term is 'buttocks'*.) But that's not what Simon said.

Grown-ups can swear as much as they like. Another reason I'd like to be one. I mean, it's not that I *want* to swear all the time, but sometimes a bad word just sort of slips out. Like when you step on a piece of Lego in bare feet, or you bite your cheek when you're eating. And if I was a grown-up, it wouldn't matter. I wouldn't get so anxious worrying about it. I could just enjoy life. If I was a grown-up driving along this *autostrada* right now, I'd be like someone on *Top Gear*, laughing and making jokes and trying to go faster, instead of gripping the door handle so tight my fingers are about to drop off.

---

* In America they call it a 'butt'.

Anyway, if the word for bottom that Simon used was bad, you should hear some of the other words he's using. From now on I'd better bleep him out like a rapper on Radio 1.

'All right, all right,' he says to the car behind us, and swerves over into the slow lane. 'Jesus. Look at that bleep-bleep go. There's going to be the most god-awful pile-up. Oh, bloody Nora. What's up with this idiot, now . . .?'

I think 'bloody Nora' is a type of old-fashioned swearing. I don't know whether to bleep it or not. Simon said it because we're now stuck behind a little grey car that's going really slowly.

I can see the two people sitting in the front waving their hands about as they talk to each other. I'm not sure which one of them is actually driving because they drive on the wrong side here, but neither of them seems to be looking at the road or holding on to a steering wheel.

'They have only two speeds in Italy,' Simon says. 'Too fast and too slow.'

And then he swerves out into the fast lane to get past the grey car. There's the PAAAAARP of a horn and he swerves quickly back again as a big, shiny black car speeds past us.

'Bloody hell,' he says. 'That bleep-bleep-bleep came up so bleeping fast I never even saw him.'

Emma's sitting in the back. not really paying attention. When she got in the car at Brindisi Airport, she put her earbuds in and said, 'I just want to finish my audiobook. It's got to a really exciting bit.' After that she hasn't really seemed to notice anything that's been going on. She did laugh when we nearly hit the other car, but I think that was because there was a funny bit in her book, not because we nearly died in a screaming inferno of twisted metal and severed limbs.

Apart from the nearly crashes, the motorway (sorry, *autostrada*) is not really that interesting. There's not much to look at except swerving cars and trees. As well as palm trees, there are lots of other ones with silvery leaves and twisted trunks. Simon tells me they're olive trees, where olive oil comes from.

'They squeeze them like grapes,' he says. 'And the juice is oil. Amazing, really, when you think about it.'

There are bushes along the middle of the motorway (*autostrada*) covered in pink and red and white flowers. Simon says they are oleander bushes.

'All parts of the oleander plant are deadly poisonous.'

Simon really does like to explain things. Especially plants.

'That's an umbrella pine . . . That's a Norfolk Island pine . . . That's a date palm . . . Those are eucalyptus . . . Oh, look, a dead dog.'

Eventually we turn off the motorway (I won't say *autostrada* again) on to another busy road, and me and Simon relax a little. And then, after a while, we get on to a smaller road and we relax more, and soon I can see the sea.

Simon shouts out, 'Look! There's the sea!' even though I'd already seen it, as I said.

It looks warm, not like the grey sea they have in Wales. It's bright blue and all sparkly. I wish we were on the beach already and I could go for a swim. I feel really uncomfortable and sweaty, my jeans feel tight and my pants are stuck up my bottom*.

We pass a lorry parked by the side of the road selling watermelons and Simon stops suddenly.

'We have got to get one of those bad boys!' he says, jumping out of the car.

Me and Emma wait for him. He has a lively conversation with the farmer selling the melons. Simon is laughing a lot. The farmer looks slightly confused. I think Simon's speaking English. Simon pays him and brings the biggest melon ever back to the car and sits it on the back seat next to Emma.

We carry on. The road to Felix's house is narrow and full of holes. Bushes on the sides scratch the car as we go past. We pass more olive trees. Hundreds of them. Thousands. All surrounded by low walls.

---

* Or butt.

'Those are dry-stone walls,' says Simon. 'They don't use any mortar or cement. They just pile the rocks on top of each other. It's quite an art.'

Lots of the walls have fallen down.

A funny little tiny shrunken pickup-truck-type thing is coming the other way. There's a big fat man sitting in the cab. He can only just fit in. He looks like a man who's been squeezed into a tin can. The truck only has three wheels and is bumbling along really slowly, making a buzzing sound like a moped.

'That's an Ape,' says Simon (he pronounces it 'appy', like happy). 'It's basically a truck made out of a motorbike. *Ape* means bee. *Vespa* means wasp. You know what a *Vespa* is, don't you, Satan? The famous scooter. Did you know *paparazzi* is an Italian word? It comes from a character in a film who was a photographer . . .'

He carries on like this for a while, telling me about Italian words that we use in English, like *fascist* and *barista* and *prima donna* and *diva* and *bunga bunga*, and then at last he says.

'There it is. There's the house.'

Up ahead is a big square building surrounded by high walls.

'That type of building is called a *masseria*,' Simon explains. 'A sort of old fortified farmhouse. You'll see lots of them round here. The house is called Masseria Opuntia. Opuntia's a type of cactus. The prickly pear.

You can eat the fruit. It's the one you see everywhere round here with the Mickey Mouse ears . . .'

If I wasn't trying to remember everything so I can tell Mum all about it when I get home, I would have stopped listening to Simon a long time ago, like Emma has.

'Oh,' she says, looking up and taking out her earbuds. 'Are we here already? My book's just got to a really exciting bit.'

There are three cars in the dusty parking area outside the house. Simon parks in the shade of an olive tree and we all get out. I see some of the cactuses Simon was talking about growing along one wall. They're taller than me, with thick trunks like tree trunks. They have big round pads growing from them, with smaller round pads growing off them, and smaller ones off them. All covered in nasty spikes.

There's a warm smell of herbs and spices in the air, a bit like curry, and a terrible racket of insects scraping and chirping and clicking away all around us.

'Cicadas,' says Simon. 'Unbelievable that they can make such a deafening noise just by rubbing their wings together . . .'

The car is covered in scratches where the branches scraped it, but Simon rubs one with a wet thumb and it disappears.

'Just lines in the dust,' he says, and then stares at the car, thinking about something. I wonder if he's all right. Finally he swallows, sighs, turns to me and smiles.

'There's a metaphor for life if you need one,' he says. ' "Lines in the dust".' And he wipes away another one.

'Ooh, profound,' I say without thinking, and Simon stares at me like I just kicked him in his delicate parts.

I never meant to say it out loud, but I'm so exhausted I don't know what I'm thinking or doing. And now I've said it right to Simon's face. He's staring at me and looks like he might burst into tears. And then he cracks up and starts laughing so much I think he's going to be sick.

'Nice one!' He slaps me on the back. 'Come on, Satan,' he says. 'I need a drink. You grab the watermelon.'

Relieved, I strap my bag on my back and pick up the melon. It's really heavy and awkward to carry.

There's a high wall along one side of the parking area with a wooden gate in it leading to the house. Up till now I've been in a bit of a bubble – today's been totally unreal, but I know that once I go through the gate there will be people I'll have to talk to. People I don't know. Grown-ups. Teenagers.

I wish my mum was here. But not Dad. Dad would say something like, 'Go on, lad, don't be so shy, say hello . . . You have to man up!' Which would only make things worse.

I take a deep breath. Come on. How bad can it be? Maybe I can slip in unnoticed. There's no reason why everyone would stare at me.

I count to ten in my mind, take another big breath and follow Simon and Emma through the gate . . .

Carrying a giant watermelon.

Reason 4: Meeting strangers

There's a big courtyard on the other side of the wall and I can see now that there's not just one house, there's two, facing each other across the yard, and a third building at the far end that looks like a sort of outdoors room, with a vine growing over it as a roof. There's a long table under the vine with people sitting round it, chatting away to each other and eating.

Oh, bleep.

They look like a gang. My tummy does a somersault. I want to go back out through the gate. Go home. I keep my head down and pray that none of them will try to talk to me. If I'm lucky, they won't even notice me and

I can just sort of go and hide in the corner somewhere. Maybe stay there for the whole holiday. They'll never even know I'm here. I could steal food at night when they've all gone to sleep.

Simon holds up his arms and calls out, 'We have arrived!'

Everyone looks round. Some of them shout. Some of them get up from the table as Simon and Emma walk towards them. I've got no choice but to follow with my melon.

'That flight's a killer,' Simon yells. 'I'll need a second holiday to get over it. Someone pour me a small medicinal glass of *vino*. Actually, make it a big one. Actually, make it a bottle. I need a transfusion.'

'It's so lovely to be here,' says Emma, but I'm not sure anyone else hears her as Simon's still shouting about wine.

I'll have to describe the other people later, when I've made sense of them all. At the moment they're just a mass, everyone talking at once. I keep my head down, not really looking at them, trying to look inconspicuous, which is difficult when you're holding a humongous watermelon. I'm terrified I'm going to drop it and make a fool of myself.

As long as nobody tries to talk to me, I'll be all right.

And then Mrs Harper, Felix's mum, spots me.

'Everyone! This is Stan, Felix's best friend.'

'Actually,' shouts Simon, 'his name's Satan!'

I look up. Try to smile. Everyone says hi, except for Felix, who's looking at his phone. Mrs Harper makes a face at him. 'Come and say hello to your friend,' she says.

Felix puts down his phone and comes over. 'Hi,' he says. Felix is like me, only not so skinny, a bit better-looking and with better clothes. He also has a 'cool' haircut, like a footballer. Actually, I can't tell if it makes him look cool or if it makes him look like a codfish. (I don't mean it literally makes him look like a cod. Or any kind of fish. Codfish is an old-fashioned insult. The word I really want to use is rude and I'd need to bleep it. Instead, I'm going to try using old-fashioned insults so that I won't get told off. I could have called him a ninnyhammer, a fribble, a nincompoop or a fopdoodle.)

Felix is totally relaxed. Tanned. With a swimming towel wrapped round his waist. Everything is so much easier for him. He's used to being here. He knows all these people. He's had a good night's sleep. He's chilled.

And he's not carrying the world's biggest watermelon.

'What should I do with this?' I mumble.

'Oh, that's fantastic,' says Mrs Harper. 'Can you take it to the kitchen for me, lovely?'

She points to an open door in one of the houses and I set off towards it, relieved to be getting away from the people. Maybe I can wait in the kitchen for a while when I get there. Recharge my bravery batteries a little bit.

'You'll see where to put it,' Mrs Harper calls after me as I trudge on, convinced that the melon's going to slip through my sweaty hands at any moment and everyone will laugh.

How? How will I know where to put it? I've never put a watermelon anywhere before. We never have melons at home – we're not a melon family. Will they have a special melon rack?

But when I go into the kitchen it's obvious where to put it because there are already three watermelons in here, sitting on a counter. One of them with a bit cut off the end. I plonk my one down next to them and wait a moment. It's cool in here and dark after being outside. I'm alone. I can pretend I don't have to deal with anyone else. You're probably thinking exactly what my dad says to me all the time.

Stop being so bloody shy and get on with it.

But that's like saying to someone 'stop being so bloody tall' or 'stop being so bloody Welsh'. I can't change how I am, and it's not like I chose to be like this.

I'm beginning to wonder whether being kidnapped might not be a better deal. If I was kidnapped, they'd put a bag over my head and hide me in a hut somewhere where I wouldn't have to talk to anyone.

All right. That's just stupid. I know it's stupid. Being kidnapped would *not* be better than this. It would be properly horrible.

You're a total wet blanket, Stan. How did I end up with a son like you?

I try to ignore the Dad voice in my head, take a deep breath and go back outside.

I'm a bit blinded by the light and I trip over a step, but I don't think anyone notices. When I get back to the table, I have a quick look at everyone. There are several adults and a few kids, including three girls. This must be Felix's big sister, Alice, and her friends. They all look the same to me, with long, straight hair, shiny lipstick and eyebrows that look like they've been painted on with one of those machines that paints lines on the road, only with black instead of white.

They're scary.

'Show Stan where he's sleeping, Felix,' says Mrs Harper.

Felix shrugs and grunts and walks off. Good. Saved again. I don't have to join in with everyone at the table.

I follow him to the other building. We go through a tall door straight into a bedroom. There are piles of clothes everywhere, spilling out of half-unpacked suitcases like the contents of a bin after the foxes have been at it.

'This is where the girls are sleeping,' says Felix.

As well as the clothes, the room is full of brushes and combs and hairdryers and make-up and towels and bikinis and shoes and magazines all muddled up together. There are also pieces of equipment – I don't know what most of them are for. They look quite complicated and a bit scary, like torture devices, but I assume they must be to do with make-up and hair.

'That's the loo and shower in there,' says Felix, pointing to a door. 'The lock doesn't work properly, so be careful.'

I don't like the sound of that, but before I can say anything Felix is climbing some stairs that run up one side of the bedroom.

'We're sleeping upstairs on the mezzanine,' he says.

I say OK as if I know what he's talking about.

I imagine that upstairs will be a different room, but it's not. The stairs go up to a sort of half-floor with two beds, a cupboard and a small window with shutters. The area round one of the beds is covered with a worse version of the mess downstairs – shorts, T-shirts, socks and pants mixed up with headphones, leads, plug adapters, chargers, a Nintendo Switch, empty soda bottles and a pizza box with a half-eaten pizza in it.

The other bed is neatly made with white sheets and there's a little table next to it with a lamp on it.

'That's yours,' says Felix.

I put down my bag and sit on the bed. I think I ought to say something.

'It's cool here,' I say. 'Thanks for inviting me.'

'S'OK.'

'Have you been having a good time?'

Felix shrugs again. 'S'OK. It rained the other day.'

'Yeah?'

'Yeah.'

This is one of the longest conversations we've ever had.

I glance out of the window, which looks down onto a garden behind the building. I can see the pool, bright blue, with an inflatable in the shape of an ice lolly floating on it. There's a diving board at one end of the pool and sunbeds all round it.

'Nice pool,' I say.

'There was a frog in it the other day when it rained.'

'Yeah?'

'Yeah.'

Felix stands there for a while with nothing more to say and then starts back down the stairs.

'It's sort of lunchtime,' he says as he goes.

I quickly unpack my bag and put my things in the cupboard, which doesn't have anything else in it. It doesn't take me long. I don't have nearly as much stuff as Felix, but when I'm finished I'm really hot and sweaty, particularly as I'm wearing two pairs of trousers. I've got really skinny legs and if you wear two pairs of trousers they don't look so thin. Mum tried to get me to wear only one pair this morning.

'After all, Stan, once you're there you'll be in shorts or swimmers all the time, and everyone will get a good look at your spaghetti legs.'

It sucks being a boy. If I was a man, I'd have proper big legs to stomp around on.

I look out of the window again. All I want to do is jump in the pool and cool off, but I know I'll have to go and have some lunch first.

I'll have to eat. In front of strange people.

All I can think is 'bleep'. Or maybe 'bleep-bleep-bleep'.

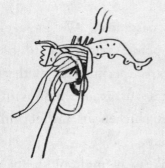

Reason 5: Weird food

You remember my emergency list? The first thing on it . . .

What to do if offered weird food.

Well. Next to talking to strange people this is probably my second worst fear. I don't like to eat at other people's houses. I like my mum's cooking. She knows what I like. We eat the same thing all the time. I take the same packed lunch to school every day. A ham sandwich, some carrot sticks, a Babybel cheese or a cheese straw, an apple and a biscuit or a bag of crisps. I don't always eat the apple. And then for dinner I always know what I'm going to have . . .

STAN'S DAILY MENU

Monday is leftovers day (I'll come back to that in a minute).

Tuesday is pasta day. We have either spaghetti bolognese or penne with tomato sauce. Although recently I've been experimenting with tuna and cheese.

Wednesday is sausage and mash with beans.

Thursday is chicken in breadcrumbs, with oven chips and ketchup.

Friday is takeaway night. Usually pizza, but I've been experimenting with curries. Chicken tikka and chicken tikka masala with plain rice are OK. Some Chinese is all right. I like prawn crackers. The best takeaway is pizza, though. Or fish and chips. Dad drives to the shops and picks up the food and we all eat together watching the TV. I like takeaway night. I get to spend a bit of time with Dad. And drink Coke.

Saturday is pie day. Which means shepherd's pie with beans. So I suppose I could just call it shepherd's pie day, although sometimes Mum makes it with beef mince and sometimes she makes it with lamb mince: 'For a bit of variety.' Dad says that technically, if you use beef mince, it's called cottage pie. 'You don't see a shepherd herding cows, do you?' As I've never seen a shepherd in my whole life, herding cows or sheep or doing anything at all, this is not really a question I can answer. And it tastes the same whether you use lamb or beef anyway.

Sunday is Sunday roast day. Which usually means roast chicken with roast potatoes and carrot sticks. I've been experimenting with peas. I haven't been getting on that well with them, to tell you the truth, but I've been sticking with it because I know it makes Mum happy.

And then we're back to Monday, which is leftovers day, as I said before, but now I hope you'll understand what I mean (it was probably quite obvious actually*).

The only time when things change is when it's a special occasion, like Christmas or Easter, or if it's someone's birthday.

If it's *my* birthday we have pizza.

And cake, of course.

So I hope you understand why I'm nervous about having lunch here. I bet it'll be weird stuff. I've only been to Felix's house in England one time. To play the new FIFA game on his Xbox last year when it first came out and we only had crisps to eat, not a proper meal. But Felix's family is posher than mine, so they probably eat posh food. There will probably be salad involved.

---

* In case it's not obvious, we eat the leftovers from Sunday. If there aren't any leftovers we have pizza from the freezer.

Today's a Saturday. We would be having shepherd's pie at home. I miss the shepherd's pie and I miss Mum and Dad, and I'm so tired I want to cry.

But I don't.

If Felix knows I've been crying, he'll never let me forget it. Me or anyone else. Felix can be a bit of a bully like that.

So I've got Dad in my left ear going, 'Stop being so shy, you great drip.'

I've got Felix in the other ear going, 'Ha, ha, Stan's a crybaby. Scared of food.'

And I've got Mum in my other ear (my final front ear?) going, 'You must be polite, Stan. Be nice to Mrs Harper and eat properly and don't mumble.'

I have to get this over with.

I take a deep breath, go back outside and over to the table under the vine, my heart beating out a loud, doomy drumbeat, like a man walking to a firing squad.

On spaghetti legs.

When I get there, I do a quick scan of the food and my heart rate slows.

It's OK! It's not too weird at all.

I mean, there are some sort of vegetable things and tomatoes, but there's also bread and cheese and ham. Some of the ham is ordinary pink ham, but some of it is dark red and doesn't look cooked. I think I'll give the weird red ham a miss.

'We're just having a light lunch,' says Mrs Harper. 'Go on, help yourself, Stan.'

I sit down. Phew. I can choose what I eat. Which means bread and cheese and pink ham.

As I eat, I try to make sense of all the people. There are the three girls down the other end of the table, giggling among themselves and sharing things on their phones. Felix's sister, Alice, is originally from China. He told me that she was adopted as a baby. She's very pretty. Her friends are too. There's a much younger girl sitting with them wearing a really wide blue hat. She looks about eight years old and she's listening very closely to every word the older girls say and laughing a lot.

Up at my end of the table are Felix, Mrs Harper and a bald man I think must be Mr Harper. He's reading a magazine and not really talking to anyone. I wish I could do that. Then there's Simon and Emma. Emma keeps saying how lovely the food is. Simon's going round the table filling everyone's wine glass. He's carrying his own glass with him and drinking from it as he goes. Every time he fills someone else's glass he refills his own. He's very loud and jolly.

Then there's a thin woman sitting next to a young black man. I think he's her boyfriend because she keeps taking food off his plate and eating it. When she does it, he pretends to be cross and slaps her hand, and then she kisses him or squeezes his leg.

Next to him is an Asian man wearing sunglasses.

There are two other women. One looks a bit like my mum and the other looks quite angry. She's wearing angry sunglasses with sharp edges and an angry dress with stripes.

I hope I learn everybody's names by the end of the holiday, and who they all are and how they fit together.

When Simon gets to me with the bottle, he asks me if I want a splash of wine. I say, 'No thank you,' but I say it so quietly I worry that he didn't hear me. Mrs Harper tells him off.

'We mustn't corrupt the poor boy,' she says. 'He's only twelve.'

'Satan's a film buff,' says Simon, making sure everybody can hear him. 'He told me the whole plot of some film about space raccoons on the way here. What was it called again, Satan?'

'*Guardians of the Galaxy 2.*'

'Oh, I love that movie,' says the black guy. 'So funny.'

'Satan wouldn't shut up about it,' says Simon, taking a gulp of wine. 'Kept going on and on until he'd told me the entire plot. I think his description of it was longer than the actual film!'

Some people laugh. I don't say anything. I don't tell anyone that Simon fell asleep and I had to talk to him to stop us all from dying. I'm more hungry than I realized and am concentrating on eating. The bread is a bit hard and chewy but tastes all right, the ordinary pink ham is good, and I found a bit of cheese that looked almost like normal English cheese so I'm doing OK. I'm even allowed a glass of Coke. There's watermelon for afters. I try a bit. It's OK. It tastes of watermelon flavour, which I've only ever had in sweets before.

The meal goes on forever, the adults all sit around drinking wine and chatting about stuff, and even though the older girls go off with the younger girl I don't know if it's polite to get down from the table. Felix is playing on his phone and ignoring me.

I start to feel tireder and tireder and think that a swim might wake me up and make me feel better. But my brain's mushy. Nothing feels real. Was I really at home this morning? Everything that's happened today has been a stress and a strain. Waking up too early, hanging around the freaky upside-down airport world, the scary flight, driving in Italy with Simon as he swerved all over the road, meeting new people, having lunch . . .

But I've done it! I'm doing OK. I've managed not to talk to anyone. I've survived lunch.

Maybe I can do this.

Maybe I can have a holiday.

Reason 6: Weird toilets

I am having a cold shower. I've read in books that's what people do to wake themselves up and clear their heads. I've jammed a chair up against the shower door so nobody can open it, but I'm still rather nervous, probably because I've had a bit of a shock.

What happened is this.

I woke up in my bed on the mezzanine feeling crap. I was really thirsty and sweaty and couldn't remember going to bed last night, but I'd been so wiped out that my mind was blank. I hadn't even undressed and my clothes were all stuck to me. I looked at my watch. It was five past eight. I didn't know what time other people would be getting up and what to do about eating breakfast.

I looked over at Felix's bed. It was empty and just as much of a mess as before. So he was already up.

I thought I'd better change my clothes so I put on a clean T-shirt. I kept my two pairs of trousers on (I wasn't ready to show my legs yet) and went downstairs. The girls were up already. I needed a wee and went to the bathroom, but when I opened the door there was a shriek. One of the girls was in there having a shower. She swore at me. I apologized.

I didn't see anything.

I really didn't.

But I wanted to die. I'd only been here a day and already I'd walked in on a girl in the shower.

I hurried outside and found people laying plates at the big table. It looked like we were all going to have breakfast together.

Mrs Harper came out of the kitchen carrying a big pan. 'Oh, you're up at last,' she said. 'Did you have a good sleep?'

I said yes, but really I didn't know. I'd certainly had a *long* sleep, but it was a bit rubbish. I didn't want to tell her I was feeling crap and sweaty and confused etc. etc. etc. That would be rude.

'Would you like a glass of water or something? Juice? A Coke maybe?'

A Coke for breakfast? I was sorely tempted (as Dad would say) but would have felt too guilty. I'd promised Mum not to drink too much Coke. And . . . *Coke for breakfast!* It was just wrong. I remembered the mad people at the airport, shopping and drinking beer and eating burgers and wearing flip-flops in the middle of the night. Holidays did strange things to people. The rules changed.

I said that some juice would be nice, hoping they didn't have some weird juice with lumps in it made out of special Italian fruits I'd never heard of. Or even juice made out of vegetables. I'd been to popular Archie's house one time (never again) and they'd had juice made out of carrots and other stupid things. The juice Mrs Harper brought me was bright red. I asked her if it was all right and she laughed.

She said it was blood orange, as if it was the most normal thing in the world and I'd know what she was talking about. Everybody was looking at me and I wondered if they were all in on the joke. *Ha, ha, blood orange – and he DRANK it! The poor fool. Now he's ONE OF US . . .*

I carefully took a sip. It tasted like normal orange. If it was a joke, there was no punchline. And nobody looked at me and nobody laughed.

The girl from the shower came out of our building. It was Alice, Felix's sister. The Chinese one.

'We have to get a new lock on that bathroom door,' she said, sitting down. 'I don't want Felix's pervy little friend crashing in on me all the time.'

'It was an accident,' I mumbled. 'I didn't know you were in there.'

'Yeah, *right*.'

It *was* an accident! If I hadn't been so tired and confused, I would have knocked. I stared at the table. I knew I was blushing. They all thought I was a pervert now. *Nice going, Stan. You've really got off to a good start.*

Luckily, before anyone could say anything, Mrs Harper brought out a basket of bread.

'Have some now if you want,' she said. 'I know how hungry you boys get.'

Phew. Nothing about me being a pervert.

I took some bread and chewed a bit off. There were knives and forks laid, so I thought it must be a cooked breakfast, what Dad calls 'a full English', which we sometimes have on Sundays. But it turned out to be a full Italian.

First Simon opened a bottle of wine. OK. I guess if you can have Coke for breakfast, you can have wine. As I say, people do things differently on holiday.

And I was getting the idea in my head that Simon probably drank wine all the time. Even at breakfast. And even when he wasn't on holiday.

When Mrs Harper took the lid off the big pan, I thought it was going to be porridge. I'm OK with porridge, if it's got sugar in it, but the next thing she said really freaked me out.

'Who's for soup?'

This was off the screwy scale. The thing I'd been most frightened about was happening – weird food. *Totally* weird.

Coke for breakfast.

Wine for breakfast.

And now *soup for breakfast* . . .

Mrs Harper ladled out a bowl. It looked like tomato soup, which I at least quite like and so I decided to be brave. I didn't want them all to think I was some sort of pathetic loser. Even though that's what I am.

'Stan? Soup?'

'Please.'

Everybody started eating their soup, but when I took a spoonful and blew on it one of the girls laughed at me. I didn't know why until I put the spoon in my mouth and it was cold. I don't mean the spoon. I mean the soup.

Was this all a big joke? Had they been plotting this together? Was the whole thing a setup? Let's really freak Stan out at breakfast and pretend we're all mad.

Or was this some kind of special breakfast soup that posh people had? I had to 'man up', as Dad would say. 'It's just soup, for god's sake!'

I swallowed a mouthful of the cold soup, which tasted of lots of things, not just tomatoes. I didn't want to think about what the other things might be. Then I looked down at my bowl. There was an ice cube in it.

'It's all right,' said Simon, pouring himself a second glass of wine. 'It's meant to be cold. It's gazpacho. A type of cold Spanish soup.'

I nodded, as if I already knew that. There was a weird atmosphere. The sky was dim, as if the sun hadn't been up for long. I stared at the soup. I had to eat cold soup that should be hot. I was groggy and grumpy. I was a perv.

I wanted my life to end.

'Don't eat it if you don't want,' said Mrs Harper. 'There's plenty more to come. I'm sure you like pasta.'

I do. I *do* like pasta. Everybody likes pasta. *But not for bleeping breakfast!*

After that the meal just got madder and madder. I had pasta with tomato sauce (I chose that rather than the pasta with prawns in it). The adults were all drinking wine and beer. There was salad. The sky got slowly darker. Someone lit some candles. I checked my watch again. It was after nine o'clock . . .

And then I got it.

You idiot!

I let out a snort of laughter. Felix looked at me.

I wasn't going mad. This wasn't a prank. It was *nine o'clock at night*. They weren't eating breakfast. They were eating *dinner*. I hadn't slept through the rest of the day and all the night. I must have fallen asleep on my bed after lunch and woken up in the evening!

It was such a relief that I actually ate some salad.

A Conversation with Mum

1

'You should have called me as soon as you landed, Stan. I've been frantic with worry.'

'If the plane had crashed, you'd have heard about it, Mum.'

'Don't say that. You'll jinx it.'

'How? I've already landed. I'm safe. It can't crash now. I've been here for hours.'

'Exactly. That's what I'm saying. You should have called me sooner.'

'I fell asleep.'

'Oh . . . Are you all right, Stan?'

'I'm fine. I was just tired from getting up so early and, you know, the travel and things.'

'Have you put mosquito repellent on? You don't want to be bitten.'

'I'm fine. I've not been bitten.'

'I've been frantic with worry.'

'I know, you said.'

'We shouldn't talk too long, Stan. This call must be costing a fortune.'

'Then don't keep saying the same thing, Mum.'

'Oh, Stan, don't be mean to me, I've been frantic with worry.'

'So why didn't you call me?'

'Because if you didn't answer I'd think something terrible had happened.'

'Nothing terrible has happened.'

'I love you, darling.'

'I love you too, Mum.'

'What?'

'I love you.'

'Why are you speaking so quietly?'

'In case someone hears me.'

'Oh, Stan . . .'

'I'm fine.'

'I love you.'

'I know, Mum. You said . . . I ate some salad.'

'Oh, well done, Stan. Well done. You good boy.'

'Yeah . . . Goodnight then.'

'Goodnight, darling . . .'

'Goodnight, Mum.'

'Goodnight, sleep tight. Your dad's in hospital by the way.'

'Yeah, goodnight – wait! What?'

'I didn't want to spoil your holiday. He's fine. I wasn't going to say anything.'

'What? Is he really all right?'

'He's fine. He sort of collapsed. But he's fine. He's sort of un-collapsed now. Ha, ha, ha!'

'Will he be in hospital long?'

'They're going to do some tests, and then, when they say he's all right, he'll come home. It's nothing serious. You mustn't worry.'

'But . . .'

'Really, Stan. He's fine. As I say, I wasn't even going to tell you.'

'OK . . . if you're sure.'

'I'm sure.'

'I love you, Mum.'

'I love you too, Stan . . . You will put on some mozzy stuff, won't you?'

'Yes . . .'

Reason 7: Being
beach body ready

It's the next day (this time it really *is* the next day). I didn't sleep well last night. It was too hot and I was covered in so much mosquito repellent I smelt like I'd been in a chemical attack and it was making my eyes sting. It was a total waste of time anyway, because I missed a bit. I feel like Achilles when his mother dipped him in the River Styx to make him invulnerable (I know about Achilles from the book of Greek myths I've brought to read on holiday). She didn't get his ankle wet, because that's where she was holding him, and so that's where his weak spot was.

With me it was my ear. *Inside* my ear. I didn't put any repellent inside my ear.

I don't know how the mosquito got in there without me hearing it buzzing. It must have sneaked up on me. Maybe it landed on the back of my head and crawled round through my hair, like a jungle fighter. The sneaky little git.

I only heard it when it flew off, laughing triumphantly (or at least that's what it sounded like – a tiny mwah-ha-ha-haaaa). It had got right inside my ear to suck my blood. I now have a terrible itch in there, and, even though I know you're not supposed to stick your finger in your ear (Dad always says, 'Never stick anything smaller than your elbow in your ear' – though I've seen him poking about with a cotton bud when nobody's looking), I just have to scratch it.

It doesn't really help.

I hate mosquitoes.

OK. Confession time. The real reason I didn't sleep well was that I was thinking about Dad. I kept trying *not* to think about him, and then I'd get worried that it was wrong not to think about him, like I didn't care. I even cried a little bit. When I was sure Felix was asleep.

I know what Dad would say: 'Stop making such a fuss, Stan. Boys don't cry.' But I saw him cry one time.

It was when Mum had to go into hospital to have a lump removed from her breast. He was in the living room at night. I saw him from the doorway. I didn't go in. Actually, thinking about it, I've seen him cry *loads* of times. We used to watch Disney films together when I was smaller – *The Jungle Book* and *The Lion King* and *Dumbo*. He always cried at them, and tried to hide it.

And now *he's* in hospital and I don't know what I should think. Mum was fine when she came out after her operation. The doctors said the lump was benign ('Rhymes with fine,' Dad said), which means 'not evil'. I hope Dad's had a benign collapse.

So, anyway, I woke up feeling tired and irritable and anxious, but at least breakfast was normal. No wine, no soup, no candles. I had cereal called Miel Pops, which is an Italian version of Honey Loops. And now we're at the beach and I can mostly forget about my itching ear.

The sea is very flat. I prefer a sea with waves. It's more fun: there's something to do – you can jump over the waves or duck under them, or let them wash you along, like surfing. But with a flat sea there isn't much to do, really, except stand and talk. Which is what the Italians are doing. The sea is full of them, all talking away to each other, arguing and waving their arms about, but in a friendly way. They're mostly standing up to their waists, but some of them are batting balls to each other with wooden bats as they talk. The whole beach is a babble of noise. I don't know what they're talking about because I don't speak Italian. Mum taught me only one phrase: '*Mi sono perso. Per favore, puoi portarmi in una stazione di polizia?*' Which means: 'I am lost. Please can you take me to a police station?' At least I hope that's what it means. She got it from Google Translate so it might be wrong. For all I know it could say, 'I'm a murderer – please have me arrested.'

Not all the Italians are standing talking in the shallow water. Further out I can see an old lady swimming up and down and a man with a snorkel and flippers and a speargun who has a colourful floaty ball thing tied to his ankle bobbing along behind him. I suppose it's to warn speedboats not to drive into him. There are lots of speedboats going up and down like the old lady, but much faster. One is pulling along a sort of a parachute that takes people up in the air and flies them around a bit. Halfway round it slows down and dips them in the ocean before speeding up again. You can just hear their shrieks as their feet go in the water.

Simon says it's called parasailing.

I imagine what Dad would say . . .

'*What kind of an idiot would go up in a thing like that? It's asking for trouble. And they probably charge you about a hundred euros for five minutes in the air.*'

And I know *exactly* what Mum would say.

'Promise me you'll never do that. It looks far too dangerous.'

Yeah, well, don't worry. There is no way I am going parasailing. Imagine it! Stuck up there in the sky like a kid's party balloon. All those people looking at you. I've already explained that I never want to do anything that involves using a parachute. Especially a weird one that takes you up instead of helping you come down.

Another speedboat is pulling along a big inflatable banana that you sit on. The Italians on the banana are also all talking to each other. It looks quite fun. I ask Felix what it's called.

'A banana,' he says, and goes back to playing on his phone.

The Italians look very happy and tanned. The men wear small tight trunks and the older the men are, the smaller their trunks are, and the browner their skins. The ladies, young and old, wear bikinis. They don't mind what they look like, which is cool.

The beach is covered in sunbeds under umbrellas – millions of them – full of Italians chatting away and eating fancy food out of cold boxes.

I think they can tell that we are English. We are eating crisps, and only Felix and the girls have suntans. Plus we're all crammed on to four sunbeds to save money. I think our group, who are quite posh mostly, could afford more beds and umbrellas, but Mr Harper said they didn't want to be ripped off.

'The kids can lie on the sand.'

Mr Harper has a sunbed to himself. He's reading a magazine and listening to music on headphones.

Everyone from the house came to the beach except for Ash, the Asian man. He likes to sit in the shade and look at the news on his computer. Ash does something in IT. He has two phones (maybe three), an Apple watch, a Fitbit, a laptop that sort of works by magic when he waves his hands over it, an iPad Pro with a 5.6 million pixel, 12.9-inch screen (I know this because he has told at least five people), his own personal Bluetooth speakers, a mini drone, a GoPro, and something he calls a Gizmoid, which has flashing lights. Nobody knows what the Gizmoid does, but Ash is very proud of it.

I should be sitting in the shade as well, really. Mum told me before I left that I had to put on the highest factor sun cream I could. I brought a bottle of factor fifty with me, but it was confiscated at the airport. They said I was only allowed a 10ml bottle in my hand luggage. I think the bottle Mum gave me was about ten pints.

It's fun to be on the beach, but I am now faced with a major problem.

I'm still wearing two pairs of trousers. Jeans and tracksuit bottoms. Well, actually, it's three, I suppose, as I have my swimming shorts on underneath. I really want to go for a swim, but I don't want anyone to see my spaghetti legs.

I wonder if I could quickly strip my trousers off and run into the sea before anyone got the chance to study me properly. If I ran fast enough, my legs would be a blur and I could wade out until the water was up to my waist.

I can't spend the rest of the holiday hiding my legs, though, can I? There's only one thing for it.

Man up.

Maybe I could do it in stages. I'll take off the tracksuit bottoms so I've only got my jeans and shorts on. And as long as nobody says, 'Wow, haven't you got skinny legs?' I could go to stage two.

Yes. Do it.

I pull the tracksuit bottoms off and then walk around a bit so people can see me. Nobody says anything. Nobody even looks. Maybe I'm worrying too much.

As I'm thinking about it, Felix comes and sits down next to me in the sand.

'Shall we dig a hole?' he asks.

'Yeah, maybe,' I say. 'In a minute.'

I look over at the thin woman, who's sharing a sunbed with her boyfriend. She's hanging on to him so she won't fall off. The little girl in the big hat is with them.

'Is she their daughter?' I ask Felix.

'Who?'

'The girl in the hat.'

'I don't think she ever takes it off,' says Felix. 'That's Aria. She's Ben's daughter, but not Livia's. Ben's a musician. Livia's an actress. Mum went to college with her. I think she used to be famous. She's Livia Channing. She's in that lame Netflix series.'

'What lame Netflix series?'

'The Harry Potter rip-off thing about teenage magicians.'

'You mean *Strange Academy*?'

'Yeah. Livia plays someone's mother.'

'Right . . . I've not really watched it. We don't have Netflix.'

'Apparently she was in some film as well.'

'What film?'

'Some film about sex. Mum said it was a big thing about ten years ago.'

'Right . . . You mean a sex film?'

'No, just a film with a lot of talk about sex and snogging and that.'

'Gross.'

'Yeah. Gross.'

I lie back in the sand and look up at the sky. It's very blue and there are no clouds, only a thin trail left by a plane. *That was me yesterday*, I think, *up there in the sky. And now I'm here. On the beach. And Felix is being nice to me.*

'Were you wearing two pairs of trousers?'

'Yeah.'

'Why?'

I shrug.

'You're weird.'

Felix starts to dig a hole. Maybe he's right. Maybe I'll attract more attention wearing two pairs of trousers all the time than if I showed my spindly legs. I mean, once I've shown them, that's it.

Another plane goes over and I feel like England and the real world are a million miles away. Dad's a million miles away. I hope he's all right.

'*Of course I'm all right. Now try to enjoy yourself, Stan.*'

I take off my jeans. It feels really good. I won't walk around just yet. One step at a time. I sit there with my arms round my legs and wriggle my toes in the warm sand, feeling really brave.

Dad would be proud of me.

Any minute now I'm going to take my T-shirt off . . .

Reason 8: The sand gets everywhere

'Omigodman, this hole is well big.'

Aria has joined me and Felix to help dig our hole and build a sort of castle. I say 'sort of castle' because it's really just a big pile of sand with some feathers stuck in. But it is quite an impressive pile. I've noticed that nobody else on the beach is making sandcastles or digging holes, and the Italians are giving us funny looks.

Nobody's said anything about my legs, and they're covered in sand now so I think I've got away with it. And I'm sort of enjoying myself.

Aria hopes we'll find some coins if we keep digging, but so far we've only found shells, bottle tops, some random bits of plastic and a few cigarette butts. Aria keeps saying 'Omigodman', though, no matter what we find.

'Omigodman, not another bottle top.'

'Omigodman, a stick.'

'Omigodman, more plastic. We should collect it all up and send it to Greenpeace.'

'Omigodman, what's that? That's disgusting.'

Two young brown Italian women go past in high heels and very tiny bikinis, talking away to each other. Their bikinis are really just bits of coloured string. They stop to look at our hole and our castle. One of them says something and they both laugh. They walk on. I know I'm not supposed to, but I look at them as they walk away. I experience feelings.

'Caught you looking.'

I suddenly go all sweaty and think I must be blushing. Maybe everyone will think it's just sunburn. It was one of Alice's friends who saw me.

'He's such a perv,' says Alice.

Alice's friend comes over and sits next to us, grinning at me. I think she's called Jess. I mumble something that doesn't mean anything and get back to digging.

'It's all right,' she says. 'Everyone's looking.'

I glance round. All the adults are staring at the Italian girls as they walk away.

'Oh god,' says Mrs Harper. 'I feel so fat and old.'

Mrs Harper is wearing a one-piece swimsuit with a long piece of brightly coloured cloth tucked into it to make a sort of dress. She's also wearing a wide straw hat and very big sunglasses that hide most of her face. As far as I can see, she isn't fat and not very old. She's just sort of normal.

'I don't know why we come here,' says the angry-looking woman with the angry sunglasses. 'It's non-stop humiliation. The Italian women are all so gorgeous.'

I've looked at the Italian women around us and most of them are bigger than Mrs Harper and at least half of them are older. The only difference is that the Italian women don't seem to care what anyone thinks. They just walk about quite happily in their bikinis and their sunglasses and their clanking jewellery.

'Can I help you?' says Jess.

I shrug.

Jess smiles and joins in with the digging.

As she digs, I give her these quick little glances, sort of flicking my eyes over and back, but it's still the longest I've dared look at her. And I begin to realize that I might have got her a bit wrong.

First flick: I see that she doesn't look exactly like Alice and her other friend.

Second flick: her hair isn't as straight and she isn't wearing any make-up.

70

Third flick: she's actually younger than the other two and she's not trying to act so grown up.

Fourth flick: I think she's more my age.

Fifth flick: she looks quite nice. I might even be able to talk to her at some point . . .

'Omigodman, treasure!'

Aria has found a coin. She shows it to me with a grin as wide as her hat.

Jess takes it and rubs sand off it. 'It's fifty cents.'

'Is that a lot?'

'It's about 49p.' She gives it back to Aria.

'Omigodman, that's a fortune.'

Aria runs off to show it to her dad, Ben, who gets up off his sunbed and announces that he's taking Aria to get an ice cream.

'She wants to spend her treasure.'

'Fiddy cents,' says Aria, and she starts to sing and dance as she walks. 'It's ma birthday, it's ma birthday . . .'

Jess smiles at me. I try to smile back. I'm not sure it works. I worry that I might look mad.

Felix pushes me into the hole. 'Shall we go for a swim?' he says.

'OK,' I say from the bottom of the hole.

The sand on the beach is burning hot when you get out from the shelter of the umbrellas and we have to sort of hop and skip down to the water, making little noises – *oh, ah, eeh, ow* . . .

The water feels really cold at first, because we're so hot. But as we go in deeper it's not so bad — there's a sort of cold band that rises up my legs as I go deeper and it's OK until it gets to my trunks, when I suddenly feel cold again and experience a shrivelling sensation down below. So I dive under the water to get it over with. Now it actually feels quite warm, halfway between hot and cold, like a bath you've stayed in just a bit too long.

Emma comes swimming past, wearing goggles.

'Oh, the water's so lovely, isn't it?'

I agree politely.

Jess comes to join us and we're not quite sure what to do, so Felix scoops some sand up from the bottom and throws it at me. I throw some back. None of the Italians are throwing sand at each other. Jess joins in. I hit Felix with a handful of wet sand and he acts like he's been shot by a bullet and the sand is blood. He goes 'Aaargh' and falls over dramatically.

When we get bored of throwing sand at each other, we swim around for a bit. Then we float on our backs. I think I might be a slightly better swimmer than Felix, though Jess is better than both of us. Then we get out. I walk over to our camp and look for a dry towel. I find one that's half dry and try to shake the sand off it without flicking it on anyone. Alice still complains, though.

'What are you doing, you perv?' she moans. 'You're getting sand all over me.'

I wish she wouldn't keep calling me that, but what can I do? And she doesn't look like she has any sand on her anyway. I look for somewhere to sit down but Livia, the actress, has spotted me. She pats her sunbed and waves me over. I have no choice. I go to the bed and sit on it, my towel wrapped round me.

'So,' she says. 'You're Ollie, right?'

'Stan.'

'OK. Stan. Tell me all about yourself.'

This is the sort of moment I've been dreading. My brain seizes up. I try to think. I mean, I'm a boy and I'm at school, what is there to tell? I play *Clash Royale* on my phone at home quite a lot, but I doubt she wants to hear about that. She's a famous actress. She'll want to talk about exciting things.

Well, she's picked the wrong person.

All I can think to say is 'um'. And then I shrug.

Livia laughs. 'Is that it?'

I say 'um' again.

'Come on. I need to know all about you.' She leans very close and stares into my eyes. I want to look away but I can't. I feel hypnotized. Plus, I've got some sand down my trunks and I'm getting really itchy.

'Do you have a girlfriend?' she says.

'I go to school with Felix,' I blurt out very quickly.

'I didn't ask you that. I asked if you're seeing anyone.'

'Um. Yes. Sort of. No. Not really.'

'What does that mean? "Yes. Sort of. No. Not really." '

I don't know what it means. I haven't thought about this before. I know some girls, but they're not really interested in me. There's one called Mel at school who I sort of quite like more than the others, but I've never talked to her. Not properly.

Livia's still leaning in very close. It's scary. If I wasn't protected by the towel, my skin would be touching hers. This is an absolute nightmare. I look to Felix for help, but he's sitting on the sand chatting to Jess. He hasn't used a towel and the sand's stuck to him so he looks like a giant piece of KFC.

Livia hasn't given up questioning me.

'Do you have a girlfriend, or not really?' she asks.

'I have a friend who's a girl,' I reply. 'Does that count? She's called Mel.'

'Ah, now we're getting somewhere,' she says. 'You snog, yeah? I used to snog all the time. I'm very good at it.'

I *really* want to get back to digging that hole.

'Mel's just my friend,' I say.

'But you're a boy. All boys ever want to do is snog girls.'

This is even more embarrassing than when Dad tried to tell me about sex. Although actually there was one time when I had stomach pains and I had to do some tests for the hospital and had to do a poo into a paper cup. Then Mum had to take a sample with a stick and put it in a little plastic capsule.

Everything about that was awkward.

And there was one time I had a problem with my willy.

But we won't go into that . . .

To distract myself I start making a list in my head.

THE 10 MOST EMBARRASSING THINGS THAT HAVE EVER HAPPENED TO ME

1. This conversation.
2. Dad trying to tell me about sex.
3. Pooing into a paper cup.
4. Weeing myself in primary school.
5. The time when I got lost and I found a policeman and I was so nervous I couldn't remember my own name and then a giant snot bubble came out of my nose.
6. The time Mum sent me to a fancy-dress party dressed as a postbox because she'd forgotten to sort out a proper costume. (I was wrapped head to foot in red material with a strip of black tape across my mouth. I couldn't use my hands or speak.)
7. That thing with my willy.
8. . . .

I don't get to 8 because Livia interrupts me. She's not going to give up – 'This sort of girlfriend-not-girlfriend-who's-just-sort-of-a-friend, this *Mel* girl?' she says. 'Is she named after one of the Spice Girls?'

'What?'

'There were two Mels in the Spice Girls.'

'What's the Spice Girls?' I say. 'Is it a film?'

'What's the Spice Girls?' Livia looks horrified. '*What's the Spice Girls?* Oh god, are you going out of your way to make me feel ancient?'

Why do grown-ups always complain about being old? It sucks being young. When you're old, you don't have to worry about anything. You don't have to go to school any more, you can get a job and earn money and spend it on whatever you like, you can go to bed as late as you want, you can eat whatever you want, and you can drive a car and everything.

'Oh, fleeting fame,' says Livia. 'The Spice Girls were the biggest girl band of all time. They were massive in the nineties. Girl power.'

'I'm not really into pop music.'

'Did your mum never play you their songs?'

'She quite likes Abba.'

'You don't say.'

'I've heard of Little Mix.'

'Who are Little Mix? They sound like a type of sweet. Or leprechauns. Are they leprechauns?'

'No, they're a girl band. They were on *X Factor*.'

'Right. Forget Little Mix. You've seen *Strange Academy*, of course.'

'Yeah. Well. Um . . .'

'Isn't it great?'

'Um.'

'Hey, everybody!' Livia shouts. 'Ollie's my biggest fan. He thinks I'm the coolest because I'm in *Strange Academy*. I like Ollie.'

'I'm called Stan.'

'I like you, Stan. I'm going to find you a girlfriend.'

'OK. Um. Right . . . Thank you.'

Simon comes back from the beach cafe with some bottles of beer.

'Who's for a cold one?'

I use the distraction to make my escape. I jump up and go over to our hole and sit in it.

'I'll bury you,' says Felix.

'OK.'

We rearrange the hole so that I can sit in it, and Felix and Jess pile the sand on me from our castle. When only my head is showing, Felix starts to shape the pile of sand, covering me into the shape of a person, as if it's my head on a new body. He makes the shape of a woman with boobs and everything. He's really concentrating and working hard. He decorates the body with stones and shells and bits of plastic and seaweed. I don't mind being buried, actually, because it means nobody can see my skinny body.

'Nice one,' says Simon.

'That boy is such a perv,' says Alice.

'Oh, did you have to?' says Mrs Harper, but she laughs and takes a picture anyway. The Italian girls come back, walking the other way, chatting to each other. They stop again and laugh again when they see me.

I feel like a bit of an idiot, but at least I made them laugh.

I soon get bored of being buried so when everyone's had a good look I get up, destroying Felix's sand woman. There's still quite a big hole in the sand, and Felix and me are talking about what we might do with it when one of the Italian sunbed attendants comes over with a serious, slightly cross expression on his face and fills it in with a rake.

When he's gone, one of Mrs Harper's friends says, 'Can you dig another hole, boys, so we can get that young Adonis back over here?'

The women laugh.

Adonis is in my book of Greek myths. He was a very handsome youth who some goddesses fought over. I picture him as looking like one of the boys on *Love Island*.

He was gored to death by a wild boar, though.

That never happened on *Love Island*.

Which is a shame.

A Conversation with Mum

2

'And were you polite to everyone at the beach?'

'Of course I was polite, Mum. How's Dad?'

'You weren't all shy?'

'I was fine. I'm OK. Tell me about Dad.'

'You talked to people? You talked to the adults when they asked you things?'

'Yes. It was all fine. The beach was nice. I talked to people. Is Dad still in hospital?'

'Did you stay in the shade?'

'Not all the time, no . . .'

'Stan, you must –'

'What about when I go swimming?'

'Fair enough. Yes. You don't have to stay in the shade when you go for a swim. That would be difficult.'

'It would be impossible. Unless I was swimming under a cliff and the sun was going down behind it.'

'Don't swim under any cliffs. Rocks could fall on you.'

'I won't swim under any cliffs.'

'What did you talk to the adults about?'

'Things.'

'What things?'

'You know . . . beach things. That's all.'

'Who did you talk to? Who else is there at the house?'

'There's an actress. Livia Channing.'

'Livia Channing? *The* Livia Channing?'

'I suppose so.'

'Oh my god. You didn't tell me! You're on holiday with Livia Channing! You talked to her. What did you talk about?'

'Stuff . . . You know . . . TV. Yes. We talked about her TV show.'

'Wait till I tell Dad. He loves Livia Channing. Did you put your sun cream on?'

'Yes. So, Dad's OK then? Is he home?'

'Did you wear a hat?'

'Yes! I was the only boy on the beach wearing a hat. Italians don't wear hats. I felt like everyone was laughing at me.'

'Well, you'll be laughing at them when they all die of skin cancer.'

'I'm not sure I will. I don't think it would be very funny.'

'As long as you haven't burned. I've been very worried about you burning.'

'I'm fine, Mum.'

'I can't believe you actually talked to Livia Channing. Well. This must be getting expensive. I'd better say goodnight, Stan.'

'Mum!'

'What?'

'What about Dad? Aren't you going to tell me about Dad?'

'He's fine. Your dad's fine . . .'

'Mum! Please!'

'I don't want you to worry.'

'I'll worry if you don't tell me anything. Is he still in hospital?'

'Well . . .'

'Well, what?'

'Yes and no.'

'He's either in hospital or he's not.'

'He's in a different hospital. They had to move him.'

'Why? What's wrong with him?'

'He's got a little problem, Stan. To do with his heart.'

'He had a heart attack?'

'No . . . nothing like that. Don't be silly. He just needs a little operation.'

'How little?'

'Come on, Stan, we don't want to talk about all this. He's going to be all right. They just need to fix his pipes.'

'His pipes? What pipes?'

'His pipes, you know, his arteries, that take the blood in and out of his heart. He's got a sort of blockage thingy. Nothing serious. It's routine. That's what they said – a routine operation.'

'I'm worried about him, Mum.'

'You mustn't be, darling. I shouldn't have told you. He's going to be all right. He'll be fitter than ever once they've cleaned out his pipes. Now, let's say goodnight and forget all about it.'

'OK . . . if you want . . . Goodnight, Mum.'

'Goodnight, Stan.'

'Goodnight . . .'

A Conversation with Felix

I

'You OK?'

'My dad's not very well.'

'Bummer.'

'Yeah . . .'

'My dad's a bit of a jerk.'

'Really?'

'Yeah . . . G'night, Stan.'

'G'night, Felix.'

Reason 9: Organized pool games

Before I went to the bathroom this morning I found a big rock in the garden. I took it inside and jammed it up against the bathroom door on the inside. If someone really wanted to get in, they could push hard and probably force it open, but I'm hoping nobody would be that desperate to see me on the loo. Just in case, though, I have started singing so people know I'm in there.

I don't know that many songs. Only Abba, really, because Mum likes to sing along to them. I hope that if someone hears me singing *Mamma mia, here I go again!*' they don't think I'm showing off about doing a poo.

Simon went to the shops this morning and came back with an inflatable for the pool in the shape of a crocodile. Felix invented a game where you had to jump on to the crocodile from the board and try to stay on. The crocodile (or *'crocodillo'* as Felix called it) lasted about twenty minutes before it burst and started to sink. It's gone to the inflatable graveyard now. There's a big basket filled with things for the pool. Floats and snorkels and balls, those long foam tube things called noodles, but mostly there are dead inflatable things. They're all different shapes and colours, and all flat. There's a giant ring, a slice of pizza, a frog, a seahorse, several ordinary lilos and a weird purple thing that looks like a mutant owl that's been run over.

The swimming pool's pretty cool. It reflects the sky and the clouds and the palm trees planted round it like something out of a Hollywood film. There's a covered area down one side with a bamboo roof where you can sit in the shade, and a little building with a loo, showers, a changing room and an outdoor kitchen under another bamboo cover.

I like going in off the board. I'm quite a good diver. Better than Aria and Felix and Jess. I think I'm even better than Alice and her other friend. Although they don't really like to go in the water. They mostly like to stay on the sunbeds posing for selfies.

Felix likes to jump from the board – he doesn't seem too keen on diving.

For lunch I had pasta with tomato sauce again. Pasta with tomato sauce is easy. My ideal holiday menu would look something like this . . .

Monday – pasta with tomato sauce.

Tuesday – pasta with tomato sauce.

Wednesday – pasta with tomato sauce.

Thursday – pasta with tomato sauce.

Friday – pasta with tomato sauce.

Saturday – pizza.

Sunday – pasta with tomato sauce.

After lunch we all stayed sitting round the big table and played a game called the Water Game.

Everyone here is always playing some sort of a game. Ping-pong, table football, cards, Scrabble. One of Mrs Harper's friends, the angry-looking woman, spends all day indoors in a big room next to the kitchen doing a gigantic jigsaw puzzle.

Anyway, the Water Game is quite easy.

You fill a jug up with iced water and someone picks a category, like colours, or countries, or types of car, or African animals, or whatever. Jess was first up and she picked fruits (that wasn't meant to be a joke, like you weren't supposed to think she was picking fruit from a tree). She chose one and had to write it down and not say it out loud. When we were ready, she went round the table holding the jug over each person's head in turn and they had to say a fruit.

The first person to say the fruit that Jess had chosen would get the whole jug of water poured over their head, and we all had to say different fruits.

It was terrifying.

'Apple . . .'

'Safe.'

'Orange . . .'

'No.'

'Plum . . .'

I sat there waiting for the jug to come round, dreading my turn, praying that someone else would get soaked, desperately trying to think of the most obscure fruit in the world, but only being able to think of the obvious ones because I was so stressed.

Some people did well. We had some very obscure ones.

Durian, kiwi, ugli, lychee, pomelo . . .

I thought of grape. There was a bowl of them on the table. But then Felix said it before Jess got to me and I had to think of another one.

I thought of banana.

Clever, eh? Really obscure.

Felix's aunt Emma was before me. And when Jess got to her she said 'banana' and I cursed, but then Jess poured the water over Emma and she shrieked and everyone laughed, and I said 'yes!' louder than I'd meant to.

And then Emma became the next jug holder and chose a new category – Johnny Depp films. (I could only think of *Pirates of the Caribbean*.)

'What's Eating Gilbert Grape . . .'

'Sleepy Hollow . . .'

'The Lone Ranger . . .'

'21 Jump Street . . .'

'Edward Scissorhands . . . Aaaaaaargh! No!' (That was Alice getting soaked.)

'Yes!'

'Aaaargh, that's so cold!'

And so it went on.

In the end I did get soaked. Felix was up and chose English football teams. I don't know very much about football and the only team I could think of under pressure was Manchester United, because they're the most famous one.

And, of course, Felix had chosen Manchester United, because he's a fan. And so I got jugged. It actually wasn't that bad when it finally happened. The fear of it was worse than the actual cold water. It was sort of refreshing, even if some ice cubes went down my shorts.

After that the others mucked about in the pool with a football while I read my book of Greek myths.

As I said, everyone here seems to love playing games, and the men spent all afternoon making up a game. They tried to get everyone involved. Eventually I had to join in, and Jess and the other girls. Even Mr Harper joined in.

I didn't really know what to do. The game had really complicated rules. It was sort of a cross between volleyball, water polo, basketball and keepy-uppy. Sometimes you had to skim the ball across the water, other times you had to throw it, then there was a part where you had to hold it underwater and when someone shouted 'Polaris!' you had to let it pop up and shoot into the air and everyone had to try to catch it.

Polaris was only one of the things you had to shout out as you did certain actions or you didn't score. The shouting-out bit seemed to be very important to the men . . .

'Slide!'

'High pass!'

'Low pass!'

'Googly pass!'

'Dummy run!'

'Big bum!'

'Bonus strike!'

'Avanti!'

'Messagio gratuito!'

'Huddle up – huddle up!'

'It's the blimp, Frank, it's the blimp!'

'Bomber!'

'Snake pit!'

'Smashface!!!!!!!'

Smashface was Felix's idea. It was what you had to shout out after you'd scored or the goal didn't count. The metal pool ladder at the shallow end was one goal and a giant rubber ring was the other. But you couldn't just get the ball and try to get it between the ladder handrails or into the ring and shout 'Smashface!' – there were lots of other complicated bits to do first and special things to shout. I actually couldn't make any sense of it at all and they kept arguing about the rules anyway.

So I tried to keep out of the way and avoid the ball. I knew what my dad would be telling me if he was here.

'Join in, lad. Make an effort.'

Even though *he* never joins in anything.

But he wasn't there to tell me, was he?

He was lying in hospital waiting for an operation.

These were the thoughts I was having when the ball hit me in the head and Felix shouted, 'Bug-splat!' and screamed with laughter.

'What's bug-splat?' I asked him, rubbing my head.

'It's a new one,' he explained. 'I just made it up. It's what you shout when you hit someone in the head when they're not paying attention. Five bonus points.'

'Whoa, that's too many points,' said Simon.

'Don't make it into a violent game, Felix,' said Mr Harper, and Simon threw the ball at him. Getting him in the back of the head.

'Bug-splat!' he shouted. 'Three points.'

Mr Harper didn't look very happy about that. Simon was getting very excited. He kept saying how brilliant the game was and how it could be an actual sport, and it could be on the TV, and he'd make a fortune selling the idea.

'Everyone with a swimming pool could play it!'

Every now and then he'd get out of the pool and get beers from the fridge and he got more and more drunk as the day went on. And the more drunk he got, the more brilliant he thought the game was and the more complicated the rules got and the more shouting there was.

Then the men all had a big argument about what to call it. Ben suggested Sliderball, Ash wanted to call it Water Ball, Felix wanted to call it Smashface (even though there isn't any part of it that actually involves smashing faces), but Simon insisted they call it Pool. Which caused the biggest argument of all.

BEN: There's already a game called pool.

SIMON: That's why it's so brilliant. It's clever.

ASH: It's stupid. People would just think it was, you know, just pool.

SIMON: Yeah, but you play it in a pool. You couldn't play normal pool in a pool. That's how it's different.

MR HARPER: Maybe you could call it Swimming Pool . . .

FELIX: Yeah, or Smashface Pool. Or just Smashface.

MR HARPER: Felix, stop going on about Smashface.
Why does everything have to be about violence
with you?

SIMON: Look, I invented the game so I get to name it,
and we're calling it Pool.

ASH: We all invented it.

SIMON: I did most of the work.

And so on. I left them to it and one by one everyone
else drifted away, until there was just Simon, Ben and
Ash standing there arguing. And then there was just
Simon, who practised for ages throwing the ball into
the ring. He was pretty rubbish at it.

Then Simon got out and me and Felix invented our
own game. It had much simpler rules. We stood in the
shallow end of the pool and whacked each other with
noodles until they broke.

'Now *this* game,' I said to him, '*should* be called
Smashface.'

'Yeah!' said Felix, and I got him a really good one on
the nose with my last bit of noodle. For a moment he
looked really mad at me, and also like he might cry, and
then he sniffed and laughed and shouted, 'Smashface!'
and it was all right.

★

Now me and Felix and Aria and the girls are sitting at a table by the pool wrapped in towels playing cards. Apart from the girls laughing about me being a perv all the time, it's fun. It's peaceful now that the others have gone and it's not so hot. The sky's a sort of pinky-orange colour. Birds are swooping down to take little sips from the pool. We've played a few games, including a card game with a rude name that I can't say (apparently you can also call it 'Shed').

Spending time with the girls means I can think of them as actual people now rather than just one single scary being – *the Girls*. Lily, the other big girl, is Alice's best friend. She's the daughter of the angry woman, who's married to Ash, the tech guy with all the phones. Ash isn't Lily's father, though. I am really trying hard to work out who everyone is, but it's very complicated.

I've worked out that the other woman, the one who looks a bit like Mum, is actually Jess's mum. She's a doctor and she's called Cathy. Jess's father isn't here. I think her parents are divorced. I'm starting to think that my family is boring and ordinary. I wonder what it would be like not to have a mum or dad, and then I feel bad because Dad's ill and I'm thinking about him not being there.

I tell myself he's going to be all right. I'm going to carry on being normal. With a normal family. I think that if I behave like this, as if everything's OK, then everything *will* be OK.

I play a card and Alice and Lily laugh. They're like spooky twins in a scary movie. They both dress the same and talk the same and like the same things. Lily painted Alice's toenails. Alice straightened Lily's hair (that's what one of the weird devices in their room was for). But Alice is better at cards. In fact, she's a demon.

After the game that I will call 'Shed', we played Perudo, which is a dice game. I'd never played it before and was rubbish at it. Either Alice or Lily won every game. Felix got cross, so then we played Yahtzee, which he's much better at. But Alice still won. Alice is very competitive. Then Felix threw the dice in the pool so that was the end of that.

Now we're playing a card game called Hearts.

It's fun and we're all relaxing. Apart from Felix who keeps saying he hates Hearts.

Jess is doing even worse than me. Luckily she laughs about it. She looks at me and smiles. 'You and me are going to have to practise together, Stan.'

'Like a montage in a film,' I say. 'Set to loud music. We'll do nothing except practise cards and come back stronger than anyone.'

Jess laughs.

Which is lucky. I really don't know what I was thinking of trying to make a joke. I guess Jess talked to me and I felt suddenly brave. It just came out. I never normally say things like that. I only think them.

'We'll be ninja card players,' says Jess.

I try to think of a snappy one-liner to add, but don't want to push my luck. So I just say 'yeah'.

I can't really concentrate on the rest of the game. It's a bit of a blur. Jess talks to me, I make another joke and she laughs and doesn't call me a sad loser. Even though the joke *is* a bit lame.

When we finish the game, it's nearly dinnertime and I need to change out of my swimmers. I go off before the others. I'll need a shower and once one of the girls gets in there they take hours. Plus I need time to properly barricade the door. I just know that if Alice walked in on me she'd claim it was my fault. That I'd left the door open on purpose. Just to be doubly sure I'll keep my swimmers on.

As I go into our block, an animal comes flying out and I jump back, thinking it's a giant rat or something. But it's only the cat. It must have got shut in there.

The cat lives in the woodpile at the house. It's a skinny little thing and quite nervous of people. But if you're not careful it'll jump on to the table and steal your food. It's called Pussolini. Felix's dad came up with the name. Apparently it's a sort of a joke.

I don't really know much about Felix's dad. The pool game is the first thing he's joined in with. He's always reading a magazine or listening to something on headphones or making long telephone calls while walking up and down in the courtyard. He's half bald and he shaves the rest of his hair really short. He owns a photography magazine apparently. I didn't even know that was a job. My dad's a postman and my mum's a teacher. Mrs Harper tries to fill in for Felix's dad by talking slightly too much and bustling around, making sure everyone's happy all the time. She looks quite stressed. The only time Mr Harper really says anything is to tell Felix off, like when he kicked a football into some flowers. Apparently Simon is his brother, but I've never seen them talking to each other.

Anyway. I've been trying to make friends with the cat by giving it bits of food. She particularly likes cheese. She won't take it out of my hand yet, but I'm working on it. I get her to come closer to me every time I offer her some. I like cats and think this one might be my friend one day. It's easier to talk to the cat than real people. We have a cat at home called Table. She's quite old and completely deaf. She can't miaow properly because she can't hear herself and the noises she makes can be a bit freaky. Mum says I named her Table when I was very young, though I don't remember it. She says that 'table' was one of the only words I knew. It was either that or calling her 'Dog'.

Thinking of Table I get a bit sad.

A Conversation with Mum

3

'Hi, Mum.'

'Hello, darling.'

'How's Table?'

'She's all right. She spent all night howling outside the bedroom door. She sounded like someone doing a Donald Duck impression. But at least it was a bit of company.'

'Ha . . . So how's Dad?'

'He's still having tests done. What with worrying about him and worrying about you and Table doing Donald Duck impressions I hardly slept at all last night.'

'You don't need to worry about me.'

'Thank you, darling, but I like worrying about you. What did you get up to today? Did you talk to any more famous people?'

'No. We played cards.'

'That's fun.'

'Yeah . . .'

'Have you had to spend any of your emergency money?'

'Not yet.'

'Good.'

'Yeah. So. Well. Goodbye.'

'Is that it?'

'I guess. I just missed you a bit, Mum. And Table . . . and Dad. You're sure he's all right?'

'I'd tell you if he wasn't.'

'No you wouldn't.'

'I've missed you a lot, darling.'

'I'd better go, Mum. It's dinner.'

'How much do you miss me?'

'Mum, this isn't like that stupid *Guess How Much I Love You* book – I'm not a baby rabbit.'

'It's a hare.'

'Whatever.'

'I miss you a million, Stan. How much do you miss me? Is it more than a million?'

'Mum . . .'

'How much? Is it more than I miss you, Stan?'

'I miss you twice as much as you miss me, Mum. So, even if you miss me to infinity and beyond, I'll still miss you double infinity. You can never win.'

'Is that possible?'

'Yes.'

'You're too clever for me, Stan.'

'I don't want Dad to die.'

'He's not going to die . . .'

'Are you sure?'

'Stan? Are you all right? You sound like you're crying.'

'I'm not crying.'

'You sound all muffled.'

'It's a really bad connection. Plus, this useless phone is useless.'

'OK. Bye, darling. Call me again tomorrow. Don't spend any money. Use the mozzy spray. Put your sun cream on . . .'

'Bye, Mum . . .'

Reason 10: Pedalos

Yesterday we made pizzas and today we're at the beach again. Just Mrs Harper, Aunt Emma, me and the other kids. We think about digging another hole, but the young Adonis is keeping an eye on us and giving us dirty looks. So me and Jess and Felix and Mrs Harper and Aria go out on a pedalo instead. Emma stayed behind, listening to a book and staring into space.

We're really excited as we climb aboard and start pedalling. It's fun for about a minute, until we realize it's actually quite hard work and a bit boring. Pedalos are not very well-designed boats. You have to pedal like mad and the water churns up and you crawl along really slowly and there's nowhere to actually go. We go down the beach one way and then we go back again. We go out deep and jump off it and then climb back on, which is also quite hard.

And that's it!

That's about all the fun you can have with a pedalo.

We're desperate for our time to be up so we can go back.

The same thing happened yesterday with the pizzas. What I mean is, we did something that looked like it was going to be a lot of fun and it turned out not to be.

I think you'll agree that pizzas are one of mankind's greatest inventions. Forget telescopes and clocks and the wheel and all that rubbish, the pizza is a masterpiece. Who would have thought that something so simple could be so delicious?

And so hard to make.

The thing about pizzas is, they're quite cheap. You can easily get one from a pizza place. So why waste time trying to make it yourself? And it *is* a waste of time. Last night was pizza night, but it took all day to make them so it was really pizza *day*. And they turned out rubbish. First of all we had to go to the shops to get the ingredients – flour and yeast and tomato paste and all sorts of horrible vegetables and mozzarella cheese and ham. I made sure there was some ham. Lots of ham.

Then we had to make the dough. Everybody argued about the best way to do this. Ash looked up pizza recipes on his iPad. Mrs Harper found an old cookbook at the house, but it was in Italian. Emma claimed to have made pizzas before and said she knew how to do it from memory. But she couldn't actually remember. Livia the actress said she'd help make them but wouldn't eat any as they were too fattening. Simon said you needed to add beer and made up a whole load of really weird-looking dough that he then dropped on the floor.

Anyway, in the end we had some dough. It was a right mess, sticking to everything and everyone. But that's not the end of it. Once you've made the dough you have to 'leave it to rise', which means leaving it in a bowl under a tea towel until it swells up into a big puffy ball. While we were waiting, Mrs Harper said we should prepare the vegetables. I kept well away from this part but did manage to cut up some pieces of ham with a pair of scissors. So I did my bit.

When I rang Mum later, she was quite proud of me.

'Oh, Stan, you made pizzas, well done. You're a proper chef now. You should go on *MasterChef*.'

Yeah, right, I can see that happening . . .

'*So, what's your signature dish, Stan?*'

'*Ham cut up with a pair of scissors.*'

There's an outside pizza oven here and you have to put small logs in it for the fire. It took ages for the men to get the wood going and they argued a lot. There was smoke everywhere and they used about a hundred firelighters.

Finally it was time to start cooking. The dough was divided up and the pizzas were rolled out, and once again they stuck to everyone and everything, and they came out all wonky. Simon tried spinning one around in the air like he'd seen proper pizza chefs do, and it flopped down and stuck to the top of his head and he laughed and made the pizza anyway and everyone said they weren't eating any of it as it was full of his hair.

Mrs Harper and the women had cooked the tomato sauce. I think the bottom got burnt at one point because I heard the angry woman swearing from the kitchen when we were trying to light the fire.

Then we all decorated the wonky pizzas. Felix wanted to make one with 'absolutely everything' on it. He looked up the Italian words and named it *Il Tutto*. He claimed it was going to be the world's greatest pizza. It had three types of cheese, two types of ham, salami, spicy salami, olives, onions, peppers, chillies and banana.

It looked disgusting.

Mine was ham and cheese.

But, at last, when it was nearly midnight, the oven was hot enough and Ben started cooking the pizzas. He enjoyed being the pizza chef, using the big flat metal spade thing to put them in and out. He was pretty good. He only dropped two of them on the floor.

Well. The end result was seven rubbish pizzas. Some were too thick and not cooked properly, some were too thin and had gone crispy like biscuits and were all burnt on the bottom. Some fell apart and were fed into the fire.

The last to go in were mine and Felix's. Mr Harper looked at *Il Tutto* and said there was too much stuff on it and it wouldn't cook properly. Felix argued. They both got quite angry. But Mr Harper was right. *Il Tutto* disintegrated in the oven and turned into what looked like molten lava with bits of banana in it.

Ben managed to scrape most of it out and get it on to a plate. Felix was really cross now. Mr Harper said he'd told him. Nobody ate any of it. Not even Felix's mum, who'd been saying things like 'Wow, yummy' all evening and 'You can't beat homemade food' and 'So much nicer than the pizzas from the pizza place'. And everyone else had joined in, saying, 'Ooh, yeah, yummy,' and pretending to agree with her.

There was a lot of pizza left at the end of the night.

Mine was the only one that looked almost like a proper pizza, maybe because there wasn't too much stuff on it so it was easier to cook. But it didn't taste like a proper pizza. No sirree. It tasted of flour and tomatoes and I only managed to eat one slice. But still Mrs Harper said, 'Wow, yummy,' and, 'This is great, Stan. You're so clever.'

And everyone else said, 'Ooh, yeah, yummy,' except for Felix who said it was crap. He said they were *all* crap.

Which they were.

It would have been so much easier and cheaper to go to the pizza place.

So, as I sit here pedalling like mad with aching legs, I add pedalos and homemade pizzas to my list of 'things that look like they're a lot of fun but actually aren't'. Thinking about it is taking my mind off cycling the pedalo along. And taking my mind off Dad. I don't think Mum's telling me everything. Last night when I called her again she didn't really say anything about him, which is making me worry a lot more.

But anyway. Here's my list.

10 THINGS THAT LOOK LIKE FUN UNTIL YOU TRY THEM

1. Pedalos.
2. Homemade pizzas.
3. Hammocks.
4. Inflatable killer whales.
5. Frisbees.
6. Kite flying.
7. Sleeping on the top bunk.
8. Using a laptop outdoors.
9. Picnics.
10. Fighting.

So. Let's go through the list properly . . .

1. **Pedalos.** We know about that.

2. **Homemade pizzas.** We know about them too.

3. **Hammocks.** Hammocks are stupid and uncomfortable and you just keep falling out of them. I've got bruises all down one side from when I fell out of the one at the house here. It would take a lot to get me back into one of those death traps again.

4. **Inflatable killer whales.** Simon bought one yesterday for the pool. Felix and I argued over who was going to go on it first. Felix won and I laughed as he kept falling off. I wasn't any better when I tried, though. It looked cool, but there was no way to actually sit on it without tipping over. When Simon tried, it burst and sank. So that was that.

5. **Frisbees.** Ben and Ash were playing with a Frisbee this morning and asked if I wanted to join in. I always get suckered into this one. You see some people throwing a Frisbee around and you think, *Wow! That looks amazing.* But when you join in, you quickly remember – *Oh, no, of course, I forgot, this is no fun at all!* For a start it's quite hard to throw a Frisbee to someone. Most times it hits the ground miles away and then rolls on its edge even further in the wrong direction. And then, if someone does manage to throw it anywhere near you, what do you do?

You *catch* it!

And? Yes?? Go on!!! Yes???????

That's it.

That's it? You catch it? What's fun about that? I mean, catching something?

6. Kite flying. Is there a more beautiful sight than people flying kites from the top of a hill on a bright windy day?

And is there any more boring activity than trying to fly a kite on a dull grey afternoon when there isn't enough wind? Which is what happens whenever I try.

You spend ages trying to get the thing into the air. Most times it goes up about two metres and then spirals down and crashes into the ground. Or you get someone to toss it up into the air and then you run off like an idiot with it flapping about behind you. And soon you're just dragging it along the ground. And then you spend ages trying to wind the string in and it gets all tangled and knotty.

But let's say you *do* manage to get it up into the air. Which I did once. You're so excited, you let the string out, unwinding it from the reel, and it goes up and up and up and . . .

That's it!

You're left standing there holding this long piece of string. And after a while you reel it all back in.

And go home.

7. Sleeping on the top bunk. What kid hasn't dreamed of sleeping on a top bunk? Well, we stayed at a

B & B once where there was a bunk bed in the room and I insisted on having the top.

I was King of the World!

And you know what? *It sucked.*

To get up to it you have to climb this awkward wooden ladder that digs into your bare feet. And once you're up there you feel all cramped and too close to the ceiling, like being in jail. And if you want to go to the loo or anything, you've got to climb all the way down. The difference between a bunk bed and an ordinary bed is that you're a bit higher up and it's much harder to go to the loo.

That's it!

8. Using a laptop outside. You've probably seen those adverts where really cool-looking people are lounging around in the sun, working on their laptops and smiling. Sometimes they're lying on their tummies. *Yeah!* you think. *This is the life! To be working wherever you like! In the sun! How cool is that?*

I'll tell you how cool that is.

None.

Dad has an old laptop at home that he sometimes lets me use to do my homework and I tried working outside in the summer once. It was awful. I couldn't see the screen and it was too hot to be outside and I got itchy and sweaty.

I thought, *Look at me! I'm outside. On a computer. Typing . . .*

Typing outdoors.

(Small voice) yay . . .

That's it!

9. Picnics. Don't picnics look great? Sitting outside on a lovely summer day eating lovely food. But picnics are the pits. You get grit in everything and it rains and nobody ever remembers to bring a bottle opener and you spill the crisps everywhere and ants arrive in a big long line. In the end you're basically just eating a meal . . . on the ground . . . outside . . .

That's it!

10. Fighting. Fighting in films looks really cool, doesn't it? Like, say, in a Marvel film where superheroes are flying all over the place, kicking butt and knocking over skyscrapers. In films you can get hit a hundred times and hammered into the floor and thrown through a building and you'll be OK.

Well, real life is not like that.

I know this. And I'll tell you why. Last night as we were going to bed I had a fight with Felix. We were both waiting to use the bathroom and we started arguing about which was better, *Super Mario* or *Mario Kart*. It went on for a while and then I said *Mario Kart* wouldn't even exist if it wasn't for *Super Mario Brothers* in the first place. Then Felix said *I* wouldn't even exist if God hadn't had an accident one day and dropped some pizza dough on the floor and it was so dirty and rubbish he threw it out and it turned into me. Then I said at least I knew how to make pizza and my pizza was better than his. Which NOBODY had eaten. Then he said I was a skinny loser and I said his haircut made him look like a nincompoop*.

Then he pushed me and I pushed him back. And then we grabbed each other and fell over on the hard floor, which hurt, and then we rolled around a bit, which hurt some more. We were all mixed up with the girls' things – hairdryers and shoes and underwear.

And then Alice and Lily came in and started laughing and cheering, and Alice filmed us on her phone. And after a while we just sort of stopped. Alice showed us the video. It looked terrible. So embarrassing. Nothing like a Marvel film. It was just two people flapping about in a pile of underwear.

And that's why fighting isn't as much fun as it looks.

So anyway me and Felix made up afterwards and laughed about it, but we're both pedalling away like galley slaves now and getting all hot and grumpy again, so it's a big relief when our time's up and we can pedal back to the beach and get off.

All that pedalling has made me quite hungry and we go to the beach cafe, where I get a sort of cheese and ham toastie, which is pretty good. As I eat the toastie, I

---

* Obviously this isn't the actual word I used.

listen to a DJ in a little booth playing europop hits to nobody in particular, and watch the speedboat drag people up into the air on the parachute, pull them round, dip them in the water and take them back to the beach. I'm feeling sort of loose and chilled and when Jess sits next to me she lets me have a sip of her Coke.

'Did you know,' I say, 'that apparently it's possible to jump from the top of the Empire State Building without a parachute?'

'Really?' she says.

'Yes,' I say. 'But you can only do it once.'

Jess laughs. I burp. She laughs some more.

'I like you, Stan,' she says. 'You're funny.'

Am I? Nobody's ever said that before. And that was one of Dad's jokes. Most of his jokes are pretty cheesy, but if you're in the right mood they're quite funny as well. I never thought one of them would actually help me make friends with a girl. Dad has some use after all.

Which is why it would be a shame if his operation went badly.

Damn. Just when I was feeling chilled I had to think of that.

And then Felix sits down next to Jess and steals my last bit of toastie.

'Loser,' he says, stuffing it into his gob with a big grin.

'Why are you being so mean to your best friend?' says Jess.

'Stan?' says Felix. 'He's not my best friend. He's Billy No-Mates, the king of the geeks! *Archie's* my best friend. Stan only came because Archie couldn't and Stan was the only kid in our *entire* school who didn't have anybody to go on holiday with.'

I guess I was wrong and Felix is still sore about our fight last night, even if it was totally random. Actually, I suppose I was stressed about my dad and he was stressed about his, but, even so, it's not really fair. I'm out here by myself without my family and Felix has everything – a big house in Italy, a really expensive smartphone, a Nintendo Switch with hundreds of games. I don't know why he has to be in such a bad mood all the time. Why he wants to keep getting at me.

I can't think of anything to say to him. I wish I could come back with something clever like, 'Archie told me he broke his leg on purpose so that he wouldn't have to come on holiday with you.'

Wait a minute! *I could!*

'Yeah,' I say. 'Well, Archie broke his only leg, no, I mean, he told me, you know, he told me you broke his leg, no, not you, he broke his leg so that . . .'

'Loser,' says Felix, then he drinks the rest of Jess's Coke and walks off singing, 'Loser, loser, loser . . .'

Right now I could happily bury him in the sand. I mean *completely* bury him, head and all. But then I have to remind myself that I wouldn't be here at all if it wasn't for him. And I *am* actually sort of beginning to enjoy this holiday, never mind how weird Felix is being.

And I think I might really like Jess.

Reason 11:

'Fun' family games

It's a warm evening. The stars are bright in the sky. Moths and other bugs gather round the lights on the walls. Geckos wait for them, camouflaged against the stone, and every now and then one darts over, grabs a bug and chews it up.

I would have been happy to just sit here watching the geckos, or even just staring at the stars. Dad has been teaching me the constellations. So far I've learnt two: the Big Dipper and another one whose name I can't remember.

I like doing things with Dad. We don't do it very often. I think I sort of take him for granted a bit, and he takes me a bit for granted. Like, well, you know, Dad's always going to be there so I won't go to the park with him – I'll just play on my computer a bit longer.

And now?

No!

I have to tell myself that he *will* always be there. We're going to carry on being just an ordinary family. Which we are. We don't have fights and argue all the time like some people I could mention.

So, as I say, I would have been happy just chilling tonight, but instead we're about to play another game. The worst sort. The sort where you have to do acting.

In front of everybody . . .

It's called the Hat Game. Felix and the girls and some of the adults have obviously played it a lot. I'm like Han Solo. I don't mean that I'm brave or heroic. I mean that I have a bad feeling about it.

The idea of the game is everybody puts five names into a hat. And then you divide up into two teams and take turns picking out names and giving clues to who they are. In the first round you can describe the people, but you obviously can't say their name. Then at the end of the round the names are put back into the hat and you play again, only in the second round you can only use one word as a clue. And in the third round you can't say anything – you have to do a sort of mime and act out who the people are.

We've all moved to a terrace in the corner of the courtyard where there are some outdoors sofas and chairs and we're busy writing names on slips of paper. Mrs Harper said they could be film stars, people from history, characters in books, ordinary people, people staying at the house, pets . . . 'Anyone from Donald Trump to Jesus Christ, really.'

I've been thinking hard, but I'm quite stressed and my mind is refusing to work. In the end I write down Donald Trump, Jesus Christ, Livia Channing, Pussolini (the cat) and Felix. It's hard. I mean, I must know hundreds of names of people, but under pressure these are the only five names in the whole world I can think of, and I'm the last to put my pieces of paper into the hat.

'Let's just organize the teams based on where everyone's already sitting,' says Mrs Harper. 'That'll be easiest.'

'No way!' Felix shouts. 'I'm not going on the same team as Alice!'

'How do you want to do it then, darling?' asks Mrs Harper, trying to smile but sounding a bit tired.

'Boys versus girls,' says Felix.

'Are you sure, darling?'

'Yeah, it'll make it more fun.'

This seems like a terrible idea to me. There will be trouble. Arguments, etc. I can see that Mrs Harper feels the same way. She has a worried look. And now Alice jumps up and points at Felix.

'You're going to lose, Felix. You and your dumb boys. Girls are way superior.'

'Yeah, right. Girls are useless.'

This is not a good start, but I know Felix is not going to change his mind.

The problem is, though, we only have six boys and there are nine girls. But Jess offers to change sides to even things up a bit. Alice and Lily protest, saying they need her on their team.

'We can't lose the Jess-meister!'

But Jess moves over and sits next to me.

Wow.

It's almost like she's chosen to be with me.

I want to say something to her.

But I don't.

'Right,' says Simon, jumping up. 'Shall I get some drinks before we start?'

As he goes off to the kitchen, Mrs Harper tells Mr Harper, who's still sitting at the big table reading a magazine, to come over and sit with his team so we can get started. And Mr Harper says he isn't planning on playing.

'No, you *have* to play,' Mrs Harper says a little too quickly and, although I can tell she wanted it to sound like she wasn't being too serious, it came out like she's giving him an order. I wonder why she was so keen to play this game if it's going to make her stressed. She seems even more stressed than me by the whole thing.

'It'll be fun!' she says, almost shouting. 'We're all going to have fun!'

'Great,' says Mr Harper sarcastically, and Mrs Harper gives him a hard stare like Paddington. (I like to listen to Paddington audiobooks when I go to bed at home. I'm a bit too old for Paddington but they help me go to sleep. As soon as the voice comes on, I'm out. I don't think I've ever got to the end of one.)

'Right,' says Mrs Harper, swapping her hard stare for a slightly mad grin. 'Someone tell Stan the rest of the rules?'

'It's really easy,' says Alice. 'When it's your turn, you've got two minutes to describe as many names as possible to your team-mates. If they get a name right, you keep that piece of paper and it scores for you. If they can't guess a name, it goes back into the hat and you can pick out another one. After two minutes is up, it's the turn of the other team to have a go. And we keep going until all the names in the hat are gone.'

'You've missed out the best bit!' Felix shouts, and Alice rolls her eyes.

'I was coming to it —'

But Felix butts in again.

'If you say "um" or "er",' he shouts, 'you're out and have to pass over to the other team. That's the funnest bit.' Felix gives an evil grin and cackles.

'Yeah,' said Alice. 'So, round two you're only allowed to use one word and round three you can *only* do actions. But not pervy actions, OK?'

'That's going to be impossible for Stan,' says Felix. 'Stan can only do pervy actions.'

Felix and Alice and Lily laugh. Personally I think their joke is getting a bit old.

'He sings on the loo,' says Felix. 'What kind of a perv sings on the loo?'

Mrs Harper jumps in. 'Don't be mean to Stan. You mustn't keep calling him that.' She turns to me. 'You'll pick it up as we go along,' she says. 'It's a scream. You'll love it.'

Yeah, right . . .

It'll be a scream all right. A scream of horror! I'm as nervous as a bottom on bottom-kicking night, as my dad would say. I can't think of anything I want to do less. Even wrestling with alligators seems like it would be more fun than this. I probably won't know any of the names and I'll be terrible at the acting-out bit. Everyone will be looking at me, judging me on how good I am . . . And to make it worse I'm not sure I really understand the rules. The only thing that's clear is that I'm going to have to stand up in front of everybody and make a fool of myself. And if I say 'um' or 'er' I'm out.

But that gives me an idea and a plan starts to form.

Ash sets his iPhone up to use as a timer and Alice is first to go. For the girls' team.

'OK . . . Ready . . .' Ash seems really excited. Not so much about the game, more that he gets to use his fanciest phone as a timer. It's the latest iPhone and has some sort of exclusive finish.

'Five . . . four . . . three . . . two . . . one . . . *and* . . . go!'

Alice picks a piece of paper out of the hat and she's off.

'OK, orange-coloured American president with mad hair . . .'

Everyone on the girls' team shouts 'Donald Trump' and Alice passes the paper to Lily, who's scoring for their team.

One point to the girls.

I have a secret smile, though. It's quite cool that one of my names is first out of the hat. Maybe this will be fun after all. But then Alice picks another piece of paper out of the hat and looks at it and makes a face.

'It's the same as the last name,' she says.

'Donald Trump!'

Her team cheers. It seems I'm not the only person to put Donald Trump in.

Alice is still going.

'OK, so, he's an American rapper married to Be—'

'Jay Z,' says Lily, before Alice has even finished saying Beyoncé.

Another point.

'OK, so he was a pirate, I think –'

'Captain Jack Sparrow!' shouts Livia.

'No. He was named after what he looked like –'

'Long John Silver!' shouts Emma.

'No! He had a hairy face . . .' She mimes a beard on her chin.

'Blackbeard!' Aria shouts.

'Yes. OK, so, she's a singer and she's married to Jay Z . . .'

'Beyoncé!' Aria again.

The girls quickly get Nigel Farage, the Queen, Boudicca, Batman, Florence Nightingale and Peppa Pig, and Alice hasn't said 'um' or 'er' once.

Very impressive.

'Seven seconds left,' says Ash. Alice quickly grabs another name and then shrieks with laughter.

'He's a perv!'

'Stan!' shouts Mrs Harper.

'Yes!'

The timer goes off.

'That was amazing, Alice,' says Emma. 'How many points, Lily?'

'Eleven! Eleven points.'

'Yay!'

Alice sits down, beaming. She looks properly happy for the first time this holiday.

Reason 11 (part 2): 'Fun' family games

First up for our team is Felix. He gets ready. Dr Cathy is using her phone as a timer for the girls' team. It's an ordinary phone. It doesn't have an exclusive finish.

'Go!'

Felix looks at the first three names and frowns. He obviously doesn't know who they are. He shakes his head and throws them back into the hat. Then he finds one he knows.

'He was German . . .'

'Adolf Hitler!' shouts Jess.

'Yes.' Encouraged, Felix takes another name. 'He's a racing driver.'

'That's one of mine,' says Simon.

'So who is he then?' says Ash.

'Michael Schumacher.'

'No,' says Felix. 'He's English.'

'Lewis Hamilton!' shouts Simon. 'I put him in too.'

'He's a footballer,' says Felix, looking at another piece of paper. 'Plays for Argentina.'

'I expect it's Lionel Messi,' says Mr Harper with a slightly bored voice.

'Yes . . .'

Felix gets two more (Napoleon and the Incredible Hulk) before letting out an 'er', and then he swears and sits down in a bad mood.

'You did really well, darling,' says Mrs Harper, and Felix shrugs.

'I'd have done much better if people hadn't put in such dumb names.'

Next up for the girls' team is Emma. She looks as excited as a little girl at a party.

'I'm so bad at this,' she says.

'No, you'll be fine,' says Livia. 'Just don't say "um", or "er".'

'OK. I'll try . . . Right – don't say "um" or "er" . . .'

Ash has his phone ready. 'Marks – set – go!'

'Yes . . .' Emma looks at the first piece of paper for a long time, thinking, and then says 'yes' again, and then 'no'. She picks out another name and reads it slowly.

'I know this one,' she says. 'It's a big monkey.'

'Caesar out of *Planet of the Apes*,' says Alice.

'No. Bigger.'

'King Kong!' says Cathy.

'Yes. Er . . .'

'Out!' yells Felix really loudly and aggressively. 'She said "er".'

'Rats,' says Emma. 'I told you I was bad at this.'

Simon gets up. 'Me next,' he says, and empties his wine glass. And now he laughs, although nobody has said anything funny. He's a bit wobbly.

'Go on, darling,' says Emma.

'Ready – go!' says Dr Cathy.

'Right . . . OK . . .' Simon picks a name out of the hat. Squints at it. 'Yes, right . . . He's a man and his name is a thing that opens and closes, but there's more than one of them, and he sounds a bit like the guy from the Psycho motel, mosquitoes are scared of him, he's trying to get rid of them all, or make them unable to mate or something, did he fly a car to the moon or was that the other guy? Yes, he's not him, he's not the guy who runs Uber, no, it was PayPal, wasn't it? Well, it wasn't him . . . this is the other one, his first name is the same as Shakespeare's . . . but he's not Shakespeare . . .'

You have to picture him doing what looks like a weird sort of dance while he's saying all this, miming things nobody can understand. Everybody is staring at him boggle-eyed. What's he talking about? I don't think Simon really understands how the Hat Game works, but at least so far he hasn't said 'um' or 'er'. Which is a bit of a miracle.

There's a long silence. Simon is hopping about, and then he laughs.

'You'll never get it!' he says as if that's a good thing.

'Could it perhaps be Bill Gates?' says Mr Harper in a bored voice.

'Yes!'

Simon's nuts. All he had to say was 'He founded Microsoft and is the richest man in the world'.

His other clues are even more random and cryptic and nobody gets any of them. Simon seems to be enjoying himself, though, and he's certainly entertaining in a weird sort of a way. But we're not doing very well here and I can see that Felix is getting cross. He *so* wants to win.

Next up for the girls is Livia. I can hardly look at her. The memory of our awful conversation on the beach is still stuck in my mind. And I'm really embarrassed that I put her name in the hat. Will she know it was me? Will she think I'm even more of a superfan?

'You're an actress,' says Dr Cathy. 'You'll be great at this.'

Livia smiles before looking at our team and throwing down a challenge.

'Get ready to crash in flames, losers!' she says. 'This one's for all the women of the world!' And she picks out her first name.

'Yeah. Right. OK. He was gay.'

'What?'

'He wore tights.'

'We need more.'

'He was a famous archer.'

'Jeffrey Archer,' shouts Emma.

'No.'

'Thingummy from the Archers . . .' Emma won't give this one up. 'Ian Craig!'

'No.' Livia rolls her eyes. 'His enemy was the Sheriff of Nottingham. God, wasn't Alan Rickman fabulous as the Sheriff of Nottingham?'

'The Sheriff of Nottingham,' Emma shouts.

'No. The bloody archer!'

'Robin Hood,' says Alice.

'Yes.'

'Robin Hood was gay?' says Emma.

'Well, he hung out with his merry men.'

'Next one! Next one! Quickly!' Alice is getting as impatient as Felix.

'OK. Right,' says Livia, looking at another name. 'She's a singer. Had a famous brother. She famously showed her boob at the Superbowl.'

'Janet Jackson!' says Dr Cathy.

'Yes . . . He's that rapper.'

'Which rapper?'

'Erm . . .' Livia is flapping her arms. 'You know . . .'

'Jay Z!'

'No, no, she's out! She said "erm".' Felix is very firm about this.

'Never mind,' says Emma. 'Who's next?'

'Stan! Go on, Stan.' Felix pushes me to my feet. 'You're up next. And try not to do anything dumb. Don't be a loser for once. We need the points.'

'OK.'

Everyone is staring at me. I feel totally stupid. It's time to put my plan into action. Dr Cathy counts me down. I pick out a piece of paper. Look at it.

It says 'Gandhi'. I know who Gandhi is and in my head I say, 'Indian political leader who led his country to independence.' But out loud I say, 'Um.'

'No!' Felix holds his head in his hands. 'You idiot!'

'Oh. Bad luck, Stan,' says Mrs Harper.

I sit down. Felix mutters 'loser' at me.

I smile to myself.

Nailed it.

My plan went off perfectly.

Reason 11 (part 3):
'Fun' family games

The girls are well ahead after the first round. We all went up three or four times. Alice was definitely the best on their team. Ash was best on ours. I was definitely the worst. Every time it came to my turn I just said 'um' or 'er' and got to sit down without making a fool of myself.

Unless, now that I come to think about it, saying 'um' or 'er' and crashing out every time might be considered making a fool of myself. Oh god. I've been a total idiot, haven't I? I could have got a lot more points for our team if I hadn't bottled it, and it might have actually been less embarrassing, but I've made my choice and I'm stuck with it now.

Ben was OK. Dr Cathy was OK. Aria did OK considering she didn't know who any of the people in the hat were, except for the names she put in, but the problem was *we* didn't know who most of *them* were.

I'd certainly never heard of . . .

- Mr Stampy Cat. Who is apparently a cartoon cat that plays Minecraft on YouTube.
- Someone called Suga who's in a K-pop band.
- Hissy. Aria's pet cat.
- Princess Saggypants. Someone Aria just made up.

The one name she put in that we all knew was Donald Trump. In fact, his name was in seven times. I think nearly everybody put him in.

The names kept going round and round until someone shouted the right answer and by the end everyone recognized them all, even if we hadn't got a clue who they were when we started.

There were still arguments, though. Lots of arguments.

'Who put in Henry Carter Blessing?' Alice asked when we'd finished, looking around accusingly at the adults. 'Who the hell is he?'

'Henri Cartier-Bresson,' said Mr Harper with a snooty superior voice, 'was a photographer.'

'That figures.'

'Yes, so you've learnt something new, Alice,' said Mr Harper with a hint of sarcasm. 'Isn't that exciting?'

'And what about Tyler Brûlé?'

'He's a magazine publisher.'

'Well, he has a stupid name.'

'As stupid as Lady Gaga?' This was one of the names Alice put in.

'Lady Gaga's cool.'

Mr Harper played quite slowly. Taking his time picking the names out, raising his eyebrows, sighing and then giving us the clues in his bored voice as if he could hardly be bothered. I can see what it's like when somebody doesn't join in properly and I wish I'd been more like Jess. She tried really hard. She didn't know a load of the names to start with but by the end was pretty good.

So now it's round two, where we're only allowed to say one word, and Alice is up first again.

Ash says, 'Go.' Alice picks out a name, flops her hand over her head like a mad wig and says, 'President.' Her team all shout 'Donald Trump' and she smiles in triumph.

Next name. She mimes pulling a bow and arrow and says, 'Archer.'

'Robin Hood!'

Now she mimes someone with a droopy bottom and points to Aria.

'Omigodman, Princess Saggypants!' Aria shouts, and we all cheer. Well, most of us. Felix doesn't. He's looking grumpy, but, you know what, this is actually *fun*. I decide I'm going to join in properly now.

'Photographer.' Alice points at her dad.

'Henri Cartier-Bresson,' says Lily. Skills. Well remembered.

Once again Alice wins them loads of names. And they stay ahead as we go on. But the game gets more and more competitive. There's shouting and arguing and angry discussions about the rules. My moment of bravery has passed and I'm beginning to get quite anxious so when it comes to my go I change my mind and decide not to be brave. I stand up, pick out Batman and say . . .

'Um.'

Nobody says anything. I look around.

'Go on!' shouts Felix. 'You're allowed to say "um" or "er" in this round.'

Damn. I'm going to have to do this properly.

I say, 'Superhero.'

'That's two words,' shouts Livia.

'No, it's not,' Felix shouts back. ' "Superhero" is one word.'

I carry on, making bat ears with my fingers.

'Batman!' Jess gets it.

Yes. It actually feels good to score a point.

Another name – Adolf Hitler.

I make a little moustache with my finger, do a Nazi salute and say, 'Dictator.'

'Hitler.'

That's two points. I whizz through now, not even thinking about everyone looking at me, just wanting to win the game.

'Wizard . . .' Miming glasses.

'Harry Potter!'

Three.

'Agent.' Posing with a gun.

'James Bond.'

Four.

'Singer.' Miming a microphone.

'Jay-Z.'

I shake my head and then do something I thought I'd never do in front of anyone – let alone a scary mix of kids and adults most of who I don't really know – I run my hands up and down my body, making curvy woman shapes. But quite a lot of female singers' names are in the hat . . .

'Beyoncé . . .'

'Lady Gaga . . .'

'Adele . . .' Simon yells, his voice suddenly high-pitched, like a weird creature in a video game.

Yes! Big cheers. I'm on a roll.

I get nine names before my time is up and my team-mates slap me on the back. I sit down, beaming. I can do this. I'm too into the game for it to be embarrassing. The game is bigger than me. I want to win.

The atmosphere has changed. Everybody's on the edge of their seats, everybody except Mr and Mrs Harper, who both look like they just want to get this over with, and Simon, who keeps laughing for no reason at all.

Livia's up again. She picks a name out. Somehow I know what she's going to say.

'Gay . . .'

'Robin Hood!'

'No.'

'Livia thinks all men are gay,' says the angry woman and Livia mimes Gandalf on the bridge of Khazad-dûm, holding one hand on his staff and the other stretched out with the palm up to stop the Balrog.

'Gandalf!' shouts Mrs Harper.

'Sir Ian McKellen,' shouts Alice.

'Yes!' says Livia, and she picks another name.

'Don't say gay!' Mrs Harper shouts.

Livia mimes someone playing tennis.

'Sister.'

'Serena Williams.'

'Yes.'

'Singer . . .' Livia mimes a woman singing, swinging her hips about.

'Beyoncé!'

'Madonna!'

'Adele!'

And then suddenly Livia lifts up her T-shirt and flashes everyone.

I can't quite believe it's happened at first. Nobody can. Someone screams. Several people laugh. Ben says, 'Livia!' Aria shrieks, 'Omigodman!' And Alice says, 'Janet Jackson.' And they win the point.

I'm still in shock, but Livia grins in triumph and picks out another name.

'*Mission Impossible.*'

'That's two words!' (Felix.)

'It doesn't matter.' (Mrs Harper.)

'Yes it does. It's the rules.' (Felix.)

'Tom Cruise.' (Emma.)

'No – you can't have it – that's cheating.' (Felix.)

'Time's up.' (Ash.)

'Can we have it?' (Livia.)

'No!' (Felix.)

'You cannot!' (Felix. Louder.)

'She said two words!' (Felix. Very loud. Quite angry.)

'You guys are such sore losers.' (Alice.) 'You can't bear to be beaten by a bunch of girls.'

'You can only beat us by cheating . . .' (Felix.)

Somehow I don't think this is going to end well.

Reason 12: Stupid family arguments (often as a result of playing 'fun' family games)

'Are you OK?' I say.

'I guess,' says Felix.

'Why did you wee in the courtyard like that?'

'I couldn't think what else to do.'

Me and Felix are in our beds with the lights off. The girls are asleep downstairs and we're talking quietly.

'It was quite funny really,' I say.

Felix says nothing.

I'm so glad this evening is over. Because everything went horribly wrong, just as I feared. The game got more and more tense, everyone getting really wound up and tired. It was taking so long it felt like we'd been playing for hours.

In the last round we weren't allowed to say anything at all. People were miming things, waving their arms and beating their chests and making grunts and weird noises like a bunch of apes – and getting very frustrated if their team-mates couldn't tell who they were supposed to be.

Simon fell asleep.

Luckily for him, because he missed *the incident*.

When we went to bed, people were already calling it Hatgate.

It was Mr Harper's go and he made a big deal of hauling himself up out of his seat, yawning and looking at his watch.

'Come on, Dad,' said Felix, desperate to win.

Dr Cathy counted him down.

He silently mimed singing at a microphone.

'Jay Z,' I shouted.

'Yes.'

He mimed mad hair.

We all shouted, 'Donald Trump.'

'Yes.'

He did a mime that could have been anything.

'Will Smith?' I said, although it was a long shot.

'Yes.'

Another vague mime.

'Florence Nightingale.'

'Yes.'

'Wait a minute,' said Alice. 'We've had Florence Nightingale already this round.'

'She must be in more than once,' said Mr Harper, picking another name out of the hat.

'No, wait,' said Alice. 'She's not. Pause the timer.'

'Oh, come on, Alice,' said Felix.

'Florence Nightingale is only in once,' said Alice. 'I put her in. I'd know if someone else had put her in as well.'

'You've obviously made a mistake,' said Mrs Harper, though it wasn't clear who she was talking to.

'Dad,' said Alice, looking at the last name that her dad had dropped on to our scoring pile. 'This is Ryan Gosling.'

Emma had been looking at the names in her team's pile. 'Look – we've got Florence Nightingale in *our* pile. That's weird.'

It wasn't weird at all. Mr Harper had obviously been cheating. He smiled and yawned and shrugged. 'Come on, I was just trying to get this game over with. It's in danger of going on all night. It's no big deal.'

'We've been playing for ages. You can't mess it up now,' said Alice, sounding like she might cry.

'It *is* getting quite late, actually,' said Mrs Harper with one of her desperate smiles.

'Yes, but Dad's cheating,' said Alice. 'That so sucks.'

'Does this mean you've been cheating all through the game?' says Livia, who seemed as cross as Alice.

'Look,' said Alice, going through our names. 'He's just been pretending that people were guessing right. There's no Will Smith, there's no Jay Z. He's ruined the whole game.'

'What does it matter, Alice?'

'We were winning and now you've made it crap, Dad.'

'That really is pretty low,' said Livia.

'He didn't mean anything,' said Emma.

'How could you do that?' said Mrs Harper. And it looked like she might cry now. 'We were having such fun. You've spoiled it all.'

'News alert,' said Mr Harper. 'It's just a bloody game.'

'You see what I have to put up with?' said Alice, looking round at Lily, and then she turned on her dad. 'You don't care about anything we do. You don't care about anything. You don't care.'

'Someone picks names out of a hat,' said Mr Harper sarcastically. 'It's not like anyone's going to die.'

'But it's cheating, Dad!'

'Oh, Ian knows all about cheating,' said Livia, and she gave Mrs Harper a 'significant look'. I figured that Ian must be Mr Harper's name.

'You really can be a miserable sod sometimes, Ian,' Livia went on. 'That was such a *male* thing to do.'

'Oh, I was wondering when somebody would drag it down to that,' said Mr Harper.

'I don't how Ruth puts up with you.' (Ruth must be Mrs Harper's name.) 'You're a jerk.'

'That's not fair,' said Mrs Harper, sticking up for her husband now.

'Whose side are you on?' said Alice. 'He's made this whole evening horrible.'

Soon everybody was shouting at everybody else, like a bunch of kids in a school football match. And then Emma said, 'Oh my god!' and we looked round to see her staring at something.

Felix was standing in the middle of the courtyard, facing away from us, having a big wee. Everyone fell silent. Mrs Harper and Alice both said, 'Felix . . .'

And his dad said, 'What the hell do you think you're doing?'

Felix finished, did up his zip and came back over as if nothing had happened. Some people laughed. They all started talking about it and the argument was forgotten.

The game was over. It was decided that the girls had won, but there was no celebration. The adults tidied up and we all went to bed.

And now only me and Felix are awake.

'I hate it when my parents argue,' says Felix. 'I needed to distract everyone. That whole stupid fight wasn't really about the game, was it?'

'I don't know,' I say.

I really don't. I'm not used to this. But I do think the adults were taking what Felix's dad had done way too seriously.

'Do your parents argue?' Felix asks.

'No. They just don't speak to each other properly for days, and go really, really polite. It's pretty horrible.'

'Arguing's worse,' says Felix.

'Maybe when my parents aren't speaking to each other I should wee on the living-room carpet?' I say.

Felix grunts. Then he goes quiet.

'I don't think my parents like each other any more,' he says after a while. 'I'm scared Dad's going to leave Mum. I don't want things to change.'

This is definitely the biggest conversation me and Felix have ever had. He knows more about what's going on than he pretends. Maybe he likes to hide behind his phone. He's upset and I don't want him to be.

'Thanks for asking me to come on holiday with you,' I say.

'S'all right . . . This might be the last year we come here.'

'It was only an argument over a game.'

'No it wasn't.'

Before I can get him to explain what he means, a beam of light moves over the ceiling and we can hear a car driving into the car park.

'Who's that?' I say.

'That'll be Uncle Mark,' says Felix.

'Who's Uncle Mark?'

'He's my mum's brother. They own this place together. Mum's always happier when he's here. Much less stressed. Uncle Mark's OK . . . Tomorrow will be better.'

Reason 13: They don't have proper breakfasts abroad

When I wake up the next morning, Felix is still asleep. The girls are still asleep. I can hear them snuffling and snoring downstairs. I get up and go down as quietly as I can — and it looks like *everyone* is still asleep. It's very quiet after the excitement of last night.

I go over to the kitchen to find something to eat and see that actually I'm not the only person up. There's a man there boiling an egg. He smiles at me when I come in. He's got wavy hair with silver streaks in and is wearing a faded T-shirt and shorts. He looks very at home, as if he's been here for weeks, but I've not seen him before. I guess this must be Uncle Mark. Another strange person I'll have to get to know.

'So, who's this then?' he asks in a friendly way. He seems like he might not be too scary.

'I'm Felix's friend, Stan.'

'Hello, Stan. I'm Mark. Have you had breakfast?'

'Not yet.'

'What about Felix?'

'He's still asleep.'

'Do you fancy waking him up and coming to the cafe with me? I'm going to get a coffee and a *cornetto*.'

I'm not sure what to say to this. I think about it slightly too long and then nod and say, 'Sure, OK.'

'You're not sick of *cornettos*?'

I shrug.

'Have you been to the cafe every morning?'

'No. We haven't been there at all yet.'

'That's terrible. What *have* you done since you've been here?'

'Stuff,' I say lamely.

'Have you been to dive off the rocks?'

'No.'

'Have you been into Otranto to see the skulls?'

'No.'

'What about going into town at night? You must have done that?'

'No.'

'Not been to any *festas*?'

'We've been to the beach,' I say.

'How was that?'

'Crowded.'

'You're telling me. So what did you do at the beach? Did you go on the banana boat or the parachute thing?'

'No.'

'What *did* you do?'

'We dug a hole.'

Mark laughs.

'The Italian man filled it in,' I say.

'We need to get you out,' says Mark. 'You need to have some fun, not be stuck here with a bunch of boring old farts all day.'

'I'm having a nice time,' I say. 'I like the pool.'

'Yeah. The pool's good. Now, you go and get dressed and grab Felix. I'll eat this egg and we'll go.'

Felix moans when I wake him up, but when I mention going to the cafe and having *cornettos* he jumps out of bed and starts to dress.

When we get outside, Mark's waiting for us.

'I can't believe you haven't taken your very good friend Stan to the cafe yet, Felix,' he says.

'Dad can never be bothered to take us.'

'What about your mum?'

'She's always too busy making breakfast for everybody else.'

'Well, let's just us three go. You'll like the cafe, Stan. They do the best *cornettos* in Italy.'

Mark's rental car is fancier than any of the others. I don't know much about cars, but it's pretty obvious even to me. It's not exactly a sports car but it's a whole different shape to the rest of them. Better looking. Felix is well impressed. He's more into cars than me.

'Wow, cool, an Alfa,' he says.

'The rental place upgraded me,' says Mark. 'I think it was all they had left. I wasn't going to argue.'

'I call shotgun,' says Felix, getting into the front, and I squeeze in the back. The seats are red leather. There isn't a lot of room.

Before we set off, Mark asks Felix if he wants to put some music on.

Felix is never without his phone and there's a USB lead to plug into it. Mark fiddles with a sort of TV screen in the middle of the dashboard, pressing it and swiping it, while Felix does the same with his phone and soon some loud music comes on. Mark opens all the windows and starts the engine. It sounds like something out of a film. We drive off and cruise through the olive groves with the song blasting out and the roar of the engine bouncing back off the drystone walls.

We're the sort of people that Dad complains about.

When I think about Dad, I feel bad that I didn't ring Mum last night, but the game just went on too long. And I haven't had a chance to ring her yet this morning. She'll be 'frantic with worry'.

I'm trying not to think about it too much or I'll be frantic with worry too.

I tell myself that if Mum hasn't rung, then there's no news. Which must be good.

I'll ring her from the cafe if I can find a private bit where no one will hear me. God. What kind of a monster am I? I'm more worried about people overhearing me than I am about my dad.

Mark's nodding his head and tapping his fingers on the steering wheel in time to the music as we go. It's hot with the window open and my hair's blowing about. I look out and watch the bushes whipping by and wonder about those *cornettos*.

Wine for breakfast. Soup for breakfast. Coke for breakfast. Now ice cream for breakfast. Ah, well. We're on holiday. I wonder if I'll ever be as chilled as Uncle Mark. Like I fit in here. Like I belong. Just hanging out. Casual.

Yeah. Sure. I'm cool. I'll have an ice cream for breakfast.

I wonder if I'll ever be that person.

Well, today I'll try to pretend that I am. I mean, I could certainly eat an ice cream right now. And I'm *going* to. Mum's not here to stop me. Dad's not here to make fun of me.

'*What kind of an idiot eats an ice cream for breakfast? You're like someone out of some awful reality-TV programme, Stan . . .*'

I like my dad. I really do. But I sometimes think that I'm the way I am because he's always saying these things, making me all self-conscious. And with him not being here I don't have to behave how he wants me to.

Is that bad? To be sort of glad he isn't here, when he's in hospital?

I mean, it's not like I want him to die.

Stop it, Stan! Don't have bad thoughts!

When we get to the cafe, I get out of the car like the sort of cool kid who does what he likes and eats ice cream for breakfast. I'm wearing sunglasses and everything.

The cafe is in a small square surrounded by old crumbling buildings. There's a church, a bakery, a fish shop and a little supermarket with coloured plastic strips hanging in the doorway to keep the flies out. There's also a bicycle repair place where a very old man is fixing a puncture while a skinny Italian man in full professional cycling gear stands waiting for him, drinking coffee out of a tiny cup. He's wearing way-too-tight shorts, a clingy multicoloured top covered in logos, fingerless gloves, a helmet and bright blue, mirrored sunglasses.

I wish I had the guts to wear such a ridiculous outfit in public. Like it was the most normal thing in the world.

We get to the cafe and Mark orders our breakfast. I'm all ready to tuck into my ice cream when I discover that in Italy a *cornetto* isn't an ice cream at all. It's a type of pastry with creamy custard-type stuff in one end and creamy chocolate-type stuff in the other. So, just like we never actually had Coke for breakfast, or soup for breakfast, or wine for breakfast (although I *have* seen Simon having wine for breakfast), I don't get ice cream for breakfast.

The *cornetto* pastry is pretty good, though.

Actually, it's *very* good.

Too good.

I could eat two of them. I could eat ten of them. I could spend the whole day here just eating *cornettos*. I want to come to this cafe every morning and have a *cornetto* and I feel a bit sad when I think about all those missed mornings when we could have come here and didn't.

I know what Mum would say – '*They'll make you fat.*' But I can't seem to get through to her that I'm actually very thin.

I realize that it's not just Dad. I'm a little bit glad Mum's not here as well. Which is weird, when I was so homesick before. It's a good feeling not having someone watching you all the time, worrying about you, loving you . . . Sometimes it's nice to be just . . .

Well . . . *just a boy.*

'Have you been out on the bikes?' Mark asks us. He's also watching the Italian cyclist in the daft outfit.

'No,' says Felix. 'They've all got punctures.'

'Someone could have helped you get them mended. We'll fix them up.'

'Cool.'

'Honestly, guys, we need to pump up your holiday. How about after lunch we go to the beach and you can have a go at parascending? You'd be up for that, wouldn't you, Stan?'

Would I? Thoughts swirl around my brain. What are the health and safety regulations like out here? And what about paying for it? Mum said I wasn't to let Felix's family pay for everything and look like a scrounger. But I *do* have the emergency money. Is this an emergency, though? Well, it does involve a parachute, which you only use in an emergency . . .

'You don't look very sure,' says Mark. And I realize I've waited far too long to reply. Mark looks at me. 'You know what Ian Fleming said? *Never say "no" to adventures. Always say "yes", otherwise you'll lead a very dull life.* What do you reckon?'

'Yeah,' I say. 'Sure.' Although I've got along very well so far by always firmly saying no to adventures.

'Who's Ian Fleming?' Felix asks, with his bored, sneery voice. As if Ian Fleming must be a real ninnyhammer.

'He created James Bond,' I say. I know this because Dad's always going on about him.

'But he wrote that line about adventures in *Chitty Chitty Bang Bang*,' says Mark.

'That's a lame book,' says Felix.

'Yeah, well, never mind that,' says Mark. 'Do you want to go parascending?'

'Can I do the banana boat instead?'

'You can do both.'

Mark asks if we're ready to leave, but there's Wi-Fi at the cafe and Felix wants to download a new game to his phone. The Wi-Fi's quite slow so we have to wait a while.

Mark looks at some emails and asks me if I want to use the Wi-Fi at all. I shrug and say I'm OK. I'd love to go on the internet, but the truth is I can't access it from my phone, so I have to keep it hidden all the time.

Everybody at the house has a smartphone except me. The person with the smartest phone is of course Ash. As well as the latest iPhone, he has an Android phone with a bendy screen that he says you can't even buy in the shops yet. He told everyone that as an 'early adopter' and an 'Instagram influencer' he gets sent new gadgets to try out all the time. He also has a portable modem dongle thing that gives him his own fast internet. It turns his laptop into a personal Wi-Fi hotspot as well, so when he's around and using it everybody wants to be his friend.

I just have a stupid phone. Nobody would ever want to be my friend because of my phone. Mum got it for me just before we came away. She thought that if I came to Italy with a smartphone it'd be a disaster. She said she'd heard stories of people going abroad and using their phones and getting charged hundreds and thousands of pounds for their data use.

'We'd have to sell our car,' she said.

'Or you,' said Dad.

So I can only use my phone for making calls.

Which reminds me.

I'd better call Mum.

A Conversation with Mum

4

'Hi, Mum.'

'Stan? Is that you?'

'What other twelve-year-old boy is going to ring you up?'

'Why didn't you ring last night?'

'We were busy and then it got too late. Don't tell me – you've been frantic with worry.'

'Don't be cheeky. I *have* been worried. But mainly about your dad.'

'Why, what's happened? Has he got worse? He's not dead, is he?'

'No, no. Nothing like that. It's just they're going to operate on him this afternoon . . .'

'On his heart?'

'Yes.'

'That sounds serious. Will they have to . . . you know . . . cut him open?'

'No. They're going to put in a stent.'

'What's a stent?'

'It's like a little sort of rubber ring thingy. What they do is they stick a tiny camera up his leg –'

'His leg?'

'Yes. In the artery in his leg and they poke it all the way up through his body to find where the artery's blocked and then they stick this little ring thing, the stent, up his leg and push it along to where the blockage is, and when it's in place they inflate it and it opens out the artery, so the blood can flow through easily. Isn't that clever?'

'It sounds weird.'

'It is weird. It's crazy. Like something from a science-fiction film.'

'Is it safe?'

'They say it's routine . . . but there's always a risk . . . The main thing is they don't have to cut his ribs apart and do open-heart surgery. That'd be awful. Just awful.'

'Yes. It would.'

'Are you sure you're all right, Stan? You're very quiet.'

'I'm at a cafe. There are people here. I've moved to another table, but I don't want them to hear.'

'All right. I understand . . . Is it a nice cafe?'

'Yes. We're having breakfast.'

'What are you having? Do they do a full English?'

'No. I'm having an Italian breakfast.'

'Don't make yourself sick.'

'I won't . . . bye, Mum.'

'Bye, love. Have a lovely day and don't worry about your dad.'

'I'll try.'

'It's routine. Just a camera up his leg. A little plastic ring. And – pop! He's good as new.'

'Yeah . . . bye.'

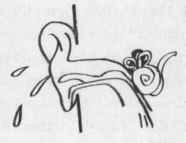

Reason 14: Water in your ears

When we finish at the cafe, Mark pays up and we go to the bakery. It's very small and dark inside. Mark buys a loaf of the hard chewy Italian bread that I'm actually growing to like. He also buys a bag of little biscuit-type things called *taralli*. We've had some at the house. They look like little curls of dried cat poo but taste quite nice.

Mark asks if there's anything else we need as we go back out into the bright sun. Felix says we've run out of crisps. So Mark buys a giant bag in the supermarket. He also gets some fresh vegetables, some slices of ham, some cheese and a couple of bottles of wine.

It's nice just poking around the little town in the sun, not in a hurry, nothing to do, just being lazy and relaxed and peaceful. The only sound is the flip and flop of my flip-flops. I think all shoes should be named after the sound they make. High heels should be called clip-clacks. Heavy boots should be called clomps or scuffs. Wellington boots should be called flumps. Trainers should be called . . . Actually, trainers don't make any sound at all really, do they? No wonder Americans call them sneakers.

Yeah, I know what you're thinking – why am I thinking about shoes at a time like this? When my dad's having a camera shoved up his leg in hospital. Well, there's nothing I can do about it, and it doesn't seem real. And . . .

And if I think about shoes, it means I'm not thinking about stents. I'd never heard of stents before today and now if I'm not careful they'll be *all* I can think about.

He's going to be all right.

When we get back to the house, a few people are up and Mrs Harper is busying about the place getting breakfast ready. Dr Cathy, Emma and the angry woman are helping her. Ash is sitting in his usual spot at a little round table in the shade. Every morning he gets up late, sits there with a cup of coffee, gets out his dongle and fires up his iPad. Then he stays there all day looking at stuff on the internet. Mainly news, I think, but now and then he laughs, which makes me think he might be watching videos on YouTube of small children being chased by chickens.

Mostly, though, it's news, and he tells everyone what he's watching as if he's some sort of special holiday news announcer.

'There's an earthquake in Turkey, pretty serious . . . Wow, that's awful, a big smash on the M11, twenty-seven cars involved . . . A ferry's sunk in Hong Kong . . . Two more ministers have resigned . . .'

He even does the weather.

'There's going to be storms at the end of the week . . . There are massive forest fires near Sydney . . . All the cars in Sternatia – which is only about twenty kilometres from here – have been wrecked by giant hailstones the size of tennis balls . . . Hundreds of people have died in flooding in Bolivia . . .'

As we come over, he looks up from his screen and sees Mark. They say hello and Ash tries to tell him about a shooting in America. Mark suddenly looks really worried.

'Oh my god,' he says. 'Is it too late? Can we stop it?'

'What do you mean?'

'Can we stop the shooting?'

'No, no, it happened, like, a few hours ago.'

'So we can't stop it?'

'No.'

'What *can* we do?'

'What do you mean?'

'OK, it's obviously difficult – we're here in Italy thousands of miles away, but there must be *something* we can do? Perhaps we can get guns banned in America?'

'I doubt it,' says Ash with a little laugh, not sure how seriously to take Mark.

'Can we turn back time and get over there and stop it from happening?'

'Yeah, right . . .'

'Just tell me, Ash – what *can* we do about it?'

'We can't do anything about it.'

'So why are you telling me about it? Do you know somebody involved? Somebody who's been shot?'

'No. I just like to know what's going on in the world.'

'There are hundreds of millions of things going on in the world right now,' says Mark. 'Every second of every day on every part of the planet. Why do I need to know about *this one*, when there's nothing I can do about it? And why do *you* need to know about it? *At this very moment?* I come here to get away from all that. It's nothing to do with me. Anything important I can deal with when I get back. So right here, right now, I don't need to know about it. If you want to feel like you're plugged into the beating heart of the universe, fine. But keep it to yourself, yeah?'

'Sure. I just like to be in the know.'

Mark stops, as if he's about to say something, and then walks off towards the kitchen without saying anything.

Ash looks at me and shakes his head and goes back to his computer. 'Wow,' he says. 'A man in Japan has eaten his neighbour . . .'

Me and Felix muck about in the pool for the rest of the morning with Jess and Aria. We have some races, we see who can go for the longest underwater, we play a game where we try to push each other off a lilo, and then we try to teach Aria how to dive. She keeps freaking out at the last moment and flopping on to her front with a shriek. Jess suggests she tries aiming through a big rubber ring and, after several tries where she chickens out, she eventually does it and dives hands first through the ring. We all cheer and after that Aria can do it over and over without any trouble.

I notice that Felix still won't dive at all. I wonder whether he can even do it?

Afterwards we all lie on sunbeds, drying off in the sun. And then we play Perudo. I can't concentrate, though, because one of my ears is blocked with water and I can't get it out.

Before lunch I go to our room and try to deal with it.

Here's a list of all the ways I know to get trapped water out of your ear. Start with number one and work your way down to number six. If number six doesn't work, you'll need to get your head amputated . . .

HOW TO GET WATER OUT OF YOUR EAR

1. The Sink Plunger.
2. The 'Doh'.
3. The Pogo.
4. The 'Why, Oh, Why?'
5. The Lumberjack.
6. The Not Very Exciting Spray.

Right, here goes . . .

1. The Sink Plunger. To do this you stick a finger in your ear so that it's wedged in tight and then pull it out quickly. The theory is that the suction will drag the water out. This doesn't work. Also, I think there is a danger that you will suck your brains out before you suck any water out, but it doesn't stop me trying. Also, as I've said before, you're not supposed to stick your finger in your ear.

2. The 'Doh'. This is a variation on the Homer Simpson face palm. But, instead of slapping your forehead, you hold your open palm out to the side of your head and bang your temple hard against it.

This hurts a lot.

And doesn't work.

Move quickly on to . . .

3. The Pogo. You jump up and down with your head tilted to the side. (This doesn't work.)

4. The 'Why, Oh, Why?' Next, you lie on your side on your bed and whack your head repeatedly on a pillow, with your blocked ear facing down, like somebody in a film who's done something awful and wants to get rid of the memory. This doesn't really work, but as you're already on your bed you can move on to the next method, which is more drastic . . .

5. The Lumberjack. You stand on your bed, shout 'Timber!' and then fall sideways so that your head hits the pillow. With luck, the momentum (we've been doing momentum in science at school) will force the water to keep moving once your body has stopped and it will gush out of your ear.

This doesn't work either.

6. The Not Very Exciting Spray (this is the only method that actually works). You ask a responsible adult (such as Mrs Harper in my case) if they have anything for getting water out of the ear. If you're lucky, they have a special spray. You spray it in your ear and in a few minutes the blocked water has been 'dispersed', which basically means it's gone.

The reason you don't start with method number six is because there's no magic moment of ear-popping freedom with the spray. At first you don't even think it's worked, and then a little while later you realize, *Hey, my ear isn't blocked any more.* Where's the fun in that? The magic moment when one of the other methods miraculously works and the water is dislodged is, well, it's magic. You hear the drop of water rolling through your ear like a giant boulder and then – WHOOSH – it's like a dam bursting. You can hear again, and delicious warm water trickles out of your ear. It's one of the best feelings in the world. Well worth the pain of all that head-battering.

Anyway. I make the most of my new super hearing and sit with Jess and Aria at lunch telling knock-knock jokes and trying to ignore everyone else. Because Felix has his head down over his phone and there's something weird going on with Alice and Lily and the adults. Everyone's still talking about Hatgate, and how awful Mr Harper was. Livia's the worst. She won't leave it alone. It seems a shame to be in this nice place having a nice lunch and spoiling everything with these bad feelings. If I can stay chilled, if I can just hang out by the pool and not get anxious or stressed, then why can't they? I'm the one with something serious to deal with. A lot more serious than cheating in a silly game. They're grown-ups – they're supposed to behave in a what-do-you-call-it? Well, in a grown-up way.

After lunch we hang out by the pool again and I get ambushed by Livia again. At first I think she's going to draw me into the Hatgate discussions, but instead she says, 'Ollie, I've been thinking about your girlfriend.'

'What girlfriend?'

'You know – I said I'd find you a girlfriend.'

'Oh, yeah . . . I'm called Stan by the way.'

'Whatever. I've found you one. The perfect girlfriend.'

'Right . . . Who?'

'Lily.'

'Alice's friend, Lily?'

'Yes. She's beautiful.'

'She's, like, four years older than me. Practically an adult.'

'Hmm. I suppose she is a *bit* older than you . . . OK. I'll keep thinking. I'm good at this sort of thing.'

'Right.'

When she's gone, Jess comes over and asks me what we were talking about.

'Nothing really.'

'Your lips were moving.'

'She asked me if I'd seen . . . the suntan lotion.'

'Right.'

Jess dives in the pool and I wonder why I didn't tell her what we were really talking about.

Reason 15: Do you know how many people die on holiday every year?

We're getting ready to go to the beach. After lunch Mark said that he'd take us kids, and then everyone else said they'd like to come too. Even Ash. And he's never been to the beach before. I wonder if he'll bring his iPad. It's important that we all know whether there's been any explosions or natural disasters or outbreaks of swine flu in Mongolia.

As everyone was rushing about, Ash said he'd help get everything ready and went to sit in his car.

Mrs Harper's getting quite 'hot and bothered' (as Mum would say) trying to get everybody herded up. The girls keep going in and out of their room, doing their make-up, changing their outfits, forgetting their swimming things, forgetting their phones . . .

'You won't need your phones!'

Mr Harper is in the loo. Livia and the angry woman are talking about him in loud whispers. Simon has disappeared. Felix is sitting playing a game on his phone.

'Felix! Have you got your shoes?'

'Yeah.'

Emma's by the pool listening to her audiobook.

'Sorry – are we going? My book's just got to a really exciting bit.'

Mrs Harper tells me to get some beach towels from the laundry room. I've not been in here before. It's full of cleaning stuff, mops and buckets and brooms and plastic bottles of chemicals, and there are shelves piled up with towels and sheets and a big washing machine in the corner.

And Simon.

I didn't expect to find him in here. He looks a bit startled. He quickly hides something, picks up a towel and waves it at me.

'I'm beach ready!' he says, and laughs as he goes out. There's a smell of alcohol.

Now Felix is in the loo. Lily's looking for her favourite top. Emma's lost her sunglasses. Mr Harper is wandering up and down having a conversation with someone on his phone about money. Ash is still in his car. Mrs Harper is locking a door, but there's a voice from the other side and she has to unlock it to let Dr Cathy out.

'Sorry. I was getting my book.'

There's a shout of 'Omigodman!' and I look over to see Ben and Aria playing table football.

'Are you coming?' asks Mrs Harper.

'Yes. One minute,' says Ben. 'This is the championship final!'

We all finally get out to the car park and Mrs Harper organizes everyone into different cars. I end up sandwiched between Felix and Jess in the back of Mark's Alfa. I tell Jess about the cafe and the *cornetto* and she says she'd like to come with us tomorrow if we go there again for breakfast.

Cool. We're having another conversation. Like friends. I wonder if Jess is my friend now. I'd be more relaxed if I wasn't covered in sun cream, though, all sweaty and sticky. I feel very aware of my bare legs next to hers. I tell her that me and Felix are going up on the parachute as if it's an easy thing to do and not UTTERLY

TERRIFYING. (I must think of an excuse before we get to the beach so I can get out of it.)

Jess asks if she can do it too.

'You can all have a go,' says Mark as we set off.

'I want to do the banana boat,' says Felix. Although we already know that.

'Ooh,' says Simon, who's sitting in the front with Mark, 'can I do the banana boat?'

'You're an adult, Simon,' says Mark. 'You can do what you want.'

'Great. Can I have an ice cream?'

'Very funny.'

'I'm going to have a go on the parachute as well,' says Simon. 'I once did a real parachute jump. A proper sky-dive. For charity. It was A-May-Zing. I slightly broke my ankle. But that was OK.' He sings a bit: '*This is Ground Control to Major Simon . . .*' And then he's rambling on about D-Day and someone called Douglas Bader, and then he's pointing out trees to us, and then Mark puts some loud music on.

Simon talking about skydiving has made me even more nervous. I can hear Mum's voice telling me to be careful and not do anything stupid. She's not even here and she's making me anxious!

When we get to the beach, the five of us walk along to where the speedboats are. Simon stops off at the bar on the way to get a bottle of beer. It's even more crowded here today and the disco guy is playing his music louder and shouting things out into a microphone.

'Crazy . . . Sexy . . . Cool . . . Yeah, baby . . . Dance . . .'

Everybody is still ignoring him.

We walk on. Two young Italian guys and two girls in bikinis are in charge of the parascending. The guys are only wearing small trunks. They are handsome with Italian-footballer haircuts and suntans and muscles, and there are a few other girls in bikinis hanging around them. The main girls take our money and show us a row of life vests hanging on a rack. As we put them on, we watch a teenager who was here before us get ready to go up.

So I get to see how it works.

First you put a harness on over your life vest. Then the straps go up between your legs and are fastened all around you with clips and Velcro. The harness is then fixed to the parachute that's attached to the speedboat by a long rope.

Two guys wait on the beach and hold the parachute up behind you. There are two more guys in the speedboat: one to drive and one to watch you and be in charge of the rope. To start with, the rope is coiled up on the sand, but, when the boat sets off, the rope unspools and then tightens until you have to run down the beach after the boat, like running with a kite. This makes the parachute fill up with air behind you, and by the time you reach the water it lifts you up and pulls you into the air.

Simples.

What could possibly go wrong?

I'm even more terrified now. The two guys in charge of the parachute are not paying full attention to their work. They are flirting with the girls who take the money, they are flirting with all the girls who go past, and they are flirting with two girls in the queue behind us. They even try to flirt with Jess, even though she's my age. They're trying to speak to her in English and ignoring me and Simon and Felix and Mark.

We watch as the teenager before us is dragged out to sea before going round in a big loop. On the return journey, the boat slows down and dunks him in the water, and then, before the parachute can completely deflate and flop into the ocean, they speed up and yank him back into the air.

It's not long before they're coasting towards the beach. The boy lands in the shallow water and the young men flirt with a passing girl for a bit and then help him on to dry land.

Simon's going up first. Which is fine by me. It gives me more time to think of a way out of this. Because it is *definitely* not a good idea, despite what Ian Fleming said about never saying no to an adventure. I mean, why would anyone put their life in the hands of some half-naked Italian boys with footballer haircuts?

I can imagine the conversation I'd have if I was here on holiday with Mum and Dad.

MUM: You are *not* going up on that, Stanley – it's far too dangerous.

DAD: It's a rip-off, Stan. It's daylight robbery. They've got a very pretty little scam going on here.

MUM: It's not about the money. It's the extreme danger I'm concerned about.

ME: But if anything happened, I'd be falling into water.

DAD: From that height, when you hit the water it would be like jumping off a ten-storey building into a car park. It would shatter every bone in your body.

ME: You're not helping.

MUM: Dad's right. Hundreds of people die in parachute accidents every year.

ME: Do they?

I don't know how many people die in parachute accidents every year, but before we came away I did look up on the internet how many people have accidents on holiday. Which I know I shouldn't have done. I thought it might make me less anxious. It didn't. It had the opposite effect: 500,000 British people got into trouble on their holidays last year; 20,000 lost their passports;

3,500 of them ended up in hospital and 4,000 actually died.

Died!

On holiday.

And that's only the British people.

'*Where are you going on holiday this year?*'

'*Heaven.*'

I turn to Jess, who's smiling.

'This is going to be so cool, isn't it?' she says.

'Yeah,' I say, 'cool.' Trying to sound casual, trying to sound like I do this sort of thing every day. When what I actually want to say to her is . . .

Do you know how many people die on holiday every year????

Reason 15 (part 2): Do you know how many people die on holiday every year?

'I'll show you how it's done,' Simon says, taking a swig from his beer bottle and stepping up to be strapped into the harness. He laughs and jokes with the Italian guys, who clearly can't understand a word he's saying, and then he walks to his starting position as the guys in the boat pull two girls in bikinis aboard. They've obviously arranged to take them out for a joyride. The girls are giggling and talking very fast, and the guys aren't really bothering to keep an eye on Simon.

I can see that this could all go horribly wrong. And, to tell you the truth, part of me is actually enjoying it. As long as it's happening to somebody else.

The two guys in charge of the parachute aren't keeping an eye on Simon either. They're also flirting. With a large group of girls in very small bikinis who have just turned up. One of the guys calls out, 'Are you ready?' without looking at Simon and Simon roars, 'Chocks away! Cabbage crates over the briny, wing commander!'

Which must mean even less to the Italians than it does to me, but they seem happy.

The boat starts off. Simon's standing ready, a wobbly smile on his face, and then he realizes he's still holding the beer bottle and wanders over to where we're standing, pulling the rope behind him.

'Can you hold on to this for me?' Simon says to Mark, holding out the bottle. The rope is starting to unspool.

'You need to get back to where you were standing before,' says Mark, with a worried look on his face. An Italian family has just arrived and are setting up beach chairs and settling down between Simon and the water. The rope is looped round behind them.

'I've done proper skydiving,' says Simon. 'This is kids' stuff. One for the road, eh . . .?' He goes to take another swig from his bottle.

I'm about to say something to warn him when it *does* all go horribly wrong, just as I suspected.

It happens quickly, but somehow in slow motion at the same time. Simon puts the bottle to his lips and then the rope jerks tight, tangling up with the Italian family who start to yell and wave their arms about and jump up from their beach chairs. At the same time Simon's jerked off his feet.

He yelps – 'Steady on!' – then swears as he goes face first into the sand. Now the rope drags him right through the middle of the Italian family's camp, knocking over beach chairs and umbrellas, cool-boxes, small children, two rather large older women and an old man in tiny Speedos, who actually shouts, *'Mamma mia!'*

The young guys in charge of the parachute are yelling, but the guys on the boat aren't paying attention. Simon is ploughed through the sand, leaving a deep trench behind him, and into the ocean.

He's underwater for some time. I'm just beginning to think we'll never see him again when the parachute opens out and fills with air and shoots upwards, pulling Simon up out of the water like a fish on a hook. He's still holding his beer bottle, but he looks a bit limp and I wonder if he's perhaps drowned. But then he raises the bottle to his mouth and takes a swig and I can just hear a distant cry of 'Bombs away!'

'Cool,' says Felix.

'Bloody idiot,' says Mark.

We watch as the boat drags Simon out to sea, dangling like a puppet. He's pulled round in a big circle and then dunked like everyone else and the boat heads back. I wonder if the guys in the boat ever get bored of this. The same thing, over and over. But it beats working on a bus, I guess, where you also have to do the same thing over and over, and you have to do it on the grey grimy streets of London rather than in a speedboat in the Mediterranean with all those girls in bikinis to flirt with.

The boat returns, comes round skilfully, and Simon drops gently from the sky. He lands in the water and one of the beach guys goes running out to him to check he's OK and take the harness off him while the others deal with the parachute.

Simon staggers ashore. His chest and tummy are badly scraped and he's bleeding from a few spots. He looks a bit dazed, but then he always looks a bit dazed.

'It was OK, wing-co,' he says, 'but we took a bit of flak over the French coast.'

Then he sees me and Felix and Jess staring at him boggle-eyed.

'You'll love it,' he says. 'It's a blast.'

The father from the Italian family comes over and says something angry-sounding to Simon with a lot of hand gestures. Simon laughs and slaps him on the back and offers him his beer. The man doesn't know what to do and walks away with one last shout and an angry gesture.

I have got to get out of this. Maybe if I say that it's clearly not safe? But, when Jess says we can go up together in a double harness, I nod and get strapped in.

I can't look like a wimp in front of her.

We're soon sorted out and standing next to each other on the sand. I can tell that Jess is almost as nervous as me. After all, we've seen what happened to Simon. Even the Italian guys are nervous. They don't want any more accidents today with stupid English people. They are giving us lots of instructions that we can't understand.

My heart is racing and my mouth goes dry and then the boat's moving away and the rope's going tight and everyone's shouting and we're running across the sand towards the sea and the next thing we know we're lifted up. Up and up and up we go, the beach dropping away below us, people getting smaller.

We're in the sky. We're actually flying above the beach.

And it would be totally amazing, awesome, spectacular . . .

If one of my nuts wasn't trapped in the harness.

All my weight is on it now and it's really quite painful. My whole body is aching. But I can't say anything to Jess. She'll think I'm a perv. I mean, it's not the sort of thing you can talk about to a girl you don't know very well, is it?

Or anyone, really.

'This is so cool,' says Jess.

'Yes,' I say, my voice a bit high and tight sounding. I smile and pretend that I'm enjoying myself, which I *was* for the first few seconds before I realized I had a nut problem. I wriggle to try to release it, but it only seems to make it worse.

The pain makes me lose the last of my confidence. It looks much higher from up here than it did down there. It's like being on top of a skyscraper. Everything looks tiny and far away. I remember what Dad said about hitting the water from this height and then have to remind myself that it was only an imaginary conversation. Even so, if the harness snaps we'll plummet like stones and smack into the water as if it was concrete . . .

'Wow! Look!' says Jess, letting go of the harness with one hand and pointing. 'There's the cafe.'

I think how brave Jess is not gripping tight to the harness with both hands. It makes me feel a bit sick. But it could just as easily be the trapped nut doing that.

Jess is right. You *can* see the cafe. And you can see past it, over the dunes at the back of the beach, and the pine trees, and past them to the road, and past the road you can see all of the countryside laid out like a map.

For about one second I forget everything and enjoy the view.

'Can you see our group?' Jess asks and I scan the beach. There's all the beds and umbrellas spread out in a perfect mathematical grid. And, there, I can see Aria's gigantic hat. And the rest of our group spilling out messily from a couple of sunbeds. I point them out to Jess and she waves. Nobody sees us. They don't wave back.

I don't wave.

No way am I going to let go of the harness.

So far the speedboat has been following the coastline and now we begin to turn so that we're heading out to sea. There's a big white ship far out, a line of smoke trailing away behind it.

'Look,' says Jess. 'You can see the mountains in Albania.'

You can. It's a very clear day and the mountains are a wavy brown smudge between the sea and the sky.

'Isn't this great?'

I just manage to squeak out a 'yes', praying that this will all be over soon. Here I am, alone with a girl I like, in a very romantic setting, nobody could possibly hear our conversation, we could talk about absolutely anything, but all I can think about is the terrible pain I'm in.

'The sea looks perfect from up here, doesn't it?' she says. 'You wouldn't know it was full of plastic.'

'Mmm.'

'Me and Mum spent a day in Dorset picking up plastic from a beach there last summer.'

'Mmm.'

'We got seventeen bin bags full. We should do it here. Do you want to do it with me one day?'

'Mmm.'

'I bet we get tons. There's a lot of rubbish on these beaches.'

'Mm-mm.'

We slow down and I can feel that we're slowly dropping. I know what's going to happen next. I've seen it enough times.

Jess knows too.

'We're going for a splashdown,' she says excitedly. 'Whoo-hoo!'

Then she looks down. 'Do you see that?' she says. 'There's loads of plastic bags in the water.'

I look down too.

'Gross,' she says. 'It's terrible that the sea is so full of plastic.'

'Actually, I don't think those are plastic bags,' I say, forgetting my pain for a moment.

'What do you mean?'

'I hate to say it, but I think they're jellyfish . . .'

Reason 16: Killer jellyfish

'Oh my god! Oh my god, you're right! They *are* jellyfish!'

We both start yelling and screaming at the speedboat. 'Take us up! Take us up!'

I let go with both hands and wave my arms. The guys in the boat wave back. The girls in the boat wave back. And we carry on dropping down.

We can clearly see the jellyfish now. There must be hundreds of them. They're all grey and purple and gloopy and transparent, with long trailing tentacles.

And we're going to land right in the middle of the deadly swarm.

I can tell Jess is really scared and in a moment of madness I try a joke, thinking it might distract her.

'Never let go, Rose,' I say in a terrible American accent.

'I'm not called Rose. I'm Jess,' she says.

'No. It's from *Titanic*,' I say. 'Jack's last words to Rose.'

'What?'

'Never mind.'

Jess looks at me as if I'm bonkers. I have a horrible sinking feeling. In fact, I have two horrible sinking feelings. One because I *am* actually sinking – the other because my joke didn't go down at all well.

And the next thing I know we're in the sea up to our waists.

Jess is shrieking and thrashing her legs about. I'm actually slightly glad to be floating in the water, though, because the weight is lifted from my nut for a moment and I manage to forget all about the jellyfish and wriggle and squirm and pull the harness aside and – oh, blessed relief – my aching nut is freed.

For a sweet moment I enjoy the intense relief, but it doesn't last long. We are in a soup of jellyfish. They're all around us. It's amazing how something so slow and useless can be so scary.

And they're starting to sting.

Jess is going crazy, churning up the water like a ship's propeller and yelling her head off.

Someone shouts, 'Stop!'

Someone who sounds grown up and in charge. Sensible and fearless.

Who was it? Captain America? Superman? No. I realize it was me. Where did that come from?

Of course – it came from Mum's emergency list!

What to do if attacked by jellyfish.

I never thought it would actually happen, but I know what to do . . .

'Jess, stop kicking.'

It's all coming back to me.

'Keep still or you'll get tangled up worse.'

'It's too late,' she says, lifting up an arm. There are tentacles wrapped round it and a big blob of jellyfish hanging off her. It doesn't have any eyes, but I punch it in the closest thing it has to a face and it falls away. And then we're going up again and the guys on the boat are waving cheerfully. Jess is crying and I must say the stings on her arms and legs *do* look pretty bad, bad enough for me to forget my own stings.

But you know what? It doesn't hurt as much as a trapped nut.

Dad says that in wars sometimes when soldiers get an arm or a leg blown off, they don't feel any pain for a while because of the shock.

Maybe I'm in shock.

By the time we get near to the beach Jess has calmed down a bit, but she's shivering and shaking and my own stings are starting to burn and itch. It's like really bad stinging nettles. Actually – *ow-ow-ow* – it's much worse than that. I yell louder than Jess.

Then I try to calm myself down and remember what to do.

'Don't scratch the stings or rub them,' I say as we float down towards the water. 'In fact, don't touch them at all. When a jellyfish stings you, they release thousands of tiny barbs that hook into your skin and release venom. There are probably still bits of tentacles stuck to your skin, and touching them will only make them sting you more.'

'It really hurts.'

'Mediterranean jellyfish aren't that bad.'

'Compared to what?'

'If this was Australia, we'd both be dead by now.'

'What?'

'We'll be OK. As long as we don't get an allergic reaction, we'll be fine.'

'When did you suddenly become an expert?'

'I know everything there is to know about the potential dangers of the Mediterranean.'

We land safely and try to explain to the Italian guys in the boat about the jellyfish. When they see our wounds, they get the picture pretty quickly. They all start talking to us at the same time as they jump out and remove the harnesses.

'Rinse the stings with sea water before we get ashore,' I tell Jess. 'And remember not to touch them. The nematocysts are filled with salt water –'

'The WHAT?'

'Nematocysts – the stinging cells,' I say, splashing about in the water. 'If you irritate them, by touching them or washing them with fresh water, they'll just release more venom.'

'Stop saying venom. It makes me think I'm going to die.'

'What do you want me to call it?'

'I don't know . . . *Owwww*. Now what do we do? It still really burns.'

'Come on.'

We go ashore and walk over to Mark and Simon.

'Have you got, like, a credit card?' I ask them. 'Anything plastic with a sharp edge?'

Mark looks confused but gets out a card. As he hands it to me, he spots the marks on our skin.

'What happened?' he asks.

'Jellyfish happened,' I say, and take his credit card.

I show Jess how to carefully scrape the stings with the edge of the card to get rid of any remaining nematocysts, at the same time wondering how amazing it is that under stress the human brain is able to remember quite obscure facts and words.

Simon comes towards Jess with a towel, but she tells him to stop. Quite sharply.

'We mustn't rub the stings or the nematocysts will release more venom,' she says, and Simon and Mark look at her like she's the hero of a sci-fi horror film armed with futuristic alien science knowledge.

One of the Italian guys comes over with a spray.

'Is good,' he says, and sprays some on one of my stings. It *does* feel good. I notice it smells of vinegar. Vinegar was one of the things on Mum's list.

'It's OK,' I say to Jess. 'It's some kind of acid spray.'

'Acid!?!?!?!??!?!'

'Mild acid,' I say quickly. 'Like vinegar. It helps.'

After Jess has been sprayed, we inspect our wounds. They don't look great, to be honest. We're both streaked with red marks and spotted with nasty red circles.

Simon keeps going 'wow' and calling the marks 'welts'.

'We'll get some ice,' says Mark, looking at the worst of my stings, which goes right across the top of my left leg.

'No,' I say. 'Hot water's best. Heat deactivates the venom toxins. It's better than ice.'

Mark looks at me funny. Who knew I was such a jellyfish boffin?

'We can get some hot water from the cafe,' says Simon. 'And we'll find you some painkillers.'

'And some antihistamine,' I say, and Mark and Simon look even more impressed.

Felix has also been studying our wounds.

'They don't look so bad,' he says. I think he's a bit jealous.

As we walk into our camp, me and Jess feel really brave, like two war heroes who've just survived a terrible battle. Which I suppose we have. We feel grown up too. Not little kids any more. I guess even bad things can have good sides. Me and Jess are a team now. We've shared an adventure. I can imagine a conversation with her in, like, fifty years' time, when we're old and grey – 'Remember that time we were dunked in the middle of a swarm of wild jellyfish?'

'Oho, yes . . .'

And we'll laugh about it and our grandchildren will say, 'Please, please, tell us about it – it sounds scary.'

'Oh, we can laugh about it now, but at the time it was terrible . . . We were on this parachute, you see . . . By the way, do you know how many people die in parachute accidents every year?'

I realize that in this imaginary conversation me and Jess are married and have children. And grandchildren. I think perhaps I'm getting carried away. I can't think of any societies in the world where getting stung half to death by jellyfish is part of getting engaged.

I giggle. I think I might be getting slightly hysterical.

Not as hysterical as Mrs Harper, though. She's having a fit, her hand over her mouth. 'That's horrific. That must be so painful. What will I tell your mother?'

'It's not too bad,' I say, trying to sound brave. 'Maybe best not to tell her. I don't want her to worry . . .'

Dr Cathy offers Jess a hug, but Jess tells her not to touch her. Her mum has some antihistamine in a big beach bag, though. The bag seems to have everything you'd ever need in it.

Ben goes off to get us some ice creams and Coke as everyone crowds around us asking millions of questions, and for once I don't mind being the centre of attention. My whole body is tingling and buzzing.

Simon arrives with a bowl of hot water. Poor old Simon, nobody's interested in his wounds, even though he's scraped half the skin off his chest.

'Come on,' says Felix, once Jess and I have bathed our wounds and the hot water has taken some of the pain away. 'Let's do the banana boat! The parascending's lame. The banana boat's really cool.' He looks to Mr Harper, who's lying on a sunbed reading a book about Donald Trump. 'Dad? Can you take us?'

'Where?'

'Banana boat.'

'I don't think so. No.'

'I'll take you,' says Mark. 'Anyone else?'

Alice and Lily and Aria also say they'd like a go. I look at Jess and she shakes her head. I shake my head too. You never know. I didn't think for one second I'd need to worry about the jellyfish attack on Mum's list. It would be just my luck to get attacked by a shark next.

I watch as Mark leads the other kids off along the beach. Felix is chatting away to him about something. Mr Harper hasn't even looked up from his book. I think it's a shame that he's not taking Felix on the banana boat instead of his uncle. But it's nothing to do with me.

A Conversation with Mum

5

'How's Dad? How did the operation go? Did they put the stent thing up his leg OK? Is he awake? Are you at the hospital? Can he talk to me?'

'They didn't put a stent up him in the end.'

'So he didn't need it? That's good.'

'No. Apparently they couldn't do it. He was too bad. Too blocked up.'

'OK . . . That's not good. So what did they do?'

'They're going to operate on him tomorrow.'

'Operate . . .? You mean cut him open and fiddle with his heart?'

'Yes. He'll need a heart bypass.'

'Like a ring road?'

'Something like that. They find the bits of his arteries that are blocked and take them out and join up the good bits. It's still routine – it's just a little bit more complicated than popping a stent up his leg.'

'But he'll be OK?'

'They do it all the time. I just can't bear the thought of them cutting him open with a giant pair of scissors. I can't get the image out of my mind . . .'

'Don't cry, Mum. He'll be all right. The doctors will look after him. You said it's routine.'

'Yes – SNIFF – Yes . . . It's routine – SNIFF . . . The poor man. He's always been such a good dad. I just can't bear that he –'

'Mum . . . We went to the beach today.'

'Oh, yes . . .? SNIFF. That's nice. Did anything happen?'

'Well . . . erm . . . no. No. It was fun. Nothing happened. Nothing went wrong. I'm OK. You don't need to worry about me. We went on a –'

'What? What did you go on?'

'We went on a banana boat. It was really fun. I'm having a great time. I haven't been attacked by any sharks!'

'Oh, Stan, you do make me laugh sometimes. You cheer me right up. It's supposed to be *me* cheering *you* up.'

'Yeah. I'm OK. Nothing's gone wrong. I'm having a great time. I don't need cheering up. I just wish I could be there with you.'

'It's boring, Stan, most of the time, waiting around. You just enjoy yourself, love, and when you get back Dad will be right as rain.'

'OK. Give him my love.'

'I will. Now. You're being nice to people, aren't you?'

'Of course I am.'

'You're being polite to Mrs Harper?'

'Yes.'

'And how are you getting on with Felix?'

'Fine. We did have a bit of a fight . . .'

'Boys! Why are you always fighting? Now, you make it up to him. His family have been really kind having you out there.'

'It wasn't serious. It was a couple of days ago.'

'Still, it doesn't hurt to say sorry.'

'Sure. I love you, Mum.'

'Love you too. I'll call you tomorrow when Dad's had his operation . . .'

A Conversation with Felix

2

'Felix. I'm sorry we had that fight the other night.'

'Yeah. It was stupid. Let's forget it.'

'OK.'

'You OK? Does the jellyfish thing sting?'

'A lot. Yeah.'

'Bummer.'

'Yeah. And Felix . . .'

'Yeah?'

'My dad . . .'

'Yeah?'

'Nothing. It's just . . . He's in . . . He's in hospital. He needs an operation.'

'Bummer.'

'Yeah. Well, it's been good to talk about it.'

'Any time. And, Stan?'

'Yeah?'

'The fight we had?'

'I'm forgetting all about it, Felix.'

'Yeah . . . but I won, right?'

'Goodnight, Felix.'

' 'Night.'

Reason 17:
Bloody mosquitoes

It's five o'clock in the morning and I'm lying by the pool on a sunbed. The pool lights are on and bats are swooping over the water picking off the insects it attracts. The pool is a bright blue rectangle. The sky is purple and growing a brighter orange in the east past the line of palm trees. It looks sort of weird and luminous like a special effect in a film or like a CGI neon sky in a computer game.

Birds are starting to tweet. It feels like I'm the only person in the whole world. That all this belongs to me.

I'm out here because I can't sleep. I've been thinking about Dad, my welts are really hurting, and there was a mosquito in the room. It was getting at me all night. I had to keep the sheet off me because it irritated the welts and I'd gone to bed without using any mozzy spray. Dr Cathy had put some calamine lotion on our welts (I like the word 'welt'). It helped a little, but I was worried that if I put on mosquito repellent it might sting even more. And when I heard that familiar *zzzzzzzzzzzz* I knew I was in trouble.

I'd plugged in one of those anti-mosquito device things, but it was clear that one of the evil little gits had got in. Whenever I closed my eyes, I could hear it buzzing around. I'd lie very still, listening, as it circled nearer and nearer, and then it would dive-bomb, straight for me – *zzzzzzzzzzzzip* – and then go silent . . .

Dad once told me that in the war the Germans had these flying bombs called doodlebugs. During the Blitz they'd fly all the way over from Germany – *Neeeeeeeeeeeeee* – and you were OK as long as you could hear them. When they stopped making a noise, it meant the engine had cut out and they were going to drop out of the sky. And that was when you had to run for cover.

Well, that's how it is with mosquitoes. It's when they stop buzzing that you know they've landed on you and are about to stick their dirty little snouts into your skin and suck up all your blood. So as soon as I couldn't hear it any more I'd sit up and slap myself all over. But for hours and hours I couldn't see it.

Everyone else was asleep. Felix didn't know anything about it, and mosquitoes don't seem to bother him anyway. He just lay there on his back, his mouth wide open, snoring loudly (another reason I found it hard to sleep). There could be a whole family of mosquitoes crawling all over him, having a picnic on his face, with a barbecue and a game of football, and he still wouldn't wake up. The smallest thing wakes me up, though, and I suppose a mosquito *is* the smallest thing.

I felt I was really getting to know this one, even though I couldn't see it. I even gave it a name. Ian.

In the end I turned my bedside light on and sat there watching and waiting, like a hunter – and *I* was the trap. I heard Ian more than I saw him. Whenever I did see him, it looked like he was moving really slowly, but when I tried to swat him I always missed, clapping the thin air like an idiot. I might as well have been applauding his flying skills.

Then I armed myself with a book about octopuses. I'd finished the book of Greek myths I'd brought with me and found the octopus one on a bookshelf in the living room, which is full of books that people have left at the house.

Anyway. I got Ian in the end. I was more patient than him. I got him and I got him good. I waited and waited until he finally landed on the wall right next to my bed. I made sure he wasn't going to move and then — WHAM! – the octopus book got him, and when I took it away there was a big red splatter on the white wall.

I was too hyper to sleep after that, so I came outside and lay down on this sunbed. It's as if time has stopped and I sort of wish it would stay like this. That the morning would never come. Then nothing bad could happen. I'd really like to ring Mum up, just to hear her voice, but if her phone rang in the middle of the night she'd probably have a heart attack and end up in the hospital with Dad.

Oh, Dad.

You'd be proud of me using my hunting skills, killing Ian. He's still stuck to my book, like a trophy.

It feels very grown up to be awake at this time. All by myself. Everyone else asleep. Watching the dawn come along. I'm going to stay out here and enjoy the new day slowly waking up around me.

Reason 18: Sunburn

I fell asleep.

And when I woke up I was lying in the hot sun. Now I'm tired and a little bit burnt with sore eyes that feel crunchy. I have to keep closing them and wiggling them around under my eyelids to keep them working properly.

I'm way too exhausted to move. It's like I fell out of an aeroplane and landed on this sunbed with a THUD, and now my half-dead body lies flat and broken and unable to get up.

Life's going on all around me and everyone's ignoring me, like a dead badger in the road. They think I'm still asleep. They've been coming and going, swimming, sunbathing, drinking coffee, chatting.

Ben and Simon are still arguing about Smashface, the pool game they invented . . .

SIMON: We should write the rules down.

BEN: But we can't actually agree on what the rules *are*.

SIMON: Maybe we should make it into an app. Would that be better?

BEN: What do you mean, an app?

SIMON: An app with the rules in it, explaining how to play. With, I don't know, an instructional video, like on YouTube. I could present it. And you could do the music. Or, even better, we should make it into a game you could play on your phone. We'd make millions. Like those golf games.

BEN: But people already know what golf is, and how to play it. Nobody knows how to play Water Ball.

SIMON: We're not calling it Water Ball. Water Ball is such a boring name. We're calling it Pool.

BEN: But there are already hundreds of pool games you can play on your phone. I mean, you know, *proper* pool.

SIMON: No. We'll get Ash to write some code or something, to make the app. He's our computer guy. We've got all the skills between us. I'm serious about this. I really think we could make a lot of money. The game's brilliant . . .

BEN: But none of us can remember how to play it . . .

As Simon and Ben walk away, I can hear more people approaching, so I keep my eyes shut . . .

ALICE: Argh! It's the perv. Asleep by the pool. Shall we tip him in?

LILY: No, don't be mean – leave him. He looks so peaceful.

ARIA: Omigodman, he looks a mess all covered in jellyfish stings. Like a diseased zombie or something.

ALICE: Maybe we need to destroy his brain?

DR CATHY: Do you girls want to come to the cafe? Me and Jess are going.

ALICE: Sure.

LILY: Cool.

ARIA: Omigodman, I love the cafe.

I wonder whether I should 'wake up' now. I'd really like to go to the cafe with Jess. Only we wouldn't all fit in the car, and . . . damn! Now someone else is going past, so I have to play dead still.

It's Livia and the angry woman, talking about Mr Harper and Hatgate. I can't believe they're still going on about that. They're like contestants on a reality show, shut away together somewhere with nothing to talk about except each other and who turned round and said what to who and what they said back and who's mugged somebody off and who's been cheating on someone . . .

LIVIA: It's just typical of how he treats Ruth.

ANGRY WOMAN: What do you mean?

LIVIA: Cheating.

ANGRY WOMAN: You think he's seeing another woman?

LIVIA: Of course he is. He's a typical man.

ANGRY WOMAN: I thought you said all men were gay.

LIVIA: Yeah, well, whatever. I'm going for my run.

ANGRY WOMAN: Aren't you going to have some breakfast first?

LIVIA: I never have breakfast. Just a coffee. All I need.

I can picture Livia in her running gear. Every morning she puts on these tight shorts that come down to her knees and a top that's a sort of cross between a T-shirt and a bra and a big pair of retro headphones and she stashes a bottle of water in her backpack and does all these stretches in front of everyone and then goes off running.

Now I can hear Emma. She's come over to talk to the angry woman . . .

EMMA: It's so lovely here, isn't it? It's just idyllic. It's so good to get away from London. You can breathe. You can let your problems go. And all the healthy food we've been eating! Simon's so much better when he comes out here. Have you noticed? He's hardly drinking at all!

The angry woman doesn't say anything to this and I can picture Emma putting in her earbuds and settling down on a sunbed in the shade with a peaceful smile on her face.
Then Ash arrives.

ASH: I'm back.
ANGRY WOMAN: I can see that.
ASH: What do you reckon? I got a watermelon.
Everyone likes watermelons, don't they?
ANGRY WOMAN: What?
ASH: Everyone likes watermelons.
ANGRY WOMAN: Have you eaten any watermelon since we got here?
ASH: Er, no, not personally ... Not yet. But now that we've got one ...
ANGRY WOMAN: Ash, if you ever went into the kitchen you'd see that it's *full* of watermelons. Five at the last count. We put slices out every lunchtime and the flies eat them and that's about it.

ASH: Well, I'm sorry I bothered. I just thought you might need some help with the shopping, so I went out and got a watermelon.

ANGRY WOMAN: You didn't go to the shops, though, did you? You got that thing from the back of a lorry, that farmer by the side of the road, like everyone else does, on your way back from the cafe ...

Ash mutters something and the two of them walk away arguing. Then I hear the voices of Mrs Harper and Felix's uncle, Mark, approaching. They're talking about someone called 'Ian' and at first I think they mean the mosquito, but when they talk about Ian driving a car I know they can't be. My Ian can't drive a car. He's a mosquito.

And he's dead.

Then I remember that Felix's dad is called Ian and I wonder if I named the mosquito after him subconsciously.

MRS HARPER: I don't know what's going on, Mark. You know what bloody Livia's like, spreading gossip. She's been saying all these things about him, but I think she makes most of it up.

MARK: Have you talked to him?

MRS HARPER: Not really. If I ever try to talk to him about anything, he just brushes me off and goes back to his magazine, or his podcast, or his book on

Donald bloody Trump he's been reading for the last six months ... I wish it was like the old days, when the kids were small ...

MARK: No. You have to let kids grow up, Ruth. You have to let them live. You have to let things change. A child's life, frozen in time, so that they never got older ... I wouldn't wish that on anyone.

MRS HARPER: I'm sorry, Mark. I don't think sometimes.

FELIX: Do you know where my swimmers are?

Felix has come round to the pool. I open my eyes a tiny squint. Mrs Harper makes a smile and tries to look happy and normal. Felix is looking grumpy and still sleepy.

'They're wherever you left them, darling,' says Mrs Harper. 'You *do* tend to just drop them when you take them off and leave them where they fall.'

'They're not where I left them. I've looked.'

Mrs Harper gives Felix a hug, which he shrugs off.

'I just want my shorts,' he says.

'Come on,' says Mrs Harper. 'Let's find them.'

Mark gives his sister a quick hug.

'I've got to go into town,' he says. 'Sort out the tax for the rubbish collection.'

'Oh. Boring . . .'

They walk off. It's safe now. I sit up. Everyone here is in their own little world, with their own problems. I'm tempted to go round and give them all Dad's advice.

Man up!

But of course I don't. I stand up and stretch.

I realize I'm still in my pyjamas. Well, they're not exactly pyjamas, they're the clothes I sleep in – a T-shirt and shorts. So nobody could tell I slept half the night out here.

I'm pretty hungry. Mark's gone off, so no trip to the cafe this morning. I go round to the kitchen and get myself a bowl of cereal. Simon's sitting at the breakfast bar, drinking coffee and checking something on his phone. He looks red-faced and red-eyed and as tired and dried out as I feel.

He looks at me when I sit down with my cereal.

'Oh, to be twelve again,' he says. 'I think I might have a bowl of that cereal. I don't think I can handle anything any more challenging.'

I watch him as he tips out a bowl of cereal, pours on some milk and starts to eat. He looks like a very big boy.

Ash comes in and sees him.

'Cool,' he says. 'Honey Loops. I'm having some of that.'

Soon all three of us are eating cereal together like a bunch of kids.

And then Ben joins us.

I can't tell if this is cool or creepy.

Reason 19: Squids, octopuses, etc.

Dad has a crap joke that he always uses whenever anyone asks him if he likes seafood.

'Seafood?' he says. 'I love seafood. I'm on a seafood diet. I see food and I eat it.'

This joke always makes Dad laugh. And I almost repeated it just now when Mark came back from town and asked me if *I* liked seafood. I didn't actually use Dad's 'joke', because – and this probably won't come as a surprise to you – I *don't* see food and eat it. I prod food around my plate with a fork and peer at it and wonder what excuses I can make not to eat it. And that's just normal food. Seafood is something else. Seafood looks like dead aliens. So I stop myself from repeating Dad's stupid joke and Mark's still standing there waiting for me to reply and what I want to say is . . .

'Seafood? Are you nuts? Of course I don't like seafood! "Sea" and "food" are two words that just don't go together. I never look at the sea and think, *Yum, I'd love to eat something out of that!*'

Instead I just shrug and mutter, 'It's OK.'

'How would you like some seafood for lunch?'

'I'm OK,' I tell him. Which is a polite way of saying, 'No way! I'd rather eat my own head.'

(I read a horror story once where a surgeon is shipwrecked on a desert island and he has to cut off and eat parts of his body to survive. It was horrible.)

'Come on,' says Mark. 'I want to eat out. There's a great little seafood restaurant I'll take you kids to. I won't ask the adults. Trying to get that lot organized is like trying to get fish to line up for a race. There wouldn't be room at the restaurant for them all anyway. The place is tiny. So, go and grab Jess and Felix and we'll go and get some lunch.'

OK. Right. We'll be going with Jess. That changes things. I've been thinking about Jess a lot since our adventure with the jellyfish. I like hanging with her. In my wildest dreams I imagine her being my girlfriend and this would be like going on a date with her. Although, of course, Jess won't know that. She'll just think we're going out to eat seafood together, along with Felix and Mark. She'll have absolutely no idea that we're actually on a date. But when Mum asks me what I did today I can say, 'I went on a date with Jess.' Mum'll like that. She'll be, like, 'Oh, I'm so proud of you! You're getting over your shyness.'

So I'll be brave. I'll go to a seafood restaurant. I just won't eat any seafood when I get there. In fact, maybe I won't eat anything at all. That might be simplest.

But when I find Jess by the pool, reading a Malorie Blackman book, all my bravery disappears. What if she doesn't want to come? Then I'll be going on a date with Felix. Which is a whole different thing.

I take a deep breath and walk over to her.

'Mark's going to take us out for lunch,' I say.

'Cool,' she says, and puts down her book. Just like that. Maybe that's how easy it would be to ask a girl out on a date for real.

Maybe you just say: 'Would you like to come out for lunch?'

And they say: 'Cool.'

Could life really be that simple?

I find Felix on his bed, looking at his phone, and tell him the plan. Secretly I'm hoping he'll say he doesn't want to come, so it will just be me and Jess. It's his call.

Felix makes a face and asks me which restaurant. I tell him I don't know, and he makes a big huffing-and-puffing deal of hauling himself up off the bed and going downstairs to find Mark.

Mark's in the courtyard, getting beach towels off the washing line.

'Where are we going?' Felix asks.

'That seafood place on the cliff,' says Mark. 'Where you can swim off the rocks. Then we can have a nice lunch. I'll buy you all Cokes.'

'OK.'

So we all go off in Mark's Alfa. Jess is sitting in the front with Mark. I'm in the back with Felix, who's listening to something on his headphones, staring out of the window. I stare out of the other window, watching the endless olive trees and identical drystone walls whizzing past, wondering how anyone could ever find their way around here without getting lost and worrying about the seafood restaurant.

Despite Dad's joke about seafood, I don't think he's ever actually been to a seafood restaurant. He's certainly never taken us to one. Unless you count fish and chips. He's always telling me not to be fussy about food, but he eats the same thing all the time, just like me. He's not what Mum would call 'an adventurous eater'. He's still less fussy than me, though, and now here I am going to a seafood restaurant. In Italy. This is crazy. What am I doing? What am I going to eat? Can you only get seafood in a seafood restaurant?

I know one thing. I am never going to eat squids.

Squids were not designed to be food. You see a sausage – you want to eat it, don't you? A sausage is designed to look tasty. It's brown for a start. All the best food is brown. I mean, you see a burger – you want to eat it. You see a plate of chips – you want to eat them.

You see a squid – you run screaming.

Squids are hideous slimy monsters. Even thinking about them gives me the creeps. Squids were on Mum's list of holiday emergencies.

What to do if attacked by a giant squid.

Well, I can tell you what to do. If you're Italian, you eat it! The Italians are definitely 'adventurous eaters'.

And squids aren't necessarily the worst thing I might be forced to eat. What about octopuses? Felix told me they even eat sea urchins round here.

SEA URCHINS!

I make a list in my head . . .

10 THINGS I WON'T EAT IN
A SEAFOOD RESTAURANT

1. Squid.
2. Octopus.
3. Sea urchins.
4. Jellyfish*.
5. Mussels.
6. Those tiny fish you're supposed to eat all of – bones and guts and fins and heads and all. Whose idea was that?
7. A big fish with its head still on.
8. In fact, anything with its head still on. With eyes. Like prawns.
9. Prawns (with or without their heads).
10. Any seafood.

In fact, I suppose I didn't need to make a list. I could have just said number ten – 'Any seafood.'

What was I thinking of?

I know what I was thinking of.

I was thinking of Jess.

---

* I think the Japanese eat jellyfish. They're even more adventurous eaters than the Italians. But, seriously, my first thought when the parachute dropped us down towards that swarm of jellyfish was definitely not 'Ooh, yum, lunchtime!'

Our date.

It's all a bit confusing.

I'm thinking about Jess and I'm getting confused.

This boy–girl thing is complicated.

I'm distracted from my confusing, complicated thoughts by Mark passing one end of the USB cable to Felix. 'Come on,' he says. 'Don't be antisocial. Stick this in your phone.'

Felix grunts and sighs but plugs his phone in and soon loud music with a man shouting over the top of it comes out of the speakers.

'I like this,' Mark says, and turns it up even louder. 'I couldn't tell you what it is, though.'

'It's Numbskulla,' says Felix. 'He's a grime artist.'

I know what Dad would say if it ever came on the radio in our car (just before he turned it off): 'He's a *grim* artist, more like.'

I try not to feel sad thinking about Dad. I still haven't heard from Mum and I'm scared to ring her. Dad doesn't talk to me that much, but I miss him. I miss being somewhere normal, like home. With normal people. And normal food.

But at the same time I'm going on a date with Jess and I'm super excited. Life didn't use to be this complicated and confusing. It was easy when I was young, at primary school.

I'm an old man now.

I think it's best if I try not to think about Dad.

Or squids.

Or octopuses.

Or any seafood.

I concentrate on the countryside as we bomb along with the windows open and the music blasting out. The grass is dry and brown with rocks sticking up everywhere. We pass a big herd of shaggy sheep with long ears and dirty wool. Or is it a flock?

Actually, I think they might be goats.

And there's a shepherd with them. Or maybe a goatherd. So I can tell Dad about that when I get back.

'*I saw my first shepherd on holiday. It looked quite biblical.*'

'*Ooh, profound.*'

They're gone now, whatever they were. If Simon was driving, he'd tell us all about them, what cheese they make from their milk and so on. Mark doesn't say anything. He just taps his hand to the beat on the doorframe where his window is open.

And now there's the sea, a strip of bright blue that blends into the sky.

When we get to the coast, we drive along a windy road through pine trees. Then we're out on a headland where there's the ruin of an old farmhouse and a lookout tower. I try to imagine what it must have been like here when the buildings were first built, being always on the lookout for invaders and pirates, guarding your sheep (or goats) from raiding parties. It must have been very stressful. Wondering if when you got home from working in the fields all day in the hot sun your family would still be alive. There's a lot of bad things going on in the world today, but at least in England we're safe. We don't have to worry about pirates and invaders and losing our sheep. I think the world is a better place without wars and people always fighting. Though I suppose there's always a war going on somewhere.

The coast road is quite busy with Italians going to and from the beach, and we have to squeeze through a couple of small towns, where the cars scrape past each other in the narrow streets. Then we come to a bay where the road curves round it. The water's full of people – swimming, sitting in boats, lying on lilos, snorkelling, standing chatting . . .

We find a car park and leave the car under a shady awning. It's really hot when we get out. We grab our towels from the boot and walk out on to a headland. There's a sort of shack here built on the rocks and someone's cut steps down to the sea. We pick our way to the water where there's a flat rock you can dive off. It's covered with Italians using holes in the rock as ashtrays. They've fitted sun umbrellas into other holes and they're all talking away. It's like a rock full of seals in a David Attenborough documentary.

Except seals don't smoke so much.

We find a bit of space. I have my trunks on under my shorts so I don't have to do any embarrassing changing in front of people.

It's brilliant fun diving off the rocks. They're not very high up, but it still feels like I'm in an action movie when I fly out over the water and splash in. Jess comes in after me. Mark's next. Felix is still sitting on the rocks.

'Come on, Felix,' Mark and Jess shout.

Felix just shrugs. He can pretend that he's too cool for the pool, but I know really. I know he's not a very confident swimmer. Maybe he's scared of diving off rocks.

I don't mind if he wants to wimp out. That's his problem. I swim around with Jess. Mark goes on ahead, doing the crawl. And when none of us are looking we hear a splash. Felix has dived in. Actually, I think he jumped. I've still never seen him dive.

So me and Jess and Felix goof around, splashing each other. The water has bits of plastic floating in it, trapped here in the bay. It's a bit like I'm still in a David Attenborough documentary. A depressing one about the end of the world. I try to imagine what it would be like to be trapped with a piece of plastic round my waist like a baby turtle.

Dad told me recently that when they cut whales' bellies open they're full of all sorts of plastic crap.

And squid . . .

No. I mustn't think about Dad and I mustn't think about squid.

Dad. Dad. Dad. Dad. Dad. Dad . . .

Squid. Squid. Squid. Squid. Squid . . .

I imagine a shoal of them swimming underneath me, their long tentacles waving around, searching for me. I'm getting into such a panic I can't even remember if Mum actually told me what to do if attacked by one.

'Shall we get out now?' I say to Jess and Felix.

'It's fun,' says Jess.

Something wraps round my leg and for one terrible moment I think it's a tentacle. I'm about to scream when I realize it's a plastic bag. But I'm still totally freaked out.

'I'm getting out,' I say.

Who's the wimp now?

I swim back to where we dived in. This date is not going well. I climb up the slippery seaweed-covered rocks and lie down on my towel in the sun.

Safe.

I can hear Felix and Jess laughing.

I feel a little bit jealous.

But I'm alive! I've survived an attack by a giant squid.

Well, an attack by a plastic bag.

I know that what I'm really scared of isn't being pulled under by a monster from the deep. It's about food. That's what I've always been scared of.

Forget sharks and parachutes and kidnapping, food is what terrifies me most in the world. I'm scared of eating it. I'm scared of one type of food touching another type. I'm scared of getting food on me. I sometimes have actual nightmares where cartoon vegetables are dancing round me, singing, 'Eat me! Eat me! Eat me!'

So, don't think about Dad. Don't think about squid. Don't think about food.

As I'm lying there, not thinking about Dad, squid or food, the others come out of the sea and we all laze around, drying off. Mark reads a book. Felix doesn't even look at his phone. He's enjoying himself for once. Maybe because he got over being scared of jumping in. Maybe because he's with me and Jess and not sitting all alone by himself thinking about things too much. And I know what that's like.

The three of us just talk. Me and Felix and Jess. And it's chilled. Felix talks about his mum and dad, how at first they didn't think they could have kids, which was why they adopted Alice.

'And then there was a miracle,' he says slightly sarcastically. 'Mum did get pregnant, and they had me. I just sometimes wonder why Dad bothered. He doesn't have any interest in me.'

'Was he always like that?' I ask.

'Nah. He was fine before. We used to have a great time out here. He'd play with me. Make things. He taught me to swim. He was going to teach me to di–' He stops himself. 'He was going to teach me all kinds of stuff.'

I think I know what Felix was going to say. His dad was going to teach him to dive. But I don't say anything. I wonder if I should tell him any more about *my* dad. But I don't want him to think I'm, like, 'Hey, you think your life's bad, my dad's about to have a heart operation . . .'

Because it's nice talking. When Felix is like this, I imagine he *could* be my best friend. He can be nice and funny and interesting. I suppose if you're going to be friends with someone, you have to accept them in all their different moods. It's just that Jess doesn't ever really seem to get moody.

And she's always nice to me.

Which is new.

Reason 19 (part 2): Squids, octopuses, etc.

Once I'm dry I pull my shorts on over my swimmers and get into my T-shirt and sliders. My swimmers aren't really dry and I know I should take them off and change properly, but I'm too embarrassed.

We go up the rocks to eat and my heart is pounding, like I'm an SAS agent going on a deadly mission, rather than just some dumb fussy kid going to a seafood restaurant.

We get to the shack where there are tables set up under a sunshade. None of the tables match, nor the chairs. Jess says this is a hipster thing. I wouldn't know. We sit down and a waitress brings us some menus. Mark talks to her in Italian and she smiles at him.

I realize I'm actually quite hungry. I look at the menu. It's in Italian. Mark asks if we want him to order for us all.

'Have they got anything that isn't seafood?' I ask.

'It's a seafood restaurant, dumbass,' says Felix.

'They do have some things like bread,' says Mark.

'Cool,' I say. 'I'll just have bread. I'm not that hungry actually.'

'They do chips,' says Jess.

'I'll just have chips then. Chips and bread.'

'God, Stan,' says Felix. 'Are you trying to get into *The Guinness Book of Records*, or something, as, like, the world's fussiest eater? You are such a baby.'

'It's all right,' says Mark. 'I know what it's like. I used to be a fussy eater.'

Does he know? Was he really a fussy eater, or is he just saying that to make me feel better?

'But, honestly, you can't just have chips and bread,' says Mark, smiling. 'I'll order some stuff.'

Please don't. Because I'm not going to eat any of it . . .

The waitress comes back with some fizzy water and bread and a glass of pink wine. Mark orders some things in Italian. At least I think that's what he's doing. He might be asking her about the weather, or telling her that I'm a fussy eater and asking her to gross me out with the weirdest food they've got, or he might be trying to chat her up for all I know.

I wriggle in my seat. The top of my legs and my bum are sore from sitting in wet shorts.

Jess says she'll have prawns. Which is brave. And Felix says he'll have spaghetti with clams. Which is crazy. As far as I'm concerned, clams are things that trap divers by their flippers in comics. And drown them.

Mark's looking at me, frowning in the bright light.

'So, come on then, Stan,' he says. 'What'll you have? You can't just have chips. Look at this . . . We're in the most beautiful spot by the Mediterranean, on a glorious day with the sun glinting on the sea. You're not in London now. You're not at home now. You have to make the most of it. Be a little adventurous.'

Oh, right, *be adventurous*, shall I order sea urchins? Or jellyfish? Or squid? Maybe shark. Yes! A live shark! A great white plonked on the table, snapping at me with its three rows of teeth . . .

And then I see another waitress go past with a big plate of crispy battered rings that look like they might be fried onion rings or special Italian doughnut-shaped chicken nuggets. Whatever they are, they look delicious.

'I'll have some of them . . .' I blurt out, pointing. 'With chips. Can I have them with chips?'

'Of course. Good choice.' Mark says something to the waitress. She smiles again and goes away.

Now that I can relax I can enjoy being here on my date (if you ignore Mark and Felix – and the fact that Jess doesn't know we're on a date). It really *is* a nice place, as Mark said. With the boats on the water and the hot sun and the glamorous people with suntans and jewellery, and, yes, the sun glinting on the sea, it's like something out of a film. A James Bond film. I have a sort of feeling that I shouldn't be here, that I don't deserve this. That I'm dreaming about someone else's holiday. And I know that if Archie hadn't broken his leg, I wouldn't be here, I'd be at home in dirty old London. We don't go out to eat very often. Dad always says it's too expensive and that the cheap places are junk. We've had Indian (good), Chinese (OK), fish and chips (seafood that's OK to eat) and burgers (easy). I can't wait to tell Mum about this when she phones. I might lie about what I eat, though, and make it sound more exciting and dangerous.

'Yeah, it was nice, I had whale tongue and octopus brains . . . and chips.'

By the time the waitress brings the food I'm starving. My plate of battered rings looks great and smells great. I quickly tuck in to some chips, then try a crispy ring. It's good. It's *very* good. Sort of half chickeny and half fish-and-chippy. I eat a couple more and then I pick up another ring and see something peculiar underneath it. I look more closely. It looks like a bunch of battered tentacles attached to a rubbery lump.

'What is this, by the way?' I ask, trying to sound casual and James Bond-like.

'Duh. What d'you think?' says Felix as if it's really obvious. 'Squid. It's what you ordered.'

'Oh yeah . . .' I say.

Squid.

I've ordered squid.

I've *eaten* squid.

The ONE THING I wasn't meant to do.

OK. I have two choices now. I can run screaming to the toilets and throw up or I can act cool. Like James Bond.

'Ah, Octopussy, I'm terribly sorry, but I seem to have eaten your cousin, Dr Squid . . .'

'How is it?' asks Mark.

I look at Jess. She's busy pulling the head off one of her prawns.

I will be a man.

I will be James Bond.

I will act cool.

'OK. Yeah. It's nice.'

And the thing is. It *is* nice. It's really tasty. If I hadn't found the tentacles, I'd never have known. I could have quite happily scoffed the lot and asked for more. I just need to rearrange my brain.

It makes sense really. People wouldn't eat things if they tasted disgusting.

'I love squid,' says Jess.

'Do you want a bit?' I say.

'Yeah, sure. Do you want some prawns?'

'No, that's OK.'

'Go on. They're yummy.'

She puts a prawn on my plate. At least it's out of its shell and she's taken the legs off. And the head. So there's no eyes staring back at me . . . '*How could you? I have a wife and kids . . .*'

'Give us a bit of squid then,' says Jess. 'But no tentacles. I'm not very good with tentacles.'

'They're the best bit,' says Felix, and he nicks some tentacles off my plate and sticks them in his mouth, so that they're sprouting out between his lips, then he sucks them in and chews them up.

Jess goes 'Eeuuuurgh' but then she laughs.

'Do you like the tentacles?' she asks as I pass her a battered ring.

'Yeah,' I say. 'They're OK.'

And do you know what I do? I spear some tentacles with my fork and put them in my mouth and I eat them.

And they taste OK. I just imagine they're chips. Skinny, curly chips.

And after I've eaten the tentacles I eat the prawn. And the prawn tastes good too. And Jess smiles at me and I feel like a Greek god. OK, maybe not a god – one of the heroes, like Achilles, or my favourite, Odysseus.

Or, actually, right now I'm Perseus. I have saved Jess from the sea monster – and I have eaten it! Tentacles and all!

A thought comes to me. Maybe all human progress has been because someone wanted to impress someone else. To make the other person notice them. To make the other person like them. To make the other person want to go out on a date with them.

Ooh, profound . . .

Reason 20: Global warming

'Do you like the wind?'

We're on the roof of one of the buildings. They all have flat roofs with low walls round them and there are stone stairways to get up there. A bit like in a castle. Mark has brought me up to see the solar panels and he's standing by the wall facing into the wind, his hair blowing around his head, silver and grey, just like the leaves of the olive trees that are also twisting in the breeze.

It all started when we were coming back from the seafood restaurant. Me and Jess and Felix were having an argument about the environment and plastic and climate change. Felix was trying to wind Jess up by saying he didn't care, that he liked plastic straws and sunbathing and didn't care if all the pandas died out because he thought pandas were idiots. I was on Jess's side and I said I thought we had to do whatever we could to stop things getting worse, and that things like solar panels were a good idea, even though I don't know much about them.

That was when Mark joined in.

'When we get back, I'll show you *our* solar panels,' he said, and now here we are. Just me and him. On the roof. Looking at solar panels. This day has certainly taken some unexpected turns.

Actually, it turns out I *am* quite interested in solar panels. I've never seen one up close before. It's like being in the future. There are several rows of them up here, fixed to frames and tilted to always be facing the sun.

Mark told me that they have two different types. One type heats the water. They have thin plastic tubes in them full of liquid that gets superheated in the sun and then goes through a big water tank downstairs. The other type are photovoltaic panels that generate electricity.

'Don't ask me how,' Mark told me. 'But they do. We're nearly self-sufficient in energy. There's plenty of sunshine here. Sunshine and wind. This part of southern Italy's famous for it. They could generate so much solar and wind power here . . .'

And that was when he walked over to the wall and stood there looking all manly like a prince in the Middle Ages standing on a castle turret watching the enemy approach, and asked me that question.

'Do you like the wind?'

I think it must be a trick question. Of course I don't like the wind! Who likes the wind? It's irritating. It blows things around in an irritating way. It makes an irritating noise. I mean, I guess it keeps you cool when it's hot, but only in an irritating way. Usually it just makes you cold. And up here, right now, it's making my hair go all over the place, like Mark's, and I have to keep swiping it out of my face. Mark looks sort of cool. Maybe the trick is to face completely into it, so that your hair blows backwards away from your face. I try that, but I don't think I look cool like Mark. I think I probably look like someone who's stood too close to an explosion.

'*I* like the wind,' says Mark. 'It makes me feel . . . *alive.*'

'Ooh, profound,' I say.

Damn! Idiot! I've said it out loud again. Just like I did with Simon when we arrived. I only meant to think it.

Mark turns to me. Luckily he laughs just like Simon did.

Phew.

'Sorry. Am I being pretentious?'

'No. It's all right,' I say. 'It was a joke.'

'I'm an old fool, standing up here banging on about the wind. But I do like it. It *does* make me feel alive . . . How about you?'

I wonder. What makes *me* feel alive? It's not the wind. I like the sun. And Coke. Coke makes me feel alive. And cereal. Maybe bacon . . .

Ice creams?

'I like the wind too,' I lie, turning my face back into the blast. It's quite painful, to be perfectly honest. Bits of grit and leaves are whacking into me and I have to screw up my eyes to stop them stinging.

'It keeps you in touch with nature,' says Mark. 'It's a force we can't control. Reminds us of our place in the world. How small we are. Do you know anything about chaos theory at all?'

'Yeah,' I say, not sure where this is going. 'A bit.'

It seems that in order to have a proper grown-up conversation you have to lie quite a lot. What the hell is chaos theory?

'You know the butterfly effect?'

I do! I *do* know the butterfly effect! Yeah! I'm not a complete fraud. I think I might know what he's talking about.

'Yes,' I say, trying to sound grown up. 'It's, like, when a butterfly flaps its wings in Australia and it causes a storm in America, or Europe, or wherever.'

'Isn't that an amazing idea?'

'Yes,' I say, although, to tell you the truth, I've never really believed it.

'I love the idea that things can have unpredictable consequences,' says Mark. 'And that tiny things can have massive effects. We can't ever properly predict the wind. It's swirling all round the planet. And when it blows on you you're part of that process, part of life, the universe and everything, as the man said.'

This time I manage not to say 'Ooh, profound' out loud. Instead I say, 'Yes,' in my best grown-up voice and turn back into the wind. I try to look like some stern ship's captain staring sternly at the horizon, and spoil it by saying, 'Ow!' in a squeaky high-pitched voice when a twig hits me in the eye.

Mark stares off towards a line of giant wind turbines in the distance.

'Do you like the windmills?' he asks. Damn – another trick question. Is he trying to catch me out? Some people think wind turbines slice birds up and are ugly and noisy and ruin the view. Others think they're going to save the planet. I guess Mark is probably a 'save the planet' type of guy. He has solar panels, after all. So I say 'yes'. But I say it quietly in case it's the wrong answer.

'I think they're beautiful,' he says, and I sigh with relief. 'Anything useful and well designed is beautiful,' he goes on. 'Whether it's a car, a corkscrew, or a, I don't know . . . a garden fork.'

'Yes,' I say. I think I'm doing quite well. This is a proper grown-up conversation, and I mostly haven't said the wrong thing yet, even if I am finding it hard to picture a beautiful garden fork. Or a good-looking corkscrew.

Although I did once see a cool one that looked like a squirrel.

Or was that a nutcracker?

'I'd like to get a wind turbine for here,' Mark says.

'One of *them*?' I say, frowning at the giant turbines.

Mark laughs.

'Not quite as big as those,' he says. 'A small one.'

Damn. Made a fool of myself.

Mark turns away from the wind.

'There are going to be storms this week, I reckon,' he says. 'Storms here can be amazing. You can see the sky lit up for miles around. Do you like storms?'

I wish he wouldn't keep asking me these questions, but again I take a stab at the correct answer.

'Yes.'

'Me too.'

Phew.

'Especially when it's been so hot and dry. All the crap's washed down out of the sky and the air's fresh again, and the plants drink up all that water. Have you ever been swimming in the rain?'

'Yes.'

I haven't. Of course.

'Doesn't it feel great?'

'Oh yes.'

I wouldn't know. But, man, I'm doing well here.

'Can I say something, Stan?'

'Yeah . . .'

Now what? At least it's not another question.

'I like you. You're a smart guy. I see you, watching what's going on, listening, paying attention. Shy people are like that. They know what's happening, but they're scared to join in. Do you mind me calling you shy?'

'Well . . .' I mumble, 'I suppose I *am* shy.'

This seems like a moment to tell the truth.

'I was shy when I was a boy,' says Mark. 'But I forced myself to get over it. I forced myself to talk to people, because it was making me miserable. I forced myself to speak my mind out loud, and not hide my thoughts. Just like *you* did just now when you took the mickey out of me.'

'I didn't mean to say it . . .'

'Exactly. But why not? It was funny. Speak your mind. Don't use your shyness as an excuse to hide away. *I* learnt how to get past it. Not totally. I'm still a bit shy. If you're born shy, you always will be shy. So you have to make an extra effort.'

'Dad's always forcing me to go up and talk to people when we're out and about,' I say. 'Ask them the time or directions somewhere.'

'Well, it's not quite that simple. It's more that you've got to make an adjustment in your head. Tell yourself you can do it. Pretend to be a person who isn't shy. And when you're ready you can go up and talk to people and that's when you find out it's not so terrifying and you wonder what you were so scared of.'

'OK.'

'Can I ask you something, Stan?'

'Yeah.'

'Your dad . . . does he go up to people a lot in public and talk to them, or does he always make you do it?'

'He usually makes me do it.'

'You need to think about that.'

I don't know what he means. This is a lot to take in.

'Are you really shy?' I ask him.

'Yeah.'

'And was it easy to sort out?'

'No.' Mark laughs. 'It was *hard*. It was *really* hard. But you know the most important thing I found out? *Nobody cares.* Nobody's actually that interested in you. Nobody really notices what you do and say. You might think it, but people aren't looking at you all the time. They're not all talking about you. They're not all judging you – because they're all living in their own little bubbles and they've all got problems of their own. We all think about ourselves a lot more than we think about other people. If someone's moody or snappy with you, it's not necessarily because of something you've done. It's because of something else going on in their life. You've got to stop thinking you're the centre of the universe. It's hard. But you can do it, Stan. You're an interesting guy. You're a funny guy. Have confidence in yourself. Be brave and your life will be so much more fun. Live, Stan . . . Get out there and live . . .'

I notice that he has tears in his eyes. For a moment I think I must have said something to upset him, but then I remember what he just told me about how, if someone's a certain way with you, it's not necessarily because of something you've done. Maybe it's just the wind stinging his eyes.

He turns away from me. 'Now bugger off, Stan,' he says. 'Go and play with the other kids. You don't want to spend the afternoon stuck up on the roof with a boring old fart.'

I do what he says.

On the way downstairs I wonder whether I've changed my mind about the wind. Whether I like it now. Whether I'm a grown-up where everything makes sense and life isn't so confusing.

As I pass the bathroom, the wind slams the door shut with a huge bang and I jump like my deaf cat when you come up on her unexpectedly.

Of course I don't like the stupid wind.

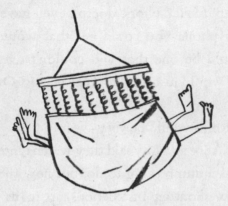

Reason 21: Something terrible is bound to happen at home while you're away

We are throwing a watermelon off the roof. It was Felix's idea. Mrs Harper said she didn't think we should, but when Felix asked her why she couldn't think of a good reason.

So me and Jess are on the roof and Felix is down below with Ash and Ben. They're ready to film it all on their phones. Felix wants to put the footage on his YouTube channel.

He has a YouTube channel. Who knew?

His phone can film in slow motion apparently.

My stupid brick phone doesn't even have a camera. The only phone you could get that would be more basic would be one that you couldn't even use as a phone. It would just be a lump of plastic. Or an actual brick.

But the bills would be very cheap.

At first Alice and Lily said they weren't interested and said it was a dumb thing to do, but now they're down with Felix shouting instructions up to us and I can see they're quite excited. They have their phones ready as well.

Simon comes over to watch. He comes too close. There's a danger he'll get brained. Jess shouts at him to stand back.

He walks backwards and trips over the edge of the terrace. He lands with a loud smack that I can hear from up here. He groans. Ben asks him if he's OK and then everyone ignores him. They're more interested in the flight of the watermelon.

'I'm OK!' Simon shouts. 'Go for it, Satan! Let the big boy go!'

'Shall we do it?' I say, and Jess nods.

We throw it off.

Down it goes and . . .

SPLAT!

HOORAY!!!!

It is much, *much* better than we could have imagined. From up here we can see a huge wide circle of watermelon brains splattered out all over the terrace. Like a bomb's gone off.

'Did you get it, Felix?' I call down.

'Just checking . . . Oh, wow! Oh, man! You gotta see this.'

Everyone crowds round his phone, totally excited. Me and Jess hurry down.

When we get there, Felix shows us the film. At ordinary speed and then in slow motion. It looks great. The others show what they got, from all the different angles.

'It's going to be epic!' says Felix.

Felix's dad comes out and sees what's happening.

'What are you doing now?' he says.

'We dropped a melon off the roof,' says Felix proudly, and he shows his dad his phone.

'What an idiotic thing to do.'

Mr Harper doesn't even look at the phone. Instead he looks round at everyone. They're all a bit sheepish. Even the grown-ups look like kids who've been told off.

'You *will* clear that up, won't you?' says Mr Harper, and he goes back inside.

Felix looks a bit miserable, like a pool inflatable that's just been burst.

'Come on,' says Ash. 'We'll upload it all on to my laptop and edit it together and add some music and sound effects and you can post it.'

'I'll do the music,' says Ben.

'Cool.' Felix cheers up a bit.

'I'll clear this lot up,' says Mrs Harper. 'I'm just happy to see the back of one of the watermelons. One down, four to go.'

The others go off and me and Jess help Mrs Harper clean up. Then Mrs Harper takes the rubbish away and me and Jess sit on the edge of the terrace and talk for a bit.

Did you see that? What I just said. About us talking? Totally casual. As if it's the most natural thing in the world. As if I do it all the time. *'Oh, look, there's Stan, talking to a girl again. What a dude.'*

We don't really talk about anything important. We just chat stuff. She tells me about her dog, Rufus, who's being looked after by a friend, and I tell her about Table, my deaf cat, and she laughs. Then she tells me about her school and I tell her about mine. She tells me what films she likes and I tell her what films I like – and then she suggests we should go and sit in the hammock in the garden behind the pool.

And we go and sit in the hammock and talk some more.

There! I've said it. As if being in a hammock with a girl is the most natural thing in the world. As if I do it all the time. *'Oh, look, there's Stan, talking to a girl in a hammock. He's a real player.'*

And I know I said before that hammocks were stupid, but this is fun. Doing things with other people makes it different. I'm going to have to take hammocks off my list of things that look fun but aren't.

Jess has a much better phone than me and we do Face Swap on it. First we swap each other's faces, which looks freaky. Though Jess says I make a good girl. I don't know if that's a good thing or not. Then we do a face swap of Jess and her mum, Dr Cathy. And that's even more freaky. Jess is like a woman and her mum's like a little weird-looking wrinkly kid. And then we put Jess's face on to a photo of the cat, Pussolini. And we laugh a lot at that. And then we find a photo of Felix and Simon that Jess took and swap their faces. That is the freakiest yet. We can't stop laughing. We laugh so much we fall out of the hammock, which makes us laugh even more.

And then we go for a swim.

And then I think about Dad and I get sad.

It must show because Jess asks me if I'm OK and I blurt out about him being in hospital. I haven't talked about it to anyone else out here. Not properly.

We go back to the hammock and lie in it wrapped in towels and I cry a bit. And she tells me about her dad who left her mum when she was little. She hardly ever sees him.

Everyone has their own problems.

My dad's going to be around. I know he is. The doctors will make him well. I'm sad and happy at the same time. We lie there for a while not talking.

And then Felix runs over and tips us out of the hammock, and this time it doesn't seem so funny. In fact, it hurts quite a lot.

'What did you do that for?' I say, getting up and brushing off the dirt from where it's stuck to my wet skin.

'Because it was funny.' Felix shrugs and walks away.

I look at Jess.

'Is Felix OK?' she says.

'I don't know,' I say, and go after him.

'Felix,' I shout, running to catch up. 'What's the matter?'

'Nothing. I'm just bored.'

'Do you want a game of table football?'

'Maybe.'

'Come on. I'll give you a game.'

We go into the courtyard where the table football is and start a game. Felix is usually really good and beats me easily, but right now he's rubbish. He's too angry and impatient. He keeps swearing and spinning the players, even though you're not supposed to. That was one of the rules he told me on the first day. He gets so worked up that he keeps letting the ball into his goal. Even scoring a few own goals.

'Are you sure you're OK?' I ask him.

'Yeah. Why wouldn't I be?'

'You seem in a bad mood about something.'

'I'm not.'

'You are.'

'You're supposed to be *my* friend,' he blurts out without looking at me. 'That's why you're here. You're my best friend but you spend all your time with Jess.'

'I'm not really your best friend, though, am I?' I say. 'I'm only here because Archie broke his leg.'

'That doesn't make any difference. You're here to be *my* friend, not Jess's.'

'You never seem that interested in me.'

'And *Jess* is interested in you, is she?' Now Felix *does* look at me.

'I don't know,' I say. 'We just like hanging out together. Talking.'

'Oh, *yeah*? Talking? I bet you want to be her boyfriend.'

'What? I just like her. She's nice.'

'Yeah. I bet you want to snog her.'

'Why are you so cross with me? Sometimes I think you hate me.'

'I hate everyone. I hate everything. You can't be bothered to do anything with me. Nobody can.'

'I'm sorry.'

I can see that Felix is about to cry and I don't know what to say.

'I'm playing table football with you, aren't I?'

'That is such a lame thing to say.'

He's right, but it was the best I could do.

'I'm sorry.'

'You already said that.'

He's very red in the face and his eyes are getting more and more watery. I don't really know what I've done wrong. And then I remember what Mark told me. Maybe this is really nothing to do with me. Maybe it's something else that's making him like this. And then I have an idea.

I walk away from the table and do a wee in the middle of the courtyard.

When I look back, Felix is laughing.

'You're a perv,' he says.

Emergency over.

For now.

A Conversation with Mum

6

'So, are you getting on better with Felix?'

'I guess . . .'

'Good. No more fights?'

'No.'

'That's good. Owww . . .!'

'Mum? Are you all right, Mum?'

'Yes. Yes. I'm fine. I just twisted my knee earlier and it's a bit sore. I tripped over Table on the stairs. She's so deaf she never hears you coming so she doesn't get out of the way, and she matches the stair carpet so you never see her. I swear, either we need to get rid of the carpet or we need to get rid of the cat. I nearly broke my neck.'

'Mum?'

'Yes?'

'How's Dad?'

'Oh, Stan, to see him lying there, with all these tubes going into him and his ribs all bandaged up and bleeding. He looks so helpless . . .'

'But the operation went well?'

'Yes, love. The doctors said it went well. Isn't that good?'

'Has he come round yet?'

'Not yet. It was quite a long operation. What they did is they took some spare bits of artery from his leg and used them to replace the blocked bits. It's amazing what they can do. We're living in an age of miracles, Stan. They say he'll be a new man. Hopping and skipping about the place . . . *sniff.*'

'So, when do the doctors say he'll wake up?'

'Soon, I hope. And when he does he'll want to have a good old chat with you.'

'He's probably lying there thinking up crap jokes.'

'Yes. Ha, ha! That's the spirit, Stan. Don't you worry, yeah?'

'I'll try. I wish he was awake now. I wish I could talk to him.'

'Soon, Stan. He's going to be fine. You'll see. So just you enjoy yourself with Felix.'

'I will . . .'

'Good boy.'

A Conversation with Felix

3

'How's your dad, Stan?'

'Yeah, he's all right.'

'Cool.'

Reason 22: Falling out with your best friend

We've had a busy day. Cafe for breakfast, then looking round the shops and a big old castle in a town called Otranto. They also had a cathedral with a weird, random mosaic floor showing the signs of the zodiac, various cool monsters, scenes from the Bible and the adventures of Alexander the Great. Even better was a chapel full of skulls. We had pizza in Otranto for lunch, then went to the beach for the afternoon. Now me and Jess and Mark are making dinner.

'Best way to get over a fear of food is to learn how to cook,' says Mark, passing me an apron. 'And you can't go far wrong with spaghetti bolognese.'

'You mean spag bol,' says Jess, putting on an apron of her own.

'God, no!' says Mark. 'Only the English would call an Italian dish "spag bol". Although there's actually no such dish in Italy.'

'Yes there is,' says Jess, all pretend serious. 'I've eaten it loads of times.'

Mark laughs. 'No, you're right,' he says, chopping up an onion. 'What I mean is the Italians don't call it that – they call it a *ragu*. Not that it makes any difference to how it tastes. You can call it what you like, really – just don't call it "spag bol".'

'What's the meat?' asks Jess, peering at a packet of mince that Mark has put on the kitchen counter.

'The local butcher ground up his own special *ragu* mix for me,' says Mark. 'Beef, pancetta, which is like bacon, some chicken livers and pork.'

I'm not sure I like the sound of chicken livers, but the mince looks all right and I trust Mark. He's right – food is less scary when you cook it yourself. After we've chopped the onions, we peel and crush some garlic, which is really smelly, then I get to rip up some basil leaves, which are also smelly. But if I can eat squid, I can eat garlic and basil. I'll show them.

Mark holds up a tomato.

'Look at that,' he says. 'Concentrated sunshine, straight from the vegetable garden. Half an hour ago it was on the vine.'

He shows me how to chop it up and I take the knife from him and carry on with the other tomatoes. Mum never lets me use a sharp knife at home. I think she worries I'll accidentally cut my head off or something.

As we're working away, Simon comes into the kitchen whistling. He's carrying a pile of lemons in his T-shirt, which he's scooped up at the bottom to make a sort of lemon hammock.

'When life gives you lemons, make lemonade!' he says, unloading them on to the counter. 'Aren't they fab? It's such a great thing to be able to pick your own lemons off the trees. I love lemons.'

He picks one up and sniffs it.

'Ahh! Amazing.' He puts it down and pours himself a glass of red wine.

'You know that phrase, don't you, Satan?' he says.

'Which one?'

'*When life gives you lemons, make lemonade.*'

'Yeah,' I say. 'My aunt has a poster in her kitchen.'

'Everyone should have the poster in their kitchen,' says Simon. 'It's such a great saying. It means when you've got something as amazing as a lemon, then make it even better and share it with the world!'

'That's not what it means,' says Mark.

'What?' Simon looks surprised.

'That's not what the saying means. It means the opposite.'

'How can it mean the opposite?'

Mark scrapes the onions into a huge sizzling frying pan full of olive oil and looks at Simon. 'It means if life throws crap at you, turn it round. Change it up and make the best of it.'

'How can it mean that? You're wrong, mate. Lemons aren't crap.'

'*You* might love lemons,' says Mark, handing Jess the wooden spoon to take over the stirring. 'But by themselves they're crap. You can't eat them like any other fruits, can you? They're not like oranges, or apples or bananas. They're sour and bitter, but with a bit of work they can be used to make something nice, like lemonade. Or you can use them in cooking . . .'

'Or for making cocktails!' says Simon, getting another sharp knife from the magnetic strip on the wall and starting to slice a lemon. 'Hence, they're fantastic! Anything that's in a gin and tonic is, by definition, fantastic!'

The onions have turned golden brown. Mark takes the plastic wrapping off the minced meat and tips it into the frying pan. As Jess stirs it into the onions, the kitchen is immediately filled with the delicious smell of cooking meat.

'You have a twisted world view, Mark,' says Simon, arranging glasses on a wooden tray. 'You've taken a beautiful saying about these wonderful God-given fruits and turned it into something dark and sinister.'

He plops a slice of lemon into each glass.

'It's not a dark and twisted world view at all,' says Mark, adding the crushed garlic to the pan. 'It's optimistic. If life deals you a bad hand, don't moan, make something better of it, see it as an opportunity – make lemonade.'

'No,' says Simon, getting slightly cross. 'My meaning is the right one. Lemons are great. Everyone loves lemons. Just smell that.'

Simon shoves half a lemon in my face and squeezes it. It smells lemony. It's a nice smell, but I wouldn't want to eat it. I ate half a lemon once for a bet and it made my mouth shrivel up.

Simon gets a bottle of gin and pours some out into each glass.

'Look at us all cooking dinner together,' he says. 'This would be a lovely moment if you didn't insist on trying to bring us all down with your weird interpretation of a beautiful saying, Mark.'

'Just Google it,' says Mark.

'Google is the enemy of good conversation!' says Simon. 'It stops anyone from having a proper, old-fashioned argument. The cut and thrust of clever wordplay, the clash of opinions . . .'

'This isn't really an argument, though, is it?' says Mark. 'I keep saying what the phrase means and you keep saying that's not what it means. We're just going round in circles.'

'It's fun.'

'No, it's not.' I've never seen Mark cross and grumpy like this before. 'Google it. I can't be bothered with this any more.'

'All right, I will.'

'I already did,' says Jess, who's looking at her phone. Mark leans over to see the screen.

'And?' says Simon. He takes a big swig of gin from the bottle, thinking nobody's looking. I'm looking. He sees me and puts his finger to his mouth – *shhhhhh* . . .

'Mark's right,' says Jess.

'We need ice,' says Simon, and he goes back to the fridge. He lifts out a watermelon that's been cut in half.

'Look at this baby!'

'We don't need that now,' says Mark, and Simon tries to put the melon back. As he does, it slips out of his hands and smashes into the bottom of the fridge, breaking one of the glass drawers. He laughs insanely and turns to us with a big grin on his face as if he's done something really clever. A magic trick or something.

'I've broken your fridge!' he shouts happily.

Mark goes over and starts to pick out broken glass. He doesn't look very pleased.

'For god's sake, Simon.'

'Come on, it's funny. I've broken your fridge.'

'What's funny about it? I'm going to have to get a new tray.'

'Yeah, but it's like . . . I mean, if it was on YouTube you'd laugh.'

'It's not on YouTube, though, is it? It's here and now in my kitchen and you've broken my fridge. Do you know what a hassle it is getting replacement parts round here?'

'It was a funny moment,' says Simon, and he looks at me. 'You thought it was funny, didn't you, Satan?'

I shrug. Not sure what to say. I don't really want to get dragged into this.

'Are we going to have an argument about the meaning of "funny", now?' says Mark, letting me off the hook. 'I say funny is when something happens that makes you laugh, and you say, "No, funny is when some drunken idiot breaks your fridge."'

'You need to lighten up, buddy.' Simon gets ice out of the freezer compartment and brings it over to the counter. 'Clink-clink-clink.' he says, dropping ice into the glasses. 'Is there any finer sound?'

Now he raises the bottle of tonic water to his ear and loosens the cap right next to it.

Sssssssssss.

'*Aaaaaah.*' He smiles at the noise it makes. 'If life gives you lemons, make gin and tonic – now there's a saying you can stick on your wall! Do you want one, Mark?'

'No thanks,' Mark snaps.

'Well, you're a right barrel of laughs,' says Simon, and he looks at me. 'We were best mates at uni,' he says, 'but Mark's changed.'

He picks up the tray of drinks. 'Yeah. If life gives you lemons,' he says again quietly, almost to himself, 'make gin and tonic . . .'

And he carries the tray outside, shouting, 'It's happy hour!'

Mark shakes his head and takes a deep breath before turning round to me and Jess with a smile.

'That was a really stupid argument,' he says. 'I'm a fool for getting dragged into it. So let's forget it ever happened. OK. Once the meat's browned, put in the tomatoes.'

We carry on cooking, and it all goes well until Felix comes in with a look on his face.

'What are you doing?' he says.

'We're making dinner,' I say.

'Why?'

'To eat,' I say, and Jess giggles.

'I don't want to eat it if you've made it,' says Felix. 'And you look like an idiot in that apron.'

'Fair enough,' I say. It seems he's in a bad mood again.

'You might have asked me if I wanted to help,' he says.

'I did, Felix. You were playing a game on your phone. Remember? You can join in now if you want.'

Felix looks at me, he looks at Jess, he looks at Mark.

'Cooking's lame,' he says, and walks out.

I take off my apron and follow him outside. 'Is this about Jess again?' I ask, catching up with him.

'I don't care about Jess.'

'What then?'

'You're spending a lot of time with Uncle Mark,' he says with a nasty voice. 'He's *my* uncle. Not yours . . .'

This is such a dumb conversation. I look round. Everyone's at the big table eating crisps and staring at us. So embarrassing. I don't say anything. I just go back into the kitchen, put my apron on and carry on cooking as if nothing's happened.

A Conversation with Mum

7

'Any news?'

'Well, the cat, let me tell you what she did –'

'Not the cat. Any news about Dad?'

'Dad's fine. Still sleeping . . .'

'But?'

'There are some . . . some complications . . .'

'What sort of complications?'

'It's very complicated.'

'I expect complications would be complicated . . . Sorry,
I didn't mean to sound like that.'

'It's all right, Stan. We're all a bit stressed.'

'Yeah.'

'Are you all right, love? You sound a bit down.'

'I'm OK. I didn't want to tell you, in case you worried, but things are a bit difficult with me and Felix.'

'How do you mean? Did you have another fight?'

'No. Not really. He's always in a bad mood. We keep arguing.'

'What will Mrs Harper think?'

'I don't know. She's Felix's mum. She can worry about him . . . So what's happened to Dad?'

'He's going to be all right, love, but he has an infection and one of his lungs won't properly blow up again.'

'His lungs?'

'When they do the operation, they deflate your lungs or something. And one of them's being a bit tricky.'

'And he has an infection?'

'Yes. He's having lots of antibiotics. He's having the best care in the world. The NHS really is fantastic.'

'He hasn't woken up at all?'

'Actually, he did sort of half wake up earlier. His eyes opened a bit and he spoke a few words.'

'What did he say?'

'He said, "I love Stan."'

'Really?'

'Or it might have been "the Isle of Man".'

'Why would he say that?'

'He's always going on about the Isle of Man. He used to say we should move there.'

'No, not the Isle of Man. Why would he say he loves me?'

'He was delirious, I suppose.'

'You mean he doesn't really love me?'

'No, I mean . . . He's your dad, Stan. Of course he loves you. Even if he doesn't often tell you.'

'When he's better, do you think he might want to have a kickabout? Play football?'

'You've never wanted to play football before.'

'No . . . I don't really like football. But maybe Dad would like it? It'd be good to do things together. It might help him recover.'

'Yes . . .'

'I don't want him to die, Mum.'

'He's not going to die . . . Don't cry, love . . .'

'I'm not crying . . . I helped cook dinner today. Spaghetti bolognese.'

'Well done, you. Was it out of a tin?'

'No! We chopped up stuff and fried the meat and everything. It was cool.'

'And how did it taste?'

'It tasted all right. In fact, it tasted *good*. It had garlic and basil in it, but luckily you couldn't really taste them.'

'Well, goodnight, darling.'

'Goodnight, Mum . . . Oh, you were going to tell me about Table?'

'Oh, yes.'

'What did she do?'

'She did a poo in my favourite hat.'

'Ha, ha, ha, ha, ha, ha, ha, ha . . .'

'I know . . .'

Reason 23: Having terrible accidents doing things you wouldn't normally do at home

Me and Felix didn't speak to each other when we went to bed, and we were both still in a bit of a mood when we woke up this morning. Everyone could see that things were a bit awkward between us so Mrs Harper suggested we go and get ice creams 'to cheer yourselves up'.

I wish it really was that simple. I wish ice creams could solve all the world's problems.

'*Mr President – the North Koreans are threatening a nuclear strike!*'

'*Offer them some ice cream . . . with sprinkles!*'

But, I don't know, maybe it'll help.

The ice-cream place is in a noisy little town with a big beach. It's really crowded inside and I get really stressed because there's no proper queue and the Italians just barge in and shout what they want. It would make Dad really angry. He's very strict about things like queues. Not that he would say anything to the Italians.

I'm thinking this isn't a great way to cheer me up, but then I tell myself not to take it so seriously and try to be more Italian. I'm not in a hurry, there's nothing else to do, and the ice creams look great. I know I'm going to get one eventually, so why not just enjoy it? So I go with it and don't actually have to wait very long at all to get served.

I have to do a lot of pointing. They have every flavour you can think of and quite a few you'd never think of – liquorice, watermelon, *frutta di bosco* (which is fruits of the forest – I can speak Italian now – well, I can speak Italian ice cream), Nutella, fig, Kinder Surprise, chilli and all sorts of ones with sweets and bits of chocolate bars mixed in. I order three scoops – Nutella, pistachio and M&M's, and the next thing I'm sitting out on the terrace with melting ice cream running down my arm, chilled.

Jess didn't like it inside because there's a shiny marble floor and everyone comes up from the beach so it's covered in sand that scrapes under people's shoes. She said the noise made her feel funny. So I got an ice cream for her as well – mango, prickly pear and lemon.

The terrace has a good view of the beach, which is the most crowded I've ever seen. There are millions of sunbeds lined up under umbrellas in perfect rows and the sea is so full of Italians talking to each other that there isn't any room to swim.

Afterwards Jess and the girls and Mrs Harper and Emma go off to do some shopping and I go back to the house with Felix, who seems to have cooled down a bit as well. Before we leave, he insists we buy something called a crêpe cake to take back with us for lunch. Crêpe cake is made from layers of pancake, cream, a sort of custard-type stuff and gooey chocolate.

Things are quiet back at the house and the cleaner is in today. A short, quiet woman in sensible trousers. She goes around the place collecting towels and sheets to wash. She has her daughter with her. A shy, quiet girl in sensible trousers.

We just have a snack lunch and when Felix brings the crêpe cake out half the people cheer and the other half groan.

Film star Livia peers at it with a disgusted expression. 'What the hell is that?'

'It's a crêpe cake,' says Felix. 'Do you want some?'

'Are you kidding?' Livia puts up her hands as if she's defending herself from an attacking bear. 'You know how much sugar and fat there is in that thing? It's positively toxic. You might just as well offer me a bowl of Novichok. I'm going to need to go for a run after lunch to work off all the pasta I've eaten as it is . . .' (She never actually puts much food on her own plate – but she eats quite a lot off Ben's. Including a bit of crêpe cake when nobody – except me – is looking.)

The crêpe cake tastes better than Novichok (not that I've ever eaten Novichok, but I imagine it doesn't taste very nice). And as I'm so skinny I need to eat as much as I can. Actually, to be honest, with all the food I've been eating I think I might have put on a little weight at last.

Mum will be pleased. I mean, she'd be more pleased if I'd put on weight by eating fruit and vegetables, but all the same.

Thinking of Mum makes me think of Dad, and I feel a bit guilty for enjoying the cake while he's being fed liquid food through tubes.

After lunch Felix asks his dad if we can go for a bike ride.

'I don't see why not.'

'The bikes need fixing,' says Felix, and his dad sighs and says, 'Well, that's that then,' and goes back to reading his magazine. Mark offers to sort them out and the three of us go over to the shed to get the bikes.

They haven't been used for a while and they've either got punctures or flat tyres or loose chains and need all sorts of adjustments made. Luckily Mark knows about bikes and says he'll show us what to do.

The bike that Felix used to ride is too small for him now, but there are some adult bikes. Mark picks out a good one, but Felix says it's his dad's bike. It's really dusty and a bit rusty.

'He won't mind if you use it,' says Mark. 'I don't suppose he'll be coming. I haven't seen him ride a bike in years.'

Felix just makes a face and gets a different bike. I pick out one for myself and Mark grabs a third one.

I like bikes. I used to have one at home. In fact, I used to have two. They both got stolen. That's what happens in London. The first one was stolen while I was actually riding it. I got jacked. I was chased by some older boys on bikes on Hampstead Heath and I ended up falling off and they took it and rode it away.

After the second bike was stolen from outside a shop, Dad said he wasn't going to waste any more money buying me another one. So it's been a while since I've ridden a bike. I'm sure I'll get the hang of it pretty quickly, though. The only fiddly bit is the gears. Different bikes have different gears that work in different ways and some of these ones look quite complicated.

The first thing we have to do is mend the punctures. Mark inspects the tyres on my bike and pulls out a nasty thorn thing.

'I call these buggers tank traps,' he says, showing it to us. It's in the shape of a little pyramid with a spike at each corner.

'They're everywhere,' he says. 'And whichever way they land they have one spike facing upwards.'

We find three more stuck into the tyres.

'I bet if you take your sliders off, you'll find loads of them stuck to the bottom,' Mark says, and he's right. There are at least five of them dug into each sole. They're really tough and vicious, but it's very satisfying pulling them out.

Then Mark shows us how to get the tyres off the wheels by jamming fork handles into the rim and sort of popping them out. Then you can take the inner tube off. Next we get a bowl of water with washing-up liquid in it and pump air into each inner tube while they're underwater until we can see bubbles coming out of the puncture holes.

After drying the inner tubes, we sand them down where the punctures are and glue little rubber patches over them. At first Felix is quite keen and helpful, but as we work away it's obvious his dad isn't going to come over and help and Felix gets all hot and grumpy again.

I try to be chatty and normal with him, but he just gets worse. We have to clean the bikes and oil the moving parts and tighten the chains, and Felix obviously doesn't like getting his hands greasy and keeps saying that this is soooooooooo boring. Even though I'm really enjoying it.

Finally we adjust the saddles and check the brakes and gears and then we're ready to go.

'Be careful with the gears,' says Mark. 'Be gentle. Don't try to change too many at the same time or you risk the chain coming off.'

Livia comes over, ready for her run. Sunglasses on. Pack on her back.

'Stan,' she says. 'I've found just the girl for you.'

Not now, I think.

'She'll be perfect. She's shy like you.'

Felix is giving me a look.

'Sofia,' says Livia as if it's the most obvious thing in the world.

'Who's Sofia?' I mumble.

'The cleaner's daughter.'

Oh, yeah, great, I can see that really working – I can't speak any Italian, Sofia can't speak any English, we're both shy, and she has absolutely no interest in me.

Luckily, before I have to say anything, Simon joins us.

'Yeah-yeah-yeah, I love a bike ride,' he says. 'Especially at this time of day. The sun through the trees is just so damned mellow. Can I come with you?'

'I suppose so,' says Felix.

Livia puts her earbuds in and points to me.

'Think about it, yeah?' she says, and jogs off.

'You can take this bike,' says Mark, handing Simon the one he's just got ready. I think he's trying to make up with Simon after having a go at him last night, a bit like me and Felix, I suppose.

'You can do that circuit we used to do,' he says to Felix. 'Past the menhir and left, left, left, yeah?'

'Yeah.'

'But, if you *do* get lost, just follow the electricity wires back here. You remember?'

'I remember,' says Felix with his 'don't go on about things' voice.

We wheel the bikes out into the car park and mount up. Ready to roll. The driveway is just dirt scattered with some loose gravel. It slopes down and curves past some trees before it gets to the road.

'Come on then!' says Simon, and he shoots off as fast as he can. 'Geronimo!' he shouts as he zooms out of the car park and bombs down the dirt track.

At the same time a car appears coming the other way. It's Mrs Harper and the girls coming back from their shopping trip. Simon swerves madly to avoid them and his bike skids in the gravel and he flies off the road into a tree.

Reason 24: Mad dogs

As Mrs Harper parks the car, me and Felix ride over to Simon. He seems all right – he's laughing – but he's a bit bruised and rubbing his shoulder and his face is bleeding.

'Well, that was stupid,' he says. 'You'd better go on without me. I think I've knackered the bike.'

We watch him pick up the bike and limp back to the car park with it.

'I wish I'd filmed that,' says Felix, the happiest I've seen him in ages. 'It was awesome. I've already got loads of hits for my exploding watermelon footage.'

'Cool.'

'Ben made some banging music for it on this app he's got.'

We ride our bikes carefully down to the road and turn left. I'm a bit wobbly at first but soon get the hang of it and go a bit faster. I even experiment with the gears to work out the best way of using them.

It's really fun, even though the road is full of holes.

A car goes past and we have to swerve out of the way. Felix nearly falls off. I look at the car and realize it's Mr Harper driving. He doesn't stop. He doesn't even slow down. He drives away in a cloud of dust.

As we carry on, Felix starts to mumble and grumble, complaining about his bike, even though he chose it himself. I offer to swap and he just mumbles and grumbles some more. I try to carry on as normal.

'So we turn left at the menhir, yeah?' I say, acting casual.

'Yeah.'

'So . . . What's a menhir?'

'It's a lump of stone.'

'What does it look like?'

'It looks like a lump of stone. What do you think?'

'Felix . . .'

'It's a lump of stone stuck in the ground. OK? About as tall as me.'

'OK.'

And then Felix swears and stops. I stop too.

'What's up?' I ask.

'These stupid gears don't work,' says Felix, getting off his bike and kicking it. 'They've made the stupid chain come off.'

I look. The chain's hanging down, all limp and greasy.

'You can put it back on,' I say, but Felix throws his bike to the side of the road.

'I'll get dirty. I just got cleaned up.'

'I'll do it,' I say, getting off my bike.

'Just leave it.' Felix is quite angry and stares into the trees. 'I never wanted to go on a stupid bike ride anyway.'

'Really?'

'I hate bikes.'

'What'll I do then?'

'You go on. It was your idea.'

I don't want to say that it was actually Felix's idea.

'I don't really know the way.'

'Left at the menhir and then left, left, left, left, left . . .'

'Still, I don't know what . . .'

'You don't know anything, do you? You're such a wimp.'

'I can't do anything right, can I?'

'No. You can't. I should never have invited you on this stupid holiday.'

'Then why did you?'

'I felt sorry for you.'

'Yeah, well, thanks,' I say sarcastically.

'But you're even more of a loser than I thought you were,' says Felix. 'I hear you every night talking to your mummy. *Oh, Mummy, I miss you. Oh, Mummy, I'm having such a horrid time. Oh, Mummy, I wish I was at home. Oh, Mummy, I can't wait to play football with Daddy in the back garden.*'

'Our garden's not big enough to play football in,' I blurt out. So angry I'm saying really stupid things.

'Yeah, that's because you're poor,' says Felix. 'You couldn't afford to come to somewhere cool like this. You're only here because of me.'

'So why did no one else want to come then?'

'They were already going on holiday with their own families.'

'That's what they told you, yeah,' I say, almost shouting now, 'but they were lying. They just didn't want to come on holiday with you, Felix, because you're so horrible all the time.'

'Not true,' says Felix. 'They can easily afford holidays of their own. Because their dads have jobs. Yours can't get a job because he's a loser like you.'

(This is sort of half true. Dad was made redundant a few weeks ago.)

'Yeah,' I say. 'Well, your dad's probably going to lose *his* job!'

(I overheard Mr Harper on the phone shouting at someone about this — at least I think that's what he was shouting about.)

'Not true!' shouts Felix, going red in the face. 'You're just jealous because you're poor.'

'Yeah, well, I may be poor,' I say, 'but at least I've got a dad who loves me.'

No. That was wrong. I shouldn't have said that. It was stupid and mean. But, before I can apologize, Felix shoves me, saying, 'I hope your stupid dad drops dead of Ebola.'

So I punch him in the chest.

Then he throws himself at me and the next thing we're rolling in the dirt by the side of the road, punching and kicking and cursing each other. It's nearly as pathetic as the fight we had before and we're soon covered in grit and snot.

We stop when Felix cuts himself on a rock.

'Now look what you've done!' he says, and starts to cry.

I get up.

'I hate you!' he shouts.

'Yeah? Well, I hate you twice as much as you hate me,' I say. 'So no matter how much you hate me, I'll always hate you more.'

Before he can say anything, I get on my bike and pedal off.

I'm going to go for a bloody bike ride. We've taken so long and worked so hard to get the bikes ready. And I don't want to go back to the house with Felix. I need to get away and be by myself for a bit.

I know the way to go. I'll just follow the road and turn left at the menhir, and then left, left, left and left again until I'm back where I started. It should be easy, but I'm quite good at getting lost. I panic and lose all sense of reason. Mum says I could get lost in a cardboard box. But I'm determined not to give up. I'll show Felix I'm not a wimp.

So I carry on and when I come to a big lump of stone (Felix's description was very accurate – it looks exactly like a lump of stone) I turn left. Now all I have to do is keep turning left until I get back to the menhir.

It feels good. I'm being brave. Adventurous. A free spirit. Grown up. The wind is in my face, the sun is blinking on and off through the trees and making everything golden. There are little vineyards planted among the olive groves and there's a smell of figs from all the fig trees everywhere, which have dropped their fruit into the road. The roads are completely flat, there are no hills round here, so it's easy going. The bike works well, the chain dropping into the different cogs with a nice clunk when I change gear, and soon I'm going quite fast.

I can feel my stress drifting away. I've left the fight with Felix a million miles behind me. There are no cars on the road. Sometimes one of the little three-wheeled Ape trucks goes past with a farmer in it who waves at me. Some men on racing bikes overtake me, zooming along, wearing skin-tight cycling outfits and little caps. I notice they all have shaved legs as well. I feel very English in my baggy shorts and sliders and Homer Simpson T-shirt.

There are a few farmers out working, tending to their trees or pruning grapevines. I pass some women walking the other way carrying baskets and chatting away to each other. Most of the time, though, I'm alone. I realize I haven't really been alone since I came out here. Except in the toilet. But that doesn't really count. It's a nice feeling. I don't have that voice in my head nagging me the whole time. Like I do when I'm with people. Always a little bit of anxiety. Always a little bit of stress.

The only time that doesn't happen is when I'm with Jess.

I've never felt that way with anyone before. Just relaxed. She makes me laugh and stops me from thinking about myself all the time.

I realize I've been wrapped up in my thoughts and not properly concentrating. It would be so easy to lose your way out here. The roads all look the same. Drystone walls, olive trees . . .

There's a crossroads up ahead. I slow down. I guess I need to go left. I turn, but then I hear a noise and see a huge white dog, as big as a house, galloping along, barking its head off.

No. It's not a dog, it's a polar bear, and it's coming straight for me. There's nothing for it. I have no choice. I turn round and pedal off along a different road, going as fast as I can.

I'm sort of terrified and yet not scared at the same time. The fear is squashed into a box at the back of my mind. I know it's there, but as long as I don't open the box it can't get out and infect the rest of my mind. Things seem sort of simple and clear.

As long as I don't panic.

I go even faster.

My heart's banging at my ribs and my lungs feel like someone's poured a scalding-hot fizzy drink into them.

I can still hear the polar bear barking. It sounds like it's getting closer. I risk looking back. There it is. Still after me. Its back legs are longer than its front legs, so it has a big advantage over me – it's always running downhill!

I pedal even faster and that's when I ride right into a swarm of killer bees. Or wasps or hornets, or some kind of giant Italian flies. To tell you the truth, I don't know what they are – I'm going too fast to tell. But they're big and slow and, because of the speed I'm travelling at, they smack into me like bullets. Battering against my face, my hands, my chest . . .

SPLAT – SPLAT – SPLAT . . .

One goes in my mouth and I spit it out. Trying not to think about it.

The killer bees are just as surprised as I am and luckily they don't have time to sting me, but when I look back I can see them swarming around the polar bear.

He's barking and snapping at them and has forgotten all about me.

So have the bees.

Yes!

But my feeling of triumph doesn't last long because now I have absolutely no idea where I am.

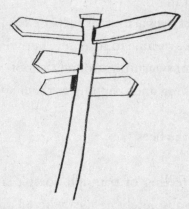

Reason 25: Getting lost

I look around. I could be anywhere. I don't know how far I've come. How far away the house is. I can't go back the way I came because the dog might still be there. And the killer bees. I'm trying to keep the panic away when a terrible thought comes to me – I might never find my way back to the house. I could end up endlessly cycling through these endless identical olive groves. I'll become a famous local legend.

'Oh no – don't go in the olive groves at night. You'll be chased by the ghost of the lost cyclist.'

That's it. If I can still make jokes, I'll be OK.

Don't panic. Be grown up. Think . . .

There are no hills or landmarks or anything to show me the way.

Except for . . .

Yes!

Idiot.

The electricity cables.

What did Mark say?

If you do get lost, just follow the electricity wires back here.

I look up. There are pylons sticking out above the trees, connected to each other with long cables. They look like great steel giants marching across the landscape. I remember seeing them when we were up on the roof. The wires pass very close to the house.

OK. Good. I can't get lost.

I cycle in the direction of the nearest pylon. Slowly, keeping my eyes peeled for danger. And when I get close I can see that the wires follow the line of the road.

I give a shout of triumph. 'Get in there!'

I just have to follow them and they'll lead me back to the house.

Only I have no idea which direction I should go. Should I follow them right or left?

I stop and get off my bike. I swear. The worst words I can think of.

It helps a little actually.

My T-shirt's soaking wet and I feel really hot, my head pounding like it might burst.

If I follow the cables the wrong way, they could take me to the other end of Italy. I could be following it for weeks. Years.

This wasn't on Mum's emergency list. What to do if lost in an olive grove after being chased by a polar bear and killer bees.

Or maybe they were locusts?

It wasn't on the list because Mum knew I wasn't brave enough to go cycling off by myself somewhere foreign where I didn't know my way around. Brave and stupid.

My breathing is going too fast, and getting faster. But I'm not going to cry. I need to calm down and think. I sit by the side of the road with my back against a wall.

There must be some way out of this.

And then I hear the noise of an engine.

There's a little pickup truck approaching. Not much bigger than an Ape. I watch as it drives up and stops. The driver has his window down. He's an old farmer with very dark, wrinkled skin. He says something to me in Italian I don't understand. I just stare at him.

'*Inglese?*' he asks. And I recognize the word. It means 'English'.

How did he know?

The Homer Simpson T-shirt, baggy shorts and sliders, I suppose. The look of someone who really doesn't belong here.

I nod and say, '*Sì. In-glay-zee.*'

'*Parli Italiano?*'

I figure he's probably asking me if I speak Italian? I shake my head and say 'In-glay-zee' again, like a parrot who can only say one word.

He says something else I don't understand. I shrug. He laughs. I must look hopeless. I *am* hopeless.

'I'm lost,' I say in English, and it's his turn to shrug.

Then he says something I recognize.

'*Sei perso?*'

It's from the Italian phrase Mum made me learn – '*Mi sono perso. Per favore, puoi portarmi in una stazione di polizia.*'

I am lost. Please take me to a police station.

'*Sì,*' I say. '*Mi sono perso.*' But I don't say the bit about taking me to a police station. I really don't want to go to a police station. What would Felix and his family think? It's too embarrassing. And the police probably wouldn't speak English either.

The farmer smiles and nods to the back of the truck.

'*Metti la bicicletta dietro.*'

'*Bicicletta?*' I say. 'My bike?' I nod to it.

He nods to it.

'You want me to put it in the back?' I point.

'*Sì, sì.*' He points.

Wow. Look at me. I'm having an actual conversation in Italian. Wait till Mum hears about this. I put the bike in the back of the truck and then he leans over to open the passenger door. I get in. I'm being rescued.

I close the door and we set off.

As we drive along, the farmer turns to me every now and then, and says something else in Italian and laughs. I nod and grin like an idiot, even though I can't understand a word of it. Italians love to talk so much they'll even talk to someone who doesn't have a clue what they're saying.

And then I have a bad thought.

Where exactly is he taking me? He doesn't know where I'm staying.

Oh god. This is not good. I've done the wrong thing. Mum warned me about this. I should never have got in a truck with a stranger. I look at him again. A squinty, sideways look. Maybe he's not a farmer at all. He has a big knife hanging from his belt. When I put my bike in the back, I saw there was a coil of rope there. Perfect for tying someone up.

He turns and sees me looking. He smiles. Showing his teeth.

I smile back. My grin so wide it's beginning to hurt.

But I'm not smiling inside. This is just awful. My mouth has gone very dry and I feel sick.

I'm being kidnapped!

Reason 26: Getting kidnapped

We rattle and bounce along the road. The truck is quite uncomfortable and I feel every bump. We take some lefts and rights and I see now that there's more than one line of electricity cables. They're all over the place. I really have no idea where we are now.

After a while we come to a little farmhouse in the middle of nowhere and the farmer turns off the road and stops outside the front door. Actually, it's more of a stone hut than a proper farmhouse.

The farmer switches off the engine and gets out. I have no choice. I do the same. It's hot. There's no shade. A big yellow dog walks round from behind the hut and looks at me. He has a pale watery eye.

The farmer pats his chest and says, 'Santo.'

It must be his name. I pat my chest and say, 'Stan.'

'Stan?'

'*Si.*'

He gabbles something else and opens the door to the hut. We go inside. There's a little sort of kitchen with old wooden chairs. It's very dark. Santo gets a bottle of something out of an ancient rusted fridge and offers it to me. Even though I'm very thirsty, I shake my head. It might be drugged or poisoned.

I frantically search my pockets. Is it there? It has to be. It might be my only hope.

There.

Yes!

I fish it out and pass it to Santo. He peers at it. Confused.

It's the picture of the fake dog that Mum gave me. If Santo thinks I have a nice pet dog at home, he might let me go.

Santo half smiles and half frowns at the photograph, then gives it back to me.

'My dog,' I say. 'He loves me. My mum loves me. My dad is dying. Please don't kidnap me. Mum will be upset . . .'

Santo nods and laughs, slaps me on the back and points to a chair.

I sit down. Is he going to tie me up?

He doesn't. Instead he scratches his head and gets out a mobile phone. Oh god, he's calling his gang. He has a long conversation, all the time glancing over at me and smiling like a wolf.

When he's finished, he makes some coffee on an old stove. I sit there, sweating. My clothes are all sticking to me.

'We're not rich,' I say. 'We can't pay you very much. You should have kidnapped Felix instead.'

Oh, that's rotten. I shouldn't have said that. But I'm very frightened. And Felix was horrible to me . . .

Santo brings over his coffee and sits in the chair facing me. He talks some more to me. After a while I hear a car arriving outside.

There are loud voices and shouts, and then three more men come in. They look like bandits, with big boots and dirty clothes. One of them has what looks like a machete. They look at me and talk to Santo and I see that another of them has a gold tooth. And a sack. A big sack. They're going to tie me up and put me in a sack.

'*Polizia*,' I say. '*Per favore, puoi portarmi in una stazione di polizia.*'

Please take me to a police station.

I don't mind being embarrassed (I obviously don't say this last bit, because I don't know how to say it in Italian, but I think it).

They just stare at me, and then start talking again, all of them at once, mixed in with laughter. I zone out. I can't understand any of it. My mind is filled with terrible images. And then I hear some words I do understand – 'Masseria Opuntia' – *the name of Felix's house.*

'Masseria Opuntia!' I say, and they look at me.

'Masseria Opuntia?' says Santo.

I nod and parrot-copy him again.

'Masseria Opuntia. *Sì.*'

'La Signora 'arper?'

'Harper! Yes. Mrs Harper. Signora Harper. You know her? That's where I'm staying.'

'Masseria Opuntia . . .?'

'*Sì, sì, sì* . . . The big house.'

Oh no. I've just made it a lot worse. If they know the house and they know I'm staying there, they must know that the Harpers are rich. They'll definitely want to ransom me now.

The three men laugh. They're drinking something that smells strong, passing the bottle around. I wonder if I should try to make a run for it – while they're distracted. I could run on foot through the olive groves. They might not be able to catch up. But what about the big yellow dog outside? He looked mean.

They could set him on me. He might chase me, and then . . .

Santo is beckoning to me to go outside. Where are they taking me now? We all go out. Even though the sun is low in the sky, it's still very bright after being in the gloomy hut.

There's a tiny battered old Fiat next to the pickup. Santo whistles to the dog and it jumps into the truck next to my bike. The other men open the car door and point inside.

No. I'm not getting in there! You can't force me . . .

They stand there, still pointing, in an 'after you' way.

What do I do?

I get in. The car smells of farm things.

The man with the gold tooth sits next to me. It's very cramped. The other new men sit in the front and we set off, Santo following in the truck. The engine is really noisy and the car fills up with exhaust fumes. I feel sick again. But at least they didn't put the sack over my head.

I dig out the picture of the fake dog again and pass it round. The men all nod and smile, just as bemused as Santo was, and then Gold-tooth says something and they laugh really loudly and then stare at me. I wonder if I should jump out of the car like they do in films.

'Please,' I say. 'I've got a cat. She's deaf. Her name's Table. She'll miss me. And I've got a girlfriend! Her name's Jess. She doesn't know she's my girlfriend. But she'll still be really upset if she never sees me again. Probably. I like her a lot. I've only just got to know her. She helps me be not so shy. And Felix. He's my best friend. Well, not really my best friend. And I don't suppose he'd actually be that bothered if I never came back. We had a fight. Forget Felix. Please. I'm only young. I'm twelve. I've got my whole life ahead of me. All those things I want to do. OK. So there's a lot of things I *don't* want to do, but, you know, like, maybe I *do* now. If you let me go, I promise I'll be brave and I'll do things. I've already eaten squid! I'll go bungee jumping! I'll wrestle alligators! JUST LET ME LIVE!'

I look out of the window. We're outside Felix's house.

'Masseria Opuntia,' says Gold-tooth.

'*Sì*,' I say. '*Grazie.*'

I get out of the car. Santo has parked and is getting the bike off the back of his truck.

'*Grazie*,' I say, and shake his hand.

He says something I don't understand, smiles and gets back in the truck. I wave as they all drive off. As if they're old friends of mine.

'*Ciao . . . ciao . . .*'

The dust settles and I'm alone on the driveway. Like nothing ever happened.

I wheel the bike up the drive and into the car park. I take a deep breath before I open the gate, getting ready for all the questions I'm going to be asked:

'Oh, Stan, where have you been?'

'We've been so worried about you.'

'We were going to send out a search party and call the police. We thought you must have been in an accident . . .'

'Or kidnapped!'

I open the gate. They'll probably be lined up ready for me.

They're not. There are a few people sitting at the big table, though. I can see Ben and Felix, Jess and Ash and Dr Cathy.

Any moment now they're going to see me and come running over.

But nobody pays me any attention. I put the bike away in the shed and go over to where they're sitting. Felix is playing a game on his phone and doesn't even look up. I can sense that he's deliberately not looking up. He's probably feeling guilty for letting me go off on my own.

Ben smiles at me. 'Hi, Stan. How was the ride, dude?'

Do I tell them? That I got totally lost and thought I was going to die?

'It was OK,' I say.

'It's lovely out there now, isn't it?' says Livia, back from her run. 'The perfect temperature.'

'Yeah,' I say.

'There's been an earthquake in northern Italy,' says Ash, who's on his iPad. 'Loads of old churches ruined.'

'Right.'

'And a dog in Kansas has beaten the world record for bursting the most number of balloons in a minute.'

I walk away from the table and go over to the kitchen to get a bottle of water out of the fridge. As I pour myself a glass, I notice that my hand is shaking.

Jess comes in, carrying a plastic bag. She must have followed me.

'You look well hot and sweaty.'

'Yeah.'

'You were gone ages.'

'Yeah . . .'

'I got you something from the shops,' she says.

'Really?'

'Some shorts. You said the other day you needed some new ones. They were dead cheap. But they're quite funky.'

She hands me the plastic bag and I take the shorts out. They're quite bright – what Mum would call 'jazzy'. I'd never have worn them before, but now they look just right.

'Thanks,' I say, and as I hold them up my hands start to shake again.

Jess stares at me. She knows something's up.

'What happened?' she asks.

'I got lost,' I say.

'No?' she says. 'Really? How badly lost? How did you find your way back?'

'Some farmer guys helped me.'

'Were you scared?'

'A bit. A lot . . . I thought I was going to die . . .'

'Poor Stan.'

She gives me a hug and I start to cry.

God, I hope nobody else comes in and sees this.

'Hey,' she says. 'It's all right. You're back now. Things are never as bad as you think.'

'I know,' I say. 'I wasn't really lost at all in the end, I suppose, was I?'

'In the end,' she says, 'I don't think you can ever *really* be lost.'

I mumble something into her shoulder where my snotty face is pressed against her T-shirt.

'What did you say?' she asks.

'Nothing.'

I have *got* to stop saying 'Ooh, profound' out loud.

Reason 19 (part 3):
Squids, octopuses, etc.

Ben and Ash did a barbecue for dinner, using olive wood instead of charcoal. They took it very seriously and I helped out, mainly so I wouldn't have to talk to anyone. Ben and Ash were only talking about wood and heat and charring and marinades and spice rubs, which was fine with me, and I kept busy fetching and carrying things for them.

It was good. We had sausages and chicken skewers and bits of lamb and pork. After we'd all cleared up, the others got ready to play cards, but I went off to read my octopus book under a light in the corner of the terrace.

I needed to be alone. And I've noticed that grown-ups don't mind if you sit by yourself if you're reading a book. In fact, they actually quite like it . . .

'Oh, isn't that great. Stan's reading a book . . .'

And you don't have to read if you don't want to – you can just sit quietly and think about things. And nobody bothers you.

So I thought about things for a bit and then I read for a bit. It's a really interesting book. I'm having to change my opinion of octopuses and squids.

Octopuses turn out to be really cool. I've been making a new list.

(And before you have a go at me, 'octopuses' is the right word for more than one octopus. Not 'octopi'.)

10 COOL FACTS ABOUT OCTOPUSES

1. Octopuses don't have tentacles. They're actually called arms. And they use them like legs to walk around on the seabed.
2. An octopus's brain, the part of it in its head, is quite small, but most of its brain is in other bits of its body, like its arms, which all have a mind of their own.

3. If you cut off an octopus's arm, it can go on doing things because of the brain bits in it (which are called neurons). And it will grow back.
4. Octopuses have three hearts and blue blood.
5. Some octopuses are poisonous. The blue-ringed octopus, even though it's only about as big as a golf ball, has enough venom in it to kill twenty-six people. And there's no antidote. And it has cool flashing blue rings. And, of course, one of the places you can find it is Australia.
6. The biggest octopus in the world is the giant Pacific octopus, which can have an arm span of up to ten metres.
7. Octopuses are masters of disguise and can camouflage themselves to exactly match their surroundings by changing the colour of their skin. They can also change their bodies into almost any shape they like.
8. Octopuses are kind of smart. They can learn how to unscrew the lids on jars — from the inside! (Look it up on YouTube — I did.) They also sometimes

use the two halves of a coconut shell as a mobile home. They carry them around and then shut themselves up inside when they want to go to sleep. An octopus called Paul also accurately predicted the winning team in all seven of Germany's World Cup matches in 2010.

9. They also have a cheeky sense of humour. A scientist was once doing experiments with three octopuses he named Albert, Bertram and Charles (A, B and C). He wanted to see how clever they were and trained them to pull a lever to get food. Albert and Bertram were fine, but Charles wasn't going along with it. He got into position in the tank, with his arms holding on to the sides, and worked away at the lever until it bent and then finally broke. He also kept pulling the light above the tank down into the water and breaking it and then squirting the scientists with jets of water if they came near him.

10. Coolest fact of all. Octopuses have no skeletons, either inside their bodies,

like humans, or on the outside, like prawns, or on their backs, like snails. The only hard part of an octopus is its beak. This means an octopus can squash its body really small and fit through openings that are only slightly bigger than one of its eyes.

And one sad fact – most octopuses only live for about two years.

This means that to an octopus I'd seem really old. I've already lived six octopus lifetimes. I think humans live maybe eighty years, if they're lucky. So, to an octopus, I'm the equivalent of being nearly five hundred years old. If I was an actual octopus, I'd be like SuperOcto, the oldest and wisest octopus in the whole universe – a sort of octopus god!

Yeah. An octopus crams a lot into its two short years. They start out as babies, then they become kids, then teenagers, then middle-aged and they have kids of their own (I won't tell you about how octopuses mate – it's weird and freaky and, if you want to know the truth, really pretty disgusting) and then they're old and then they die.

All in two years.

It makes me feel older and more grown up than I thought I was. And I'm thinking that maybe I don't want to rush ahead like I used to. I don't want to get old and die quite just yet. This growing-up thing is more complicated than I thought.

OK. I close the book. I can't put it off any longer. I have to sort things out with Felix. We haven't properly spoken since our fight.

This could be a tricky conversation.

A Conversation with Felix

4

'I'm sorry I said what I did, Felix.'

'Yeah . . . Me too.'

'We friends again?'

'Guess so.'

'Good.'

'Yeah.'

'G'night.'

'Night.'

Reason 27: Monster storms

Up till today the sky's been clear blue all the time, but this morning when I woke up it was black and I felt like there was a big weight pressing down on me. Everywhere you looked was one huge cloud, swirling and low over your head. It seemed like the wind was blowing from every direction at the same time and it actually felt cold. So cold I had to put on a jumper for the first time. There was this rumbling in the distance and bright flashes, and then, as the morning went on, the rumbling and the flashes came nearer and nearer, until you could see proper lightning bolts streaking down out of the clouds, like something out of a horror movie, and the thunder was really loud. It was quite scary actually.

And then the rain came. Like no rain I've ever seen before. Smashing into the ground, hammering on the roof, splashing off the terraces. It's so thick and heavy it looks like it's made of something solid, like metal. In hardly any time at all there were great puddles, and then pools, and now the courtyard's become a lake.

Jess and Aria and most of the grown-ups went off in the cars to look at some churches. Felix and the older girls are just sitting around in their rooms, watching films on their phones. I'm in the main building by myself. Like the last boy on Earth in a dystopian book. Even though it's eleven o'clock in the morning it's dark as night outside and it's really, really gloomy inside, especially as the lights keep flickering on and off.

There are big sofas in here and a low table full of magazines. I pick one up to take a look at it. It's really big and made of thick shiny paper. It's called *Depth of Focus* and the name sounds familiar – I think it might be the magazine that Felix's dad owns. I put on a lamp and I flip through it. It's full of all sorts of photographs. Photographs of mountains, photographs of lakes and forests and deserts, photographs of animals and cities and cars. There are lots of photographs of people, some of the people are naked and I skip past those pages in case anyone comes in and catches me looking and thinks

I'm a perv. There are pictures of skyscrapers and houses, of furniture, trees, famous people, ordinary people, wars, floods, fires . . .

The whole world is in here.

I lose myself looking at the pictures. Some are black and white, some in colour and some in really weird colours . . .

'Do you like photographs?'

I look round. Felix's dad has come in from the kitchen. He's carrying a coffee pot and a cup. I feel embarrassed at first and think maybe I'm not allowed to look at his magazine. But he doesn't seem cross. He's smiling.

'Sure,' I say. 'I suppose.'

'Well. Make the most of that magazine. It may well be the last issue.'

'Why? It's good.'

'Why? Because nobody reads magazines any more. Except me. Everything's online these days. That's all anyone's interested in. The digital world. Screens. Although they're not prepared to pay for anything they look at on them.'

He sits down on the sofa opposite me.

'Have you ever seen Felix reading anything?' he asks. 'I mean a book, or a magazine, anything . . .'

'He looks at things on his phone.'

'Exactly. That's the modern world. Not my world . . .'

He goes quiet and just sits there, staring at me and sipping his coffee. I think I ought to say something.

'I like books,' I say lamely.

'Yeah. I see you reading a lot. That octopus book's great, isn't it?'

'Yeah. Is it yours?'

'I brought it out here, yeah. I thought Felix might be interested in it . . . Needless to say, he wasn't.'

'Right.'

Mr Harper takes another sip of coffee. The thunder rumbles. The rain hammers down.

'Tell me,' says Mr Harper after a while. 'You're Felix's best friend. Perhaps you can explain something to me . . .'

'Maybe.'

'What's the matter with him?'

'What do you mean?'

'He's so miserable and bad-tempered all the time,' says Mr Harper. 'Always in a mood, never wants to help out. It's like he's . . . not interested. In *anything*. He's in his own little world. I sometimes think he doesn't like me.'

He obviously wants me to say something, but I don't know what. In the end a thought does come to me, though. The sort of thing a grown-up might say. The sort of thing Mum might say. I try it out.

'Maybe you should ask him,' I say.

'Oh, he won't talk to me.' Mr Harper waves his hand as if he's waving a fly away. 'I'm just his boring, irrelevant old dad. He has no interest in me whatsoever.'

I seem to have got into quite a heavy conversation. Two weeks ago I'd have mumbled an apology and got out of there fast, but people do things differently on holiday. It's not like the real world, and since my kidnapping I've decided to take Mark's advice and be brave.

'I think he misses you,' I say.

Mr Harper laughs quietly. 'How can he miss me? I haven't gone anywhere.'

'Can I say something, Mr Harper? Truthfully?'

'Go on.'

'I don't think you know him very well.'

'I've known him all his life,' says Mr Harper with another little half-laugh.

'If you knew him better, you'd know that I'm not really his best friend,' I say, and Mr Harper frowns at me. 'Just as a "for instance".'

Mr Harper peers at me. 'Yes. Well. As I say, Stan, I'd talk to him if he wanted to talk to me.'

'Well, you could at least try.'

'You think it would help?'

'I just think Felix would like you to do more things with him. He told me all the things you used to do together when you first came out here. Like riding bikes and teaching him to swim. You were going to teach him to dive as well . . . He still can't dive. He's embarrassed about it. And he told me how you used to play with him.'

'He's twelve. Nearly thirteen. He's too old. The only thing he plays with is his phone.'

'Twelve isn't really that old,' I say. 'Maybe it's you that's got too old to play.'

Mr Harper looks at me. I wonder if he's going to be cross and tell me off. *How dare you speak to me like that!!?!?!?!?*

Instead he just says, 'That's very profound, Stan.'

I smile. But he was saying it seriously. Not mocking me.

'You can still play with him,' I say. 'Table football. Or . . . I don't know . . . anything . . . Teach him to dive.'

Mr Harper drinks some more coffee. Thinking.

'Does your dad do things with you?' he asks. 'Does he play with you?'

'No. Not really. Not as much as he used to.'

'Would you like him to?'

'I guess so. He's a bit useless, though, basically.'

Mr Harper laughs. 'Do you think I'm useless?'

'A bit . . .'

'It's just . . .' Mr Harper fiddles with the coffee pot. 'I've got a lot of things on my mind.'

'Everybody does,' I say. 'Everybody has their own problems. I know you're worried about losing the magazine, about losing your job. But don't you worry about losing Felix too?'

'Losing him?'

'He thinks you don't like him.'

Mr Harper looks thoughtful. A bit hurt even. He looks away from me. Rubs his neck. Maybe I've gone too far. But I'm not stopping now. This is actually kind of fun. Unreal. But fun.

'Can I say something else?' I say.

'There's no stopping you.'

'Me and Felix are different,' I say. 'Our families are different. I'm scared of lots of things. But I'm not scared of the same things that Felix is scared of.'

'What scares you?' he asks.

'This,' I say. 'Talking to people. Talking to grown-ups.'

'You're quite good at it.'

I shrug. *Beginner's luck.*

'And what scares Felix?' asks Mr Harper.

'He's scared that he won't be able to come out here again. That he won't have a family any more.'

Mr Harper puts down his cup and stares at me. 'What do you mean by that?'

'He thinks you and Mrs Harper are going to split up. That you might go off with someone else.'

This time I think I really have gone too far. I should have done what I always used to do. I should have kept quiet. I should never have got into this conversation.

'Does anyone else think that?' he asks.

'Some.'

Mr Harper is still staring at me. 'How do you know all this?'

'I listen.'

'You know,' he says, refilling his coffee cup, 'this is the weirdest conversation I've ever had.'

'Me too,' I say.

He looks up at me and after a few seconds he laughs. I laugh too.

And at that moment the sun comes out. I look out of the window. The rain has stopped. The storm has passed over. I remember what Mark said about a storm washing everything clean. The day looks bright and shiny, like it's had a shower.

I get up off the sofa.

'Where are you going?' asks Mr Harper.

'I'm going to go outside and play . . .'

Reason 28: Weird bottles of stuff you'd never drink back home

Tomorrow is our last day and tonight we've all come into the local village for a *festa*, which is the Italian word for a party.

This *festa*'s in the village square, where the cafe is. They've built a stage where a band's playing crazy Italian folk music. There are stalls all around the square selling food and drink and the sort of stuff you find at tacky markets. T-shirts, cheap homemade jewellery, sweets, leather belts . . . and tambourines. Lots of tambourines. Tambourines seem to be a big part of the local music. There are three men on stage now thrashing the life out of huge tambourines. It sounds like heavy metal drumming. As well as the tambourinists, there are two women playing violins, a man with an accordion, another man playing what looks and sounds like bagpipes, and a guitarist who thrashes his guitar like he's in a punk rock band.

The noise is great. Wild and thundering.

There are more people in the crowd banging away at their own tambourines, and there are some very expensive ones for sale on the stalls as well as loads of cheap ones with paintings on them. Mostly of spiders and spiderwebs. And lots of them say 'Salento'. There are also T-shirts with 'Salento' on them and more spiders and spiderwebs.

Simon explains it to me.

'The local music here in Salento is called *pizzica*, or *tarantella*, Satan. You know, like a tarantula. The story goes that if you're bitten by a spider you have to go into a wild dance to get rid of the poison.'

There are lights blazing everywhere and it's exciting being somewhere at night that's so bright. It reminds me of Stansted Airport where there was no difference between day and night and everyone was behaving slightly mad. There's a happy party feeling, everyone's drinking and eating and talking, but mostly dancing. Young and old, men and women, boys and girls, locals and tourists – everyone's jigging about in the square. Some people know the right moves, but most are just doing their own thing.

Simon joins them, and the girls, and then everyone else. Felix dances with his mum. I hold back, but Jess grabs me and drags me into the mosh pit. I've never danced before in my life and, actually, as long as I don't think about it, it's not too hard. You just sort of hop about. Nobody seems to mind what I do. They're all just enjoying themselves.

And I am too.

Wait till I tell Mum and Dad!

'You're delirious again, lad. I know you're not a dancer.'

Every song sounds the same, which helps, because once you've worked out a way to dance you don't need to change it. Me and Jess go as wild as we can, imagining we've been bitten by spiders. I feel great. Not anxious or stressed about anything. Maybe Simon was right. Maybe you can get rid of any bad things inside you by dancing crazily. All our lot from the house seem happy.

I see Santo, the farmer that rescued me, and go over to say hello and he grins and we shake hands. The other three men are there and tonight I can see them as what they are. Just farmers. Not scary, or sinister or anything.

They all speak at once and I grin, not understanding the words, just the meaning – that we're friends and that life is good.

I introduce Jess, as well as I can, and we all have a dance together. Like it's the most normal thing in the world.

It's quite tiring, though, and after a while me and Jess take a break and go to get crêpes with Nutella in them. Afterwards we bump into Mark and he buys us souvenir Salento T-shirts. I get a red one with a mad spider on it.

I buy some presents for Mum and Dad. Some of the dried-cat-poo biscuits, *taralli*. A bracelet made of stones and shells for Mum. And a small tambourine – the cheapest I can find – for Dad. Not that he'll ever play it.

Then I buy Jess a Coke. I'm using up my emergency money, but I figure it's nearly the end of the holiday and tonight I'm being reckless. There's a small funfair set up in a road off the square, and me and Jess sit on a wall drinking Cokes and chatting and watching people on the rides, the wind blowing in their hair.

I remember talking to Mark on the roof about chaos theory – how the tiny flap of a butterfly wing creates a little draught, which makes a bigger wind, and eventually, thousands of miles away, there's a big storm. I think about how small things can happen that lead to other things happening, which lead to other things, and nobody knows how it will all end. I think about Archie breaking his leg, me coming out here instead of him, and meeting Jess, and eating squid, and not getting kidnapped . . . Who knows where it will all end?

We notice that a small crowd has gathered near the stage and the band has stopped playing, so we finish our Cokes and go over to see what's going on. It's Ben, surrounded by locals. I hope there isn't a problem, but then I see that he's shaking hands and posing for selfies and signing autographs. And then the guitarist from the band comes up to him and offers him his guitar. At first Ben shakes his head, but people push him and shove him towards the stage and he shrugs and climbs up the steps. He does a small mock bow to the crowd who all clap and cheer.

'What's going on?' I ask Jess.

'I guess he's going to sing,' says Jess.

'But how do they all know him?'

'Stan!' says Jess. 'I thought you knew.'

'Knew what?'

'Ben's famous. He's a famous singer.'

'Is he . . .? I don't know much about music. Except Dad's music. He likes dad rock. Particularly Bruce Springsteen.'

'Well, Ben's not dad rock.'

The crowd goes quiet and Ben speaks into the mike.

'I'm sorry. This is really embarrassing. I just came here to enjoy myself tonight – I've been loving the music – but do you want me to sing something?'

A big cheer goes up.

'OK. You might know this one . . .'

Ben starts singing a song and I recognize it. I've heard it being played loads of times. I had no idea it was Ben. As he sings, people cheer and then sing and clap along. Ben nods to Aria and she joins him on stage, wearing her ginormous hat, banging a tambourine and grinning. I can see her turn and say something to her dad. I can't hear her, but I know what she's saying . . .

'Omigodman!'

Now the violinist joins in as well. I can see Livia standing on the side of the stage, beaming at Ben and slapping a tambourine.

When Ben finishes, there's another huge cheer, but they won't let Ben go, so he plays another song. I recognize this one as well. Other musicians join him and the whole crowd gets dancing again.

Felix comes over, eating a lump of meat in a bun. 'Isn't this amazing?' he says.

'Yeah,' I shout above the music. 'Ben's cool.'

Felix is right. The atmosphere *is* amazing and a little bit of me feels proud that I know Ben.

'He's great,' I say to Jess. 'But I had no idea how famous he was. He seems just like an ordinary guy.'

'He *is*,' says Jess. 'Why shouldn't he be? Famous people are just people in the end. They start out like you or me.'

Ben starts another song and Jess goes off to be nearer the stage. I'm left alone with Felix.

'You know, Felix,' I say, 'I've actually had a really good holiday.'

'Good.'

'I wish *you* had too.'

'Yeah. Well. Some of it's been fun – this is fun, and doing stuff with Uncle Mark.'

'I really like him,' I say. I can see Mark by the stage, smiling up at Ben and the musicians.

'Me too,' says Felix. 'I wish I could swap him for my dad.'

'You know, Felix, maybe you should, like, *talk* to your dad . . .'

'He doesn't want to talk to me.'

'You don't know till you try.'

'Mark said the same thing.'

'Your uncle knows what he's talking about.'

'Maybe.'

'Does he have kids?' I ask.

'Don't you know?' says Felix.

'Know what?'

'It's a bit sad,' says Felix. 'Are you sure you want me to tell you?'

'I suppose,' I say.

'He had a boy called Peter. My cousin. We were the same age.'

'What happened to him?'

'He died when he was really young. Then my Aunt Sal and Mark split up.'

'That's horrible,' I say. 'That's so sad.'

'Yeah.'

There's clapping as Ben finishes and bows. I'm thinking about Mark and his boy, Peter, who would have been the same age as me.

When Ben comes off stage, he's mobbed again. Felix goes over to join him, but his dad intercepts him. I can see the two of them talking. I hope they're not having an argument.

Livia walks up. 'Wasn't Ben fabulous?'

'Yeah.'

'People are being polite with *me*, though,' Livia says. 'They can see I need my space and they're not coming up for autographs.'

'Yeah.'

'Now, Stan!' she says, excited. 'I've found you the perfect girlfriend.'

I can see Jess coming back. If I can't get rid of Livia, she's going to hear our embarrassing conversation. I can't think of anything to say, though.

'There's a young Italian girl dancing over there,' says Livia, 'and she's the most beautiful girl I've ever seen – she reminds me of me when I was young. She looks like –'

'It's OK,' says Jess, walking up and cutting her off. 'Stan's already got a girlfriend.'

'Oh. Fine. Cool.' Livia laughs and shrugs and looks a bit awkward, and then the Italian band starts up again and she dances away from us.

'Thanks for getting rid of her,' I say to Jess. 'I should have thought of making up a girlfriend.'

'I didn't make it up,' says Jess, and she laughs and takes my arm. 'You *have* a girlfriend.'

'Who?'

'Me! I'm your girlfriend, stupid.'

'Really?'

This is awesome. I was pretending to myself that she was my girlfriend, and it turns out she actually is. Who knew?

Unless . . .

'Are you joking with me?'

'No. I mean . . . I thought you wanted . . .'

'Yes! Yes,' I say. 'I *do* want.'

Jess laughs and drags me towards the small funfair. The first thing we come to is a shooting gallery. There are rows of tin cans set up with targets on them and air rifles to shoot them with.

It turns out I'm quite good at shooting. I hit a few cans and win a prize. Jess cheers. The man in charge gives me a little miniature bottle. Like a doll's bottle. Full of bright pink liquid. I drink half and Jess drinks half. It tastes of strawberry – and something else.

'I think that was alcohol,' says Jess.

'Whoa,' I say. 'Are we drunk?'

'I don't think so. It was a very small bottle.'

'Let's get another one!'

Now Jess shoots, and she's even better than me. We win another two bottles. We go to find a quiet place to sit, away from the crowds, and drink the tiny pink bottles in silence, and then Jess suddenly kisses me.

Yes. She kisses me.

I won't tell you what it's like, because it's private. I've never liked the bits in films when people kiss, but, well . . . SHE KISSED ME.

Will I tell Felix?

No.

Will I tell Mum?

No.

Will I tell anyone?

No.

It was just for me and Jess.

Afterwards we swap phone numbers and agree to meet up when we're back in London.

And the day after tomorrow that's where I'll be.

Home . . .

But I have to tell someone what it felt like kissing Jess, so I'll tell you.

It tasted of strawberry and something else and it felt like the touch of a butterfly's wing . . .

Ooh, profound.

A Conversation with Dad

'Stan?'

'Dad? *Dad?!*'

'Don't sound so disappointed, lad. Did you hope I was going to die?'

'No. I'm not disappointed. I'm amazed. I'm so happy . . . You're awake!'

'Yeah. What time is it out there?'

'It's after midnight.'

'Mum said you'd want to speak to me as soon as I woke up.'

'Oh, Dad, it's so great to hear your voice. Even if it is a bit croaky.'

'I'm a Shetland pony.'

'What?'

'I'm a little hoarse.'

'Nice one, Dad.'

'I can only do crap jokes, Stan. If I make myself laugh too much, it hurts. I've got staples all down my front. It looks like a giant zip. I'm a silly sod for letting myself get into this state, but I'm going to be all right. How about you? How are you doing, lad?'

'Oh, Dad, I went up on a parachute and I landed in a swarm of jellyfish and I got chased by killer bees and a polar bear and I got kidnapped, only I wasn't really —'

'Ha, ha! Don't make me laugh, Stan. Please. Ooooh . . . You always did have a good imagination. I've been delirious on the drugs they've been giving me for the pain, and I've been having really weird dreams, but I'm not half as delirious as you by the sound of it. What have they been putting in the water out there?'

'I drank this weird pink stuff. I think it might have had alcohol in it.'

'Sounds like you're having a whale of a time.'

'It's been great, Dad. I've had an awesome time.'

'Good. I had my doubts about this holiday. I didn't know if you'd be able to cope. But as long as you've enjoyed it.'

'Most of it.'

'Ah . . .'

'There were some bad bits. It was a bit tough at times. I was worried about you, of course, and I argued with Felix and I got homesick . . .'

'I knew you would. You were never very good at manning up.'

'Dad, it's got nothing to do with manning up! That's not it at all. It's about . . . Oh, I can't explain it. I'll tell you all about it when I get back.'

'Can't wait. I've missed you too, Stan.'

'You know, Dad, I think we're the same really.'

'What do you mean?'

'If I ask you something, Dad, will you answer me truthfully?'

'Where's this going, Stan?'

'Just say you'll be honest with me.'

'Of course I will. I've always been honest with you. If you're going to ask me if I'm really going to be all right, I am. I'm going to be fine.'

'That's brilliant, but it's not what I was going to ask you.'

'Go on, then . . .'

'Are you actually shy, Dad?'

'Shy?'

'Yes. When you make me go up and ask people directions and things, is it because, really, you're too shy to do it yourself?'

'Well . . .'

'Truthfully . . .'

'Well, yes, maybe I am a bit shy. And, if we're being honest, maybe that's where you get it from. I know I go on all the time about manning up, but I'm not sure I know what it means to be a man. Especially now. Lying here. I know what's really important in life. And it's the family, Stan. It's you and Mum and . . .'

'You and me, Dad, we can help each other from now on.'

'Good plan, Stan.'

'And we'll start by doing more things together.'

'That'd be nice.'

'Doesn't have to be anything amazing. Just, you know, football and chatting and whatever you like . . .'

'Well. Where did this all come from?'

'I think I've grown up a bit, Dad. On this holiday.'

'I think maybe you have. But it's back to your boring old life after this, I'm afraid. No more excitements.'

'There's nothing wrong with our boring life, Dad. I love our boring life. Being at home with you and Mum and Table. Just an ordinary, boring family.'

'With a dad who's got a giant zip down his front.'

'With a dad who's alive and well and normal.'

'Ooh. Normal, am I?'

'Yes. And there's nothing wrong with being normal. I don't want a dad who's a millionaire, or a pop star, or who has the latest, biggest iPhone – I just want a dad . . . like you.'

'Ooh, profound.'

Reason 29: Tomatoes, tomatoes, nothing but tomatoes!

I wake up early to find that Felix isn't in bed. Maybe he's in the loo. I hear a splash from the pool and go to look out of the window. It's not like Felix to be swimming first thing in the morning. He likes to lie in.

But there he is, climbing out of the pool. And there's his dad. Just the two of them. Mr Harper's standing by the board. He says something to Felix and shows him a diving position. Felix stands on the edge, arms stretched out above his head. His dad says something else and smiles.

And Felix dives in.

It's not the greatest dive in the world. But it's a dive. His dad laughs and claps. Felix bobs up, grinning.

I watch them for a bit. With every dive, Felix gets better and more confident. His dad even films him on his phone. I wonder if Felix will put it on his YouTube channel.

At breakfast Felix is chatty and telling jokes, and when we've finished Mr Harper rounds up all the kids and hands out baskets and buckets and containers.

'We'll be going home tomorrow,' he says. 'I want you to go and pick every tomato you can find in the vegetable garden.'

'Oh, what?' says Felix. 'It's so hot.'

'They'll just rot if we leave them,' says Mr Harper. 'And pick all the rotten ones as well. I don't want them littering the place. Strip the vines and fill up your containers. You'll be amazed how many there are if you really look.'

'Do we have to, Dad?' says Felix. It seems his good mood hasn't lasted very long. 'It's really sweaty.'

'Do it for me, Felix, yeah?'

'Well . . . OK.'

'You never know, you might actually have fun. I want every tomato you can get. We'll sort out the rotten ones from the fresh ones later.'

So me and Jess and Felix and Alice and Lily and Aria troop out into the car park, Felix complaining every step of the way, and go through a little gate into the vegetable garden, which is a bit of a tangled mess. There's an old gardener who looks after it and he doesn't seem very keen on weeding. Not that it seems to matter. It's full of brightly coloured vegetables.

Mr Harper was right – once you start digging down through all the tomato plants and poking around among the stems and leaves, you can find hundreds of tomatoes. We fill the containers, mixing the OK tomatoes up with the squashed and rotten ones, so that my hands are soon covered in sticky tomato juice. At first I think it's gross when you pick a squishy one, but you get used to it. Two weeks ago I'd never have done anything like this. I couldn't bear to get any food on me. But it's just tomatoes. And being out here, in the sun, with all this life popping up everywhere around you, and the fresh smell of the vegetables and the other kids all joking and laughing, it's fun.

Even Felix gets into it – trying to see if he can pick more than anyone else. He throws a rotten tomato at the wall where it splatters right next to Lily, who shrieks and swears at him and calls him a fribble*.

Alice tells him off. 'Dad wants all the tomatoes. Don't waste them.'

'What's he going to do with the rotten ones?'

'You know he hates mess. He wants us to tidy this place up. So let's just do it. He's pretty chilled this morning. I don't want him to go back to being in a bad mood.'

'Yeah, OK . . .'

Eventually we can't find any more tomatoes, and the containers are all full and quite heavy. We lug them out of the vegetable garden, back across the car park and go through into the courtyard, where we find the adults lined up, waiting for us. All of them, even Ash and the angry woman and Emma, who for once isn't listening to a book. They're all wearing T-shirts and swimmers or old shorts.

'Right,' says Mr Harper. 'Put the containers down, then go and get into your swimming things.'

Felix mumbles and complains, but we all go off to get changed. I ask Felix what's going on, but he doesn't know.

'This isn't a game you've played before or something?'

'I said I don't know.'

'Whatever.'

---

* She didn't really call him a fribble. She called him a bleep.

When we go back outside, we see that Mr Harper is wearing a snorkel mask.

'Right,' he says. 'We're going to play a game. You're never too old for games.'

'What game?' says Felix.

'The Tomato Game.'

'What are the rules?' says Felix.

'There aren't any. Split up into teams and choose a couple of containers for each group.'

'Then what?'

'Then what do you think?' Mr Harper picks a big rotten tomato out of a basket and lobs it right at Felix – hitting him in the chest. It explodes like something from a war movie. Felix swears. Mrs Harper laughs. Everyone else laughs. Felix looks like he might throw a wobbler, but then he laughs.

Mr Harper laughs too. 'If life gives you tomatoes,' he says, 'make a mess. That's it! Those are the rules. Split up, and, on the count of three, start throwing!'

I team up with Felix and Jess. We have two buckets and a big basket stuffed with tomatoes.

'I'm going to get him,' says Felix.

'Ready?' shouts Mr Harper. 'One, two, three – let battle commence!'

Felix lobs a big, juicy, rotten tomato at his dad and hits him right in the snorkel mask.

'Good shot,' I shout, and start throwing.

In a moment the air is thick with flying red missiles. One gets me in the side of the head and I look round to see Livia laughing her head off.

Me and Jess pick up a handful of tomatoes each and let fly. She's not laughing any more. She's standing there with her mouth wide open in a silent scream and a look of horror on her face.

'*What did you do today, son?*'

'*I threw rotten tomatoes at the famous actress Livia Channing, Dad.*'

'*Excellent!*'

Felix joins me and Livia's soon covered in red gunk. Then Mr Harper's team are on us, busy grabbing tomatoes and flinging them. I get done by a few. Some sting a little, but most you hardly feel. I've got tomato in my hair, all over my body, down my trunks, juice and bits of skin and seeds. The smell of tomato is very strong.

Any that land on us, or near us and don't totally disintegrate, we throw back. I get a couple more good hits in – on Ash and Mark. I get Ash right between the eyes and he laughs like a mad person.

Then Mr Harper runs over, picks up our biggest container and pours the contents all over Felix. Me and Jess fight back, driving him off with a barrage of flying fruit. Felix cheers. Mrs Harper comes in from the side for a sneak attack. But Alice and Lily and Aria have spotted her and are hurling everything they've got at her.

'Omigodman! She's well splattered!'

Simon's going nuts, yelling, 'Bombs away! Incoming! Grenade! Let 'em have it!' and other war-related shouts while chucking tomato after tomato after tomato. He's actually a really good shot. Ben's not so bad either. Emma, Dr Cathy and the angry woman are another team. They're not the best — they're laughing too much.

Eventually there's nothing left to throw — all the tomatoes have been smashed to bits. Everyone is weak with laughter and there's a wild and crazy atmosphere like all the rules of normal behaviour have been forgotten. The courtyard is covered with what looks like tomato sauce. And so are we. People are wiping their eyes, scraping their skin, untangling their hair.

It's Tomatogeddon!

We all pile into the pool showers and as soon as people are clean they run out and leap into the pool.

We stay there for the rest of the day, mucking about in the water, jumping, having races, floating on lilos or just sitting about in the shallow end, chatting like Italians.

And we dive. *We all dive.* Felix doesn't say anything. He just joins in. As if he could *always* dive. And nobody says anything. But I do catch Mr Harper watching him proudly. By the end of the day, Felix is even diving in off the board without thinking about it.

That evening he and Alice go off with their mum and dad to a pizza place, just the four of them. I play cards with Jess and Aria and Lily, and it's warm and fun and nice. And when, a few hours later, Felix comes back, he's talking to his parents, laughing and joking, and I think maybe he *could* actually be my best friend one day.

Reason 30: You might come back a different person

I'm on the plane, looking out of the window at the Alps. They look amazing from up here. Gigantic and still covered in snow even in the summer. I remember what Mark said to me about the wind. How it makes you feel part of the world, but only a small part. And looking at the Alps I feel very small.

And that feels nice. Knowing I'm not *that* important. Mark was right – people aren't always looking at me and talking about me. I don't need to feel so self-conscious all the time. And I'm not the only one who gets anxious. Everybody has their own worries and problems.

Soon I'll be back at Stansted, where this whole adventure began. I picture myself as a frightened little boy wandering lost in the shopping maze at four o'clock in the morning. He seems a different person to the Stan that's sitting here on the plane in his new T-shirt and shorts, sipping an iced Coke and looking at the Alps. The Stan who ate squid and shot tin cans like a special ops ninja and kissed a girl . . .

Kissing was on my duck-it list. One of the things I never wanted to do. Everything I was worried about when I was lost in the shopping maze. I remember thinking that most of the things on my duck-it list were things other people would probably have on their bucket list.

And now I've done some of them, *and they were fun*. Ian Fleming was right. Never say no to an adventure. Well, unless you don't want to. In the end just do what you want and don't think too much about it.

Yeah. This is the new grown-up Stan talking. Like someone cool with their own YouTube channel giving out advice.

Who knows . . . Maybe one day . . .

For now I'm wondering if I can turn things upside down and make my duck-it list into a bucket list.

1. Bungee jumping. OK. Bad start. I'm still terrified of the idea of bungee jumping. So I won't put it on my bucket list.
2. Anything where you have to use a parachute. Done it. The parachute part was fine. It was the jellyfish that were the problem.
3. Dancing. Done that too. The new Stan is king of the dancefloor.
4. Dancing in public. Yeah? What's the problem?
5. Going on Strictly Come Dancing. Right. I'll put that one in with bungee jumping. I never, ever want to go on Strictly Come Dancing.
6. White-water rafting. Yeah. Might be cool . . . one day.
7. Fire-eating. OK. I forgot some of the things I put on the list. I'm learning to be more 'adventurous' with my eating, but I draw the line at eating fire. The point is, it's all right not to do things if you don't want. It's your choice. Being brave is not just saying yes to everything. Sometimes you have to say no to things. Like . . .

8. Alligator wrestling. This one's like Strictly. Not to be tried out. Although, thinking about it, they could make a new TV show that might be more exciting than Strictly – Strictly Come Alligator Wrestling. I'd watch that.

9. Kissing. I kissed a girl. And I liked it. It's like dancing – best if you don't think about it too much and just do it.

10. Going on holiday with people you don't know. Well, the thing about going on holiday with strangers, is . . . by the end of the holiday they're not strangers any more – they're people you know. Ash with his daily news reports, Emma with her audiobooks, Simon who likes a drink, Mark who was really nice and treated me like a grown-up, Mr and Mrs Harper, of course, Livia the film star, Ben the musician, the girls – Alice and Lily and Aria, Jess's mum, Dr Cathy, and Jess. My new actual best friend, Jess. The only one I didn't really get to know was the angry woman. Although I got to know her enough to know that she wasn't really

angry in the end. But I'm a bit embarrassed that I still don't know her name.

11. Octopuses. Octopuses are cool. Maybe one day I'll go snorkelling and see one for real. Maybe next year. If Felix asks me back . . .

We fly across France and the English Channel and then over Essex, and everything turns grey and dull below us. Rows and rows of houses and cars crawling along the roads. We land and go back through Stansted Airport, passing excited passengers going in the other direction – on their way to holidays in the sun.

After we go through passport control, we all meet up in the place where you pick up your luggage. Some of our lot have to wait for suitcases, including Jess and her mum. So we say goodbye and kiss each other and hug, and it feels weird living so closely with these people for two weeks and now I might never see most of them again.

Except for Felix. Who's so much nicer to me now.

And Jess . . .

I have her number and she has mine. I say a proper goodbye to her and promise to call her. Then I thank Mrs Harper who tells me that Mum's sent a message saying that she's here waiting for me.

Simon comes over. His eyes are watery, like he might be about to cry. I really hope he doesn't. He shakes my hand.

'Lines in the dust, Satan,' he says. 'Lines in the dust. I hope yours is a long one, and a straight one, not all squiggly like mine.'

He smiles and I smile back and then he leans in closer. 'Ooh, profound,' he says, and winks.

I say goodbye to Jess again. I'm going to miss her. But I will *definitely* call her. And then I'm done. No more goodbyes. I go on ahead by myself, leaving the others to wait for their luggage. I go through customs and then I'm out, back in the real world.

And I survived. I survived all the things on Mum's emergency list! Well, not all of them. I wasn't attacked by sharks, obviously, or caught in a tsunami. Rabid dog? Well, there was the polar bear dog. I survived that. And kidnapping. No problem. Giant squid? Hah! I *ate* the thing. And I survived the disasters I had on my own list – weird food, weird toilets, speaking Italian, going on holiday with other people . . .

None of them were anywhere near as difficult and scary as I feared. Even Stansted Airport isn't a problem any more. In the middle of the day, coming home, it just seems sort of boring and normal. What was I so worried about? I've got through it all by myself and I'm in the arrivals lounge, walking with a crowd of passengers along a sort of wide corridor between crash barriers. There are people pushed up against the barriers, waiting to greet family and friends. And there are drivers holding up pieces of cardboard with passengers' names on.

And then I see her . . .

Mum's waiting there with my big brother, Jack. (I maybe should have mentioned him before, I suppose. But I forgot.)

Mum looks anxious, scanning the faces. She probably thinks the plane's crashed and my charred body's at the bottom of the English Channel right now, being eaten by sharks and giant squid.

She looks right past me as if I'm invisible. Maybe I've got my ultimate wish. You know, the old question – 'What would your superpower be? Flight, invisibility or massive strength?'

I always choose invisibility, of course.

And now it's as if I really am invisible. Mum doesn't recognize me. I want to run over and shout 'Mum! Mum! It's me!' but for some reason I stop and hold back.

It's at this moment I realize I love Mum very much and that I've missed her more than anything. Much more than a million. So why don't I run over to her?

There's a fairy story about a prince who goes away and comes back as a different person and nobody recognizes him. Or maybe it was in a comic. Maybe it's happened to me? Maybe I really am a new person? Not the same Stan who left for Stansted Airport all those days ago.

Stansted. It sounds like 'Stan's dead . . .' I've become a ghost . . .

Ooh, profound.

Come on. I've only been on holiday.

But I am a different Stan. I ate cold soup, and salad, and squid. I got lost and I got back all right. I spoke to adults. I told Mr Harper off . . .

And I kissed a girl.

And then Mum looks my way again. I'm sure she's seen me this time, but, no, she's looked right past me again. I wait there a moment before she turns her head back, frowns, smiles, laughs, starts to cry. I run across to her and hug her over the barrier, and Mum hugs me back.

And then I hug Jack. I've never hugged Jack before. He doesn't know what to do.

'I didn't recognize you,' says Mum. 'What's that T-shirt you're wearing?'

'Are you saying you can only recognize me from my T-shirt?'

'No. Of course not. It's just you look different. You're all brown and your hair's gone lighter and you look taller. Have you grown? And you're not so skinny. And you're wearing shorts? Shorts, Stan! Whatever next? I haven't seen your legs in years. Have they swapped you with someone?'

'Yeah. Maybe.'

'But seriously where did you get that shirt?'

'It's new.'

'My god. You bought it? Stan! Was it expensive?'

'Felix's uncle got it for me. The shorts are new as well. Someone else got them for me. I did spend some of the money you gave me, though. I brought you all presents.'

'That money was for an emergency.'

'I didn't have any emergencies.'

'Oh.'

'You sound disappointed, Mum.'

'I'm not. I'm just all discombobulated. How was it?'

'It was great. I had such a great time. But I'm looking forward to being in my own bed in my own room in my own house . . . with my own family.'

'I've got you your favourite dinner,' says Mum.

'Squid?'

'Squid? Don't be daft. Sausages and mash. And tomorrow we'll have a takeaway. You can have chicken tikka masala and poppadoms . . .'

Yeah. Tasty. I *do* like Italian food now, but the thought of something different, something spicy, sounds amazing.

'We'll drive straight to the hospital,' says Mum. 'Dad's so looking forward to seeing you.'

I give Jack some Italian sweets I got at Brindisi Airport and we go to the car park and find our beaten-up old Ford Focus. As we drive home along the motorway, I look out of the window at familiar grey England going past and already Italy feels like a dream.

'So what do you reckon, Stan?' says Jack.

'Best. Holiday. Ever,' I say.

'What were your peaks and troughs?'

I tell him the best bits: the pool and the beach and ice cream and *cornettos*, the tomato fight, dropping the watermelon off the roof . . .

(Mum: 'That sounds dangerous.')

But not the bit about kissing Jess. That's private.

'And what did you learn?' asks Mum. Always a teacher.

'I learnt how to play Perudo,' I say. 'It's a dice game.'

'OK . . .'

I've learnt a lot of other stuff as well. I've learnt a lot about how to enjoy myself. I've learnt to not be so anxious. I've learnt that I need to get on top of my shyness, because nobody else is going to help me. And I've learnt that I'm not in such a hurry to be a grown-up any more. In fact, I've added it to my list of things that look fun but actually aren't, like pedalos and Frisbee and sleeping on the top bunk . . .

Growing up . . .

You see, adults aren't really any more sorted out than us kids. They get happy and sad and scared and excited and moody and angry just like us, and, like us, they don't always know the best thing to do. And they worry about all the things that we worry about – if people will like us, if we'll make fools of ourselves, who's the most important person in the room, if we're too fat or too thin, if you like someone else but they don't like you . . .?

In the end, I don't reckon they know how to get through the day any better than we do.

And they're happiest when they're behaving like kids again. Which is maybe what holidays are all about.

Ooh, profound.

But true.

Actually, you know what, I don't think I'll say any of this to Mum and Dad.

Because, let's face it, part of being a child is protecting your parents from the harsh realities of life.

About the Author

Charlie Higson started writing when he was ten years old. After university he was a singer and painter and decorator before he started writing for television. He went on to create and star in the hugely successful comedy series *The Fast Show*. He is the author of the bestselling Young Bond books and the incredibly successful horror series *The Enemy*.

Charlie doesn't do Facebook, but you can tweet him @monstroso